Like Sparrows

Joanna Morey

ISBN: 978-1-4834-3355-4 (sc)
ISBN: 978-1-4834-3357-8 (hc)
ISBN: 978-1-4834-3356-1 (e)

Library of Congress Control Number: 2015909898

Lulu Publishing Services rev. date: 06/29/2015

For Holden

Acknowledgments

MY MOTHER SHARES A memory of when I was four years old, finding me tucked beneath a piano bench in our dining room, reading German words from one of her music books. That may have been where my love for reading began. When I was six, I handed my father a stack of wide rule paper on which I had written my first story. He gladly accepted the pages with my careful, yet shaky, handwriting, took them to work with him, bound the pages together with an industrial grade stapler, and brought home my first "novel". I've been writing ever since.

I didn't take myself too seriously when I started to write this book. It was a hobby, just as my previous written work had been. I was simply attempting to stay busy during the cold Michigan winter of 2014. After a few late nights of pecking away on my laptop I thought I had something worth allowing other people to read. The story of Abbie and Michael began to come to life so I had to run with it.

As I go through the list of people to thank, my son, Holden, is at the top. Thank you, sweet child, for pushing me to greatness. I hope I've made you proud.

Family, friends, and coworkers that took the time to put their noses in this book, thank you. All of the encouragement I received during the process kept me motivated and inspired. Some said they were honored to read it, even in its roughest state. However, I am the one that is most honored. Thank you.

Prologue

IT STARTS AS A whisper. A nudge. In some cases, a dream. A quiet voice beckoning from somewhere to take heed, to listen up, to pay attention. The little hairs that stand straight up out of our flesh, or the sensation of our blood running cold, are the indicators that we should open our eyes, look about, and possibly change our course of action. A series of inconsequential events can lead to a crescendo of disaster if we don't react.

All too often, warnings are disregarded, and whispers grow into calls of distress. It is usually in the instances of real danger that the quiet moments of caution are brought to the forefront of our minds. When we suddenly understand what our intuition was trying to explain, it's too late to turn back. If we aren't prepared to act on the whispers, if we don't move when nudged, we must prepare to act after life takes an unexpected turn. Foresight is sweeter than hindsight, but we are seldom allowed such a luxury.

Some would say that when the dust settles, all that remains are fragments of what we had hoped for. What we are ultimately left with is a life we would have ended up with all along. Others would say that their lives would have turned out differently had they not hushed the voice in the back of their minds. If only they could go back in time, right the course, and steer straight.

Part
1

1

ABBIE

RAIN. AS ABBIE PETERSON raced up the street, she fumbled through her shoulder bag for an umbrella. With coffee in one hand and a newspaper in the other, the task proved to be more difficult than she had anticipated. Frustrated, drenched, and slightly chilly, she gave up looking for the umbrella and quickened her pace. She was running late for work—again—and was hoping to sneak into the diner unnoticed.

"You're late." No such luck. Karl, her boss and owner of Kate & Karl's Place, met her at the door. He was an older gentleman, in his late sixties, who opened the diner with his wife, Kate, twenty-five years earlier.

"I know," she said as she quickly glided past him and ducked behind the counter. She swept up her long, brunette hair into a bun and tied an apron around her small waist.

"Abbie—"

"I'm sorry, Karl," she managed to say. "I loaned my bike to the neighbor boy, and he has yet to return it. He was supposed to bring it by last night, but when I went to leave this morning, it wasn't by the back porch."

"David?" Karl clarified.

"Yes, David," Abbie said.

Karl crossed his arms over his large, round belly and stroked his white beard with one hand. He said, "I lent that boy my garden rake two weeks back, and I haven't seen it since." His voice trailed off and his mind seemed to wander as he pondered the irresponsibility of a fourteen-year-old boy.

Abbie quickly got to work and left Karl alone with his thoughts. She didn't want him to recall that she had been late for work three days in a row. She had moved to the neighborhood two months ago without a job or a vehicle and met Karl and Kate Whitaker as she spent her last ten dollars on a meal at their diner. The couple instantly fell in love with Abbie's charming innocence and friendly attitude, so they offered her a job at the diner, a rental house a few miles away, and a bicycle. She did not want Karl to perceive her tardiness as ungratefulness.

Abbie Peterson grew up in southern Georgia. She was an only child, raised by her father, Henry, after her mother, Annabelle, passed away when she was three years old. At twenty-two years old, Abbie bought a bus ticket and headed to North Carolina. When she got off the bus near the diner two months earlier, she knew she had found her new home. The town was small, the people were friendly, and it was a perfect place for her to figure out what she wanted to do with her life.

As the morning turned into afternoon, the rain let up. It was only mid-May, but it was already hot and muggy. Hungry customers bustled in and out as Abbie happily took their orders while making small talk with everyone. Since moving into the sleepy little coastal town outside of Wilmington, she had gotten to know pretty much everyone who came into the diner. The customers loved her sweet Georgia charm and the way she seemed to fit right in. She was a natural beauty, although she didn't seem aware of it. Her wardrobe consisted of jeans or shorts, plain T-shirts, and flip-flops. Her hair was usually in a bun, and she hardly wore a dab of makeup. She had large blue eyes and flawless skin, and a way about her that made everyone feel special. She had come to know each person who came into the diner by name as well as the roles they played in the community. They shared many stories with her, and she shared some of her own, telling them about her father and what it was like to grow up in Georgia.

After the lunch rush had died down, she made herself a turkey sandwich, propped herself up on a stool, and ate quietly. She pulled her cell phone from her apron and texted her father: *Miss you. Love you.*

He texted back: *Me too, kiddo.*

Henry Peterson was a man of few words, but she didn't mind. Abbie and her father had always had a quiet understanding that no matter how far apart they were, they were each other's best friend. When all of her friends went off to college after graduation, she stayed behind. Part of her hadn't decided what she wanted to study, and the other part of her didn't want to leave her father all alone. He had devoted his entire life to raising Abbie and always made sure she was happy and loved, despite the fact that her mom was gone. He had never remarried. In fact, Abbie couldn't recall him ever dating anyone. But nearly four years after she graduated, she was dying to get out of Georgia, even if it meant they both had to be independent of one another.

The day she hugged her father good-bye at the bus station was bittersweet for both of them. She wasn't sure where she wanted to go or what she wanted to do, but she was excited at the same time for the opportunity to figure it out along the way. Henry was nervous, but not for her. He was afraid of being alone. Not having another person to take care of seemed to strip him of his identity of being a father. He knew Abbie would be fine. He could see a strength in her she hadn't yet discovered on her own. But she soon would. He was sure of it.

Abbie had just finished her sandwich when an old, beat-up blue pickup truck with the windows rolled down pulled into the parking lot. The truck appeared to be at least twenty years old, with rust on the bumper and a few dents on the back end. It rumbled into the parking spot, and three men who appeared to be in their late twenties hopped out. They wore T-shirts, blue jeans, and work boots, all of which were covered in dirt. Abbie assumed they most likely did construction or mechanical work. She quickly washed her hands, grabbed a notepad, and met them at the booth where they chose to sit.

"What can I get you guys?" Abbie asked as they looked over the menus. She immediately locked eyes with the man who sat opposite the other two. He had dark, messy hair, a week's worth of stubble on his face, and the most sparkling blue eyes she had ever seen. She quickly looked away as soon as he caught her gaze. The other two had sandy blond hair. One was tall, slender, and wore glasses. The other was shorter and stockier than the first. The three of them ended their conversation midsentence and looked up at her. They couldn't help but notice how attractive she was.

"Um, what do you have on special?" the gentleman with the glasses asked.

"Clam chowder," she said matter-of-factly. "Kate's recipe is the best within a hundred miles."

"Is that so?" he asked flirtatiously.

"I wouldn't lie about Kate's clam chowder," she said with a smile. "I'd get that with a turkey sandwich."

Satisfied with her answer, he closed his menu and said, "Well, that's what I'll have then."

"I'll have the same," said the shorter blond, "with a side of fries."

"Side of fries," she repeated as she jotted it down. "And for you?" she asked, pointing her pen in the direction of the man with the dark hair.

He was still gazing at her. She had caught him off guard, and he quickly opened his menu and browsed his options. "How's the country-fried steak?" he asked, slightly flustered.

"It's not as good as one you'll find in southern Georgia, but it'll do," Abbie said with a smile.

"Is that where your accent is from?" he asked, intrigued.

"Born and raised," she said. "You're going to want to eat that with Kate's mashed potatoes and gravy," she added. "They are the best."

"Sounds great," he said. They locked eyes again. Abbie hated how obviously she was staring at him, but she couldn't help it. She could tell just by looking at him that he was kind and that there was something about him that made her want to get to know him more. She tore her eyes from his, scooped up the menus, smiled, and quickly went to get their sodas.

Good grief, Abbie, it's just a guy, she thought to herself as she quietly shook her head next to the soda machine. *Get it together.* She returned to their table, drinks in hand. This time, she was careful not to stare so obviously at his striking features. The three gentlemen were laughing and joking among each other. She smiled politely as she handed them their beverages.

"So you're from Georgia?" the blond with the glasses asked, making conversation.

"Yes," she said, "I actually just moved to town a few months ago." All three of them were looking at her. Abbie suddenly regretted her messy hair and the jeans she wore for the second day in a row. She typically didn't spend too much time on her appearance, but today she wished she had.

4

The handsome, dark-haired man took a sip of his soda and said, "Do you like it so far?"

She smiled and nodded. "Yes," she said confidently. "Everyone is so friendly and down to earth." Her nerves started to ease, and she asked them, "Are y'all from the area?"

The three of them nodded in unison. "I'm Stephen, by the way," said the blond with glasses, raising his hand slightly at her, "and this is Paul," he said, gesturing to the other blond.

It was then that those brilliant blue eyes from the opposite side of the table caught hers once more, and when he spoke he said, "I'm Michael. I own a landscaping company in Wilmington. These guys work for me." He pointed to the two across from him. "We like to swing by here for lunch sometimes. My parents grew up with Karl and Kate."

"I'm Abbie," she said as she tried to drink in each syllable he had just recited. She wanted to wrap up each word only to open it up later and replay it in her mind so she would never forget what they sounded like. "Yes, they are the sweetest couple," she agreed, snapping back to reality. "Kate and Karl were so nice to offer me a job and a place to stay as soon as I got into town. You don't find people like that every day."

"Abbie!" one of the other waitresses, Meghan, called to her. "Order's up!"

Abbie quickly excused herself, scooted away from their table, and got back to work. She had neglected her other tables while talking to Stephen, Paul, and Michael. *Michael.* Abbie smiled to herself while she bustled about, serving other patrons at her designated tables. She continued to carry on a conversation with the gentlemen as she brought them their order, refilled their drinks, and brought them their separate checks. Abbie noticed the three of them were getting ready to leave, so she started toward their table, to wish them a great afternoon and, of course, to get a chance to see Michael one last time.

Just then, David, Abbie's neighbor, burst through the door of the diner. He rushed over to her, out of breath. Abbie's attention shifted from Stephen, Paul, and Michael to the boy.

"I'm so sorry, Abbie!" David blurted out as he rushed over to her. "I meant to bring your bike back last night. Honest! But, you see, the thing is—"

5

"Shh, David, it's not a problem," Abbie reassured him, looking past him, just in time to see the three of them heading out the door. Her heart sank.

"I brought it back," David said apologetically. "It's right outside. I even put air in the tires."

Abbie brought her attention back to him, smiled, and said, "Thanks, David." She explained to him that she was not upset, and then she got back to work. She ruffled his hair as she walked past him, toward the empty table where Michael and his coworkers sat. As she started to clear the table, she had noticed they left her a generous tip. Then, out of the corner of her eye, she spotted a neatly folded napkin with some scribbling on it. She reached for it, and her heart jumped out of her chest as she read:

Call me.
—Michael

His phone number was scribbled underneath. She read it several times, making sure it was real. She turned the napkin over and back again in disbelief. Abbie had nearly finished clearing the table when she looked up and saw Michael walk back through the door. She was speechless. She looked down at the napkin, and then looked back up at him as she tried to think of something to say.

Michael ran a hand through his hair, and then pointed toward the napkin, almost embarrassed. "Yeah," he said, "I was just coming to get that."

Her face fell flat. "Oh," she said. She turned a dark shade of red and quickly handed him the napkin.

"No, no, no!" Michael started. "I didn't mean it like that. Oh, gosh, I'm sorry, that's not what I meant." He had an apologetic look on his face and said, "What I meant was, I was going to take that off the table before you saw it."

She drew in her breath, turned away, quickly wiped down the table, and started to hurry away.

"No, that's not what I meant either!" Michael was at a loss for words. He touched her arm and said, "Abbie, let me start over."

She froze and looked up at him. He was standing right in front of her, barely a foot away, looking straight into her eyes. She held her

6

breath as he spoke. "What I meant was, I wanted to come back in here, toss my lame napkin note, and ask you out in person."

Abbie blinked but didn't speak. She wondered if what was happening was real. Was Michael actually standing there, hand on her arm, looking at her, smiling, waiting for her to answer him? *Answer him!*

"Abbie," Michael asked, "can I take you out sometime?"

"Yes," she answered, calmly and confidently.

"Great," he said as he slowly lifted his hand from her arm. "Can I take you out on Friday?"

"Yes, that sounds perfect," she said, trying to contain her excitement. She focused on holding her feet firmly onto the floor because she was convinced that if she moved, she would float away. She memorized his features as he spoke; his chiseled jaw, covered in just the right amount of facial hair, was wavy and messy, but perfect.

"Abbie?"

She snapped back to the present.

"Yes?"

Michael chuckled slightly and said, "Can I get your number so I can call you Friday to pick you up?"

She blinked a few times, guessed that he was repeating himself, and said, "Of course." She blushed a bit and gave him her phone number as he stood there and entered it into his cell phone.

"Thank you," Michael said as he put his phone back in his pocket. He smiled at her, his eyes twinkling, touched her arm again, and said, "I'll see you on Friday."

She smiled back and said, "See you Friday."

Michael turned and walked out of the diner. Abbie sat down on the bench at the booth and caught her breath. She was a bit shocked at what had just happened, but she was elated. With butterflies dancing in her stomach, she finished clearing the table and headed back to the kitchen. On her way, she caught the glances of two other waitresses, Tracey and Meghan. They were smiling at her, and their faces were begging for details about what had just happened with Michael. Once the three of them were in the kitchen, out of earshot of both customers and other coworkers, Tracey and Meghan squealed with delight and urged her to tell them what happened.

"Whoa, calm down," Abbie said, trying to hush them. She put the dirty dishes in the sink and began spraying them off with water. The kitchen was small, each wall lined with shelves containing boxes of nonperishables, dishes, cups, silverware, and pots and pans. Meghan hopped up on the counter by the sink, and Tracey sat on a step stool.

"Tell us everything," Tracey begged.

"We saw what happened, but we need details," Meghan chimed in, her face beaming.

Abbie grinned and shook her head, still speechless. "I don't even know if I could describe it," she said, laughing. "Do you both know Michael?" She continued cleaning the dishes, mostly out of nervousness.

"Know him?" Tracey joked, "We've both had crushes on him since we've both worked here. He's been our eye candy for going on five years. And he has *never* made a move like that."

Abbie was somewhat surprised. At twenty-three and twenty-four, Tracey and Meghan were young, attractive girls, who always seemed to be dating someone. They both were thin, had long blonde hair, and wore makeup. Both of them could be seen at the diner wearing cutoff shorts and skimpy tops. Abbie could see either of the three gentlemen she had just met asking either one of them out on a date. She started to wonder why Michael had asked her.

Meghan interrupted her thoughts. "C'mon, Abbie, what did he say?"

Abbie repeated every detail of what happened, from the time his truck pulled into the parking lot until the moment he left. They stared at her in awe as if she were describing how she rescued a puppy from being swept down a turbulent river, when all she was actually doing was telling them what Michael smelled like up close, lawnmower gasoline and fresh-cut grass, and how the kindness of his eyes matched the tone of his voice.

Other waitresses made their way back to the kitchen to unload dirty dishes gathered from tables. Abbie, Tracey, and Meghan glanced at each other and decided to get back to work before they could finish their conversation. Abbie floated around the diner for the remainder of her shift with a permanent smile beaming from her face.

Her shift ended just as the sun started to hang low in the sky. She hung up her apron, counted her tips at the front counter, stuffed them into her shoulder bag, and headed out the door. She located her bike that David had dropped off earlier that afternoon and began to pedal home. The air outside was still warm, but less thick and humid than it was earlier that day. She could hardly tell that it had rained that morning.

She headed west of the diner, pedaling slowly, shielding her eyes from the sun. Trees lined the streets she headed down, and the sound of the leaves in the wind soothed her as she breezed past. The houses she passed on her way home became fewer and farther in between as she reached her destination.

The house that she rented from Kate and Karl was fairly modest. The outside was neat and tidy with flower boxes on the windows in the front and a small garden in the backyard. It had one bedroom, one bathroom, a small kitchen, and a living room. It came furnished, with a twin bed, couch, and rocking chair, and although they were a bit shabby, Abbie didn't mind.

She parked her bike by the front porch, grabbed the mail from the mailbox, and went inside. She put her shoulder bag and the mail on the kitchen counter and walked into the living room. She plopped down on the couch, exhausted, and thought about what had happened that day with Michael. She hadn't been on a date since, well, ever.

Abbie was completely unprepared for Friday. She stood up from the couch and headed into the bedroom. She flung open her closet and rifled through her clothes looking for something to wear on her date. Dissatisfied with her choices and a bit desperate, she considered asking Tracey or Meghan if she could borrow something from them. They were, after all, just about the same size. She quickly shut that idea out of her mind, feeling as though the types of clothes they wore were not appropriate for a first date. Or for any occasion, for that matter. Instead, she decided to buy something new.

She opened the top drawer of her dresser, where a stack of twenty-dollar bills had accumulated in an envelope under a pile of clothing from extra tips she had earned so she could afford to take a few classes at the community center in the fall. She justified borrowing some of the money for a new outfit. She pulled a few bills out of the envelope and walked to the kitchen to put them in her shoulder bag. She decided she would go shopping the next day.

Abbie lay in bed as night began to fall. That day was by far the best she had had since she moved away from home. She pictured Michael, and his perfect features, and pondered what their date would be like as she drifted off to sleep.

2

MICHAEL

MICHAEL HAMMOND FINISHED UP at his last job just as the sun was going down. Ribbons of orange, pink, and yellow laced the sky, between clouds that began to grow dark. Bullfrogs sang in the marsh, and cicadae chirped in the weeds. He loaded his tools and lawn equipment in the back of his truck and slammed the tailgate shut. Wiping the sweat from his brow, he made his way to the front of his truck and waved after Stephen and Paul, who were also getting ready to leave. He got in his truck to head home. On his way he stopped at the convenience store and grabbed a couple of frozen burritos and a six pack of beer.

As Michael drove home, he focused on the hum of the tires and the rumble of the motor as he thought about Abbie. He had never met a girl quite like her. She was effortlessly beautiful, he decided, simple but not plain. Michael adored the way Abbie's smile filled the entire restaurant earlier that afternoon. Her kindness didn't remind him of the way most people were kind, out of duty, but it was born deep within her soul and radiated from her, no matter the situation. He wanted to know her. She had a goodness in her that he wanted in his life.

Michael's truck made its way to the outskirts of town, where paved roads turned to dirt. He was raised on those roads, and he knew them like the back of his hand. He had memorized every hill, every dip, every turn. Michael knew every driveway and house that he passed, as well as the families that lived in them. His truck slowed as his tires went from smooth pavement to rough gravel of his dirt road. He wound his way for a mile or so before arriving home.

Home was a large, three-story farmhouse that rested far back from the road. Michael had inherited the farm from his grandparents, Eugene and Pearl Hammond. It had been in the family for five generations. The house had a large porch that wrapped from the front of the house to the back. Dark blue shutters lined the windows of the white house. A carriage house, which once provided lodging for servants, stood nearly a hundred yards from the back of the main house, and was also white with blue shutters. It was small, with but one main living area and a washroom.

The property was picturesque. A large, red hip roof barn rose up from behind the main house, and a long wooden fence surrounded the pasture adjacent to the barn, near a garden that Michael planted and harvested every year. On the south side of the property stretched fifty acres of farmland. Mature shade trees lined the main property and provided relief from the sun in the summertime. A large pond rested beyond the house, past the barn. The far end of the property was shielded by forty wooded acres. Michael spent a good portion of his childhood exploring those woods, climbing trees, making forts, and hunting.

Michael was the only child of Clark and Elisabeth Hammond, as well as an only grandchild. He grew up in his parents' home, on a small parcel of land adjoining the Hammond Farm. Clark and Elisabeth both worked in Wilmington but preferred the small-town life in the country. Clark was an engineer, and Elisabeth, a nurse. They both had very demanding schedules, so Michael spent most of his time on the farm with his grandparents. Michael was glad to have had the experience to not only grow up on the farm, but to also call it his own as an adult. Eugene had wanted his grandson to inherit the farm ever since Michael was a young boy. Before Eugene passed away three years earlier, he told Michael to raise a family there, just as he had. Michael fully intended to do just that, but he had yet to find the right woman.

Or maybe he had. Michael pondered that thought as he pulled the truck into the drive and parked. He grabbed his beer and his burritos and got out of the truck. While gazing out at the property, he saw the sun dipping below the horizon. Nearly all of the color had dimmed from the sky. The shadows that typically cast themselves on the sides of the house and barn had drifted off to sleep. Michael stood in the driveway and recalled the good times he had on the farm when he was a child. Memories of swimming in the pond during hot summers and of sledding down hills in the winters flooded his mind. He enjoyed helping his grandfather tend to the animals and helping his grandmother bake pies in the kitchen. Eugene had taught him how to drive a tractor and milk a cow, and Pearl had taught him how to make iced tea and play the piano. Pearl passed away when Michael was fourteen, and Eugene joined his bride twelve years later. Michael kept their wishes and moved to the farm six months after his grandfather's funeral. He did his best to keep up with demands of the crops, animals, the grounds, and the house itself, as well as his landscaping business. It proved to be too much work after two short years, so he sold the livestock and rented out most of the farmland and some of the equipment to other farmers. The red barn now stood empty with the exception of a few stray cats that lived in the loft. He longed for the day that he would meet the right woman, marry her, and build the life that his grandparents had on that farm. He hoped Abbie was that woman.

Michael climbed the steps to the porch of the house and walked in the back door. His two black labs, Sam and Bull, met him in the kitchen. He knelt to the floor and gave them each a lavish amount of hugs and kisses. He played with them for a bit and then sent them both outside. They had been cooped up all day and were excited to run free.

Once Sam and Bull were outside, Michael cracked open a beer and heated up a burrito. Food and drink in hand, he walked out to the front porch. He recalled sitting on that same front porch with his grandmother, helping her shuck corn and trim green beans from the garden in the summertime while they drank lemonade. He sat down on the front stoop and took a long pull of his beer. He loved evenings like this. The smell of summer filled the air, and the sound of the country echoed a calming silence. He was comforted by the familiarity of his surroundings. Two dark figures bobbed up and down in the grass and made their way toward him. Sam and Bull were exhausted as they made their way over to him, tails wagging. Michael saved two scraps from his burrito and fed them to each one as they lay down at his feet.

"Good boys," he said to them. He scratched them both behind their ears and then rubbed their bellies. He had rescued both dogs just after he moved to the farm. The house seemed entirely too empty when he moved in, so when he saw an ad in the local paper for a free litter of puppies, he went to check it out. He only had intentions of bringing home one dog. He saw Bull first, the runt of the litter. Eight puppies lay on a blanket tucked inside a large cardboard box. Smaller than the rest, Bull climbed over his brothers and sisters and made his way toward Michael. Michael picked him up, and Bull instantly covered him in kisses. Not a moment later, Sam stumbled over the other dogs as well and sat patiently, begging Michael with his large brown eyes to take him too. Michael figured Bull needed a companion, so he took Sam as well. The three of them were the best of friends. On weekends, when Michael would drive into town for groceries, Sam and Bull rode in the truck with him. The dogs followed Michael around the farm as he tended to the gardens and the repairs on the barn.

Michael finished his beer, stood up, and headed inside. Sam and Bull followed. He grabbed another beer and cracked it open. He leaned against the island in the middle of the kitchen, took a sip, and gazed about the room. The kitchen, as well as the rest of the house, had the original hardwood floors. He had helped his grandfather refinish them five years ago. The house was filled with antique furniture that Pearl and Eugene had since they were newlyweds. Michael had incorporated a few modern pieces of décor and furniture, but for the most part, he preferred to preserve the farmhouse atmosphere that his grandparents had created.

Michael, Sam, and Bull wandered into the living room. He watched TV, flipping through the channels, not exactly paying attention to what was on, before heading to bed. He wondered if he and Abbie would ever share that same couch, aimlessly flipping through channels together. He brushed the thought from his mind and turned the TV off. The floorboards creaked beneath his feet as he ascended the stairs to the master bedroom. Michael stripped his grimy work clothes off and tossed them on the bedroom floor. Sam and Bull lay at the foot of the bed. Michael walked back out into the hallway and grabbed a towel from the linen closet. He headed down the hall to the bathroom and flipped on the light. A claw-foot tub with an overhead shower stood against the wall, next to a pedestal sink. He turned the hot water on full blast and let the bathroom fill with steam before stepping into the shower. Once he climbed into the tub, he stood and let the water pour over his head, and he ran his fingers through his hair. He allowed the steam to fill his lungs as the water beaded over his chest and back, washing the day away.

3

HENRY

THE NEWSPAPER CRINKLED BETWEEN Henry's fingers as he sat at the kitchen table while he drank his coffee. He had just gotten a text from Abbie during her lunch break at work telling him she loved him and missed him. He couldn't help but beam with pride as he thought of her. She was doing so much more with her life than he was at her age. Henry hoped she was finding everything she had gone looking for in North Carolina.

As he sipped on his coffee, Henry's mind traveled back in time to the night that he had met Abbie's mother, Annabelle. He was barely twenty-four years old, fresh out of the service, and single. A few of his friends had taken him out for his birthday. Annabelle was tending bar at the local pub, and Henry and his friends had her serve them drinks that night. She was breathtakingly beautiful. She was tan, tall, and thin, with long dark hair, high cheekbones, dark eyes, and full lips. Henry knew she was out of his league. His friends flirted with her, and she flirted back. A few times he noticed her glance his way, but he didn't think much of it. Henry and his friends drank heavily that night. He couldn't recall a time he had been so drunk. Annabelle had called a couple of cabs for them just before the bar had closed, as she helped him and his friends stumble their way outside to wait for their rides home. While they waited, Henry managed to vomit on the concrete next to Annabelle. Embarrassed and feeling terrible, he uttered several apologies while she simply laughed and helped him sit down on the curb. Henry would later learn that she was always this gracious. He lifted his head, looked at Annabelle and slurred, "I don't know how I could ever repay you for your kindness."

She smiled and said, "You can take me out to dinner." He promised he would as the cabs arrived to take them home. Annabelle laughed and shook her head as Henry and his friends rode away.

Henry nursed a hangover the following day. Despite feeling lousy, he showered, got dressed, and headed out to find Annabelle. The pub wasn't far, so he decided to walk. He wanted to apologize for his actions the night before. Henry saw her, before she saw him, wiping down tables and looking even more beautiful than he had remembered her from the previous evening. "Annabelle?" he asked, getting her attention.

Annabelle stopped what she was doing, set her washrag down, and turned to look at him. "Hey, there!" she said enthusiastically. "How are you feeling?" she joked.

Henry blushed and smiled. When he spoke, he said, "Annabelle, I wanted to apologize about last night. I honestly never drink like that, and it obviously got out of hand. I'm so sorry about the scene we caused."

She smirked and asked, "So you came by to apologize?"

"Yes," he said sincerely.

"Hmmm," she said flirtatiously. "Here I thought maybe you had come by to ask me to dinner."

By this time, Henry's face was a deep shade of red. "I didn't know if you were serious last night or not," he stammered.

She stood there, one hand on her hip and an eyebrow raised, waiting for him to ask.

Henry straightened up and said, "Annabelle, I'd like to take you out to dinner. Would you do me the honor?"

She smiled, picked up her washrag, and got back to work. Her eyes stayed on him, and she said, "My shift ends at eight. Pick me up then. I like steak."

A smile spread across his face. He nodded at her and said, "Sounds good. I'll be here at eight o'clock." He left the pub and walked back home, this time with a slight spring in his step. Henry picked up Annabelle promptly at eight. He obliged Annabelle's request for a steak dinner. She did most of the talking that night. He loved listening to her. She was young, twenty years old, outgoing and strong, sharp but imaginative.

Henry fell in love with her that night. He walked her home, and she leaned in to kiss him. They said good night, and she stole his heart.

They went out twice more that week, and saw each other every day the week after that. Annabelle was crazy about Henry, and he was madly in love with her. After they had been dating for a month, Henry purchased a ring and asked Annabelle to marry him. She said yes. They were married six months later at her parents' home in Savannah. One year later, Abigail Elise Peterson was born. Henry and Annabelle were head over heels in love, not only with each other, but with Abbie. Abbie taught her parents about patience and joy. A love grew between the three of them that was bigger than Henry could have imagined.

By the time Abbie was a year old, Annabelle started to experience headaches. They grew worse over time, often leaving her in bed for days at a time. Henry encouraged Annabelle to see a doctor, but she was too stubborn. One evening, Henry came home from work to find Annabelle lying on the floor, unconscious, with Abbie crying on the floor beside her. He scooped up both girls in his arms, trying to calm Abbie and, at the same time, wake his wife. He called an ambulance, which showed up minutes later. The three of them were rushed to the hospital. Once Annabelle was conscious, Henry and Abbie were able to see and talk with her. She seemed fine but sleepy. A doctor had come in awhile later and asked Henry to sit down. He held Abbie on his lap, and she played with the buttons on his shirt.

"Mr. Peterson, Mrs. Peterson," the doctor said, acknowledging them. The doctor spoke delicately of Annabelle's condition and explained to them that she had experienced a seizure caused by a massive malignant brain tumor. Panic spread across Henry's face as he looked at his wife. She looked calm, even serene, but a tear spilled down her cheek. The doctor went on to explain that the cancer was very advanced and that she was terminally ill.

Henry begged Annabelle to seek a second opinion and to undergo whatever treatment was available to her. He couldn't lose her. Abbie was barely two years old at the time, and the thought of his daughter living without her mother shattered his entire world.

Although Annabelle was at peace with her diagnosis, she fought for her life. She fought for Henry. She fought for Abbie. The chemotherapy and radiation put her through unfathomable amounts of agony and sickness, but she continued to fight. Her hair fell out, and her skin grew pale, and still, she fought.

The three of them spent the majority of a year in and out of the hospital. Henry had remortgaged their home to afford Annabelle's treatment and worked double shifts when he could get them. Family members pitched in to care for Abbie. Annabelle could feel the burdens lying heavy on her husband.

Henry recalled one day at the hospital in particular. He and Abbie lay sleeping on a cot in Annabelle's room. It was barely dawn, but Annabelle was awake, watching her family sleep. Henry could feel her eyes on him, and he slowly roused himself awake.

"Hey," Annabelle said sweetly.

"Hey yourself," he smiled back. He saw something different in his wife that day. Surrender. He could tell, just by looking at her, in the dim light of the hospital room, with the covers pulled up around her frail body, that she was done fighting. In that moment, he gave her a knowing look and said, "I love you, Annabelle."

She blinked back tears and smiled. "Come here," she whispered. She pointed at Abbie, asleep, and said, "Her too." Henry picked up their daughter, and she nestled into his shoulder. Annabelle slowly sat up, and Henry handed Abbie to her. "I want to show you something," she said.

Henry sat down next to his wife and daughter. Annabelle combed Abbie's hair with her hands. The child yawned and rubbed her eyes as she woke up and sat in front of her mother. Annabelle took three sections of Abbie's hair in her hands, turned to Henry, and calmly said, "You're going to need to learn how to braid."

Tears filled Henry's eyes. "Annabelle—" he choked.

"Shh. Watch." And she continued to braid Abbie's hair. Henry nodded while he sobbed next to them, reassuring his wife he could braid their daughter's hair. When Annabelle had finished, she took Henry's hand in hers and said, "Please take me home."

So Henry took Annabelle home. She was able to be kept comfortable and pain-free. She spent most of her time in bed, but occasionally was able to sit in a chair by an open window. One night Annabelle and Henry lay beside each other, whispering in the dark. They reminisced about how they first met, their wedding day, and the day Abbie was born, as well as other important moments that they had shared. Annabelle's breaths became heavy, and Henry knew the time had come to say

17

good-bye. He kissed her mouth, her forehead, and her eyelids while he placed his hand upon her cheek. Annabelle yawned, and Henry helped her roll onto her side. With her back toward him, he held her close and she fell asleep. Henry stayed awake all night. When Annabelle's body started to shake, Henry assured her that he was right there with her. He continued to hold her, long after she had left her body, and cried until morning.

The following weeks were a blur. The only thing that he would remember vividly was Abbie's face crumpling when he had told her that her mother had gone to heaven. Looking back, it was unclear to Henry how he and Abbie made it through the first year without Annabelle. At first, he felt as though she wasn't truly gone, but was on a vacation, or in the next room. Henry hadn't truly acknowledged that she was not coming back until the visitors and the do-gooders had stopped coming around, when meals were no longer sent over, and when the phone stopped ringing. A few times he had spoken her name aloud out of habit. The silence that echoed back at him was deafening.

Henry fell into a deep depression, and he found it very difficult to take care of Abbie. He was able to perform the motions of getting her dressed every day, serving her breakfast, or taking her for walks, but, deep inside, the void he felt drove a wedge between him and his daughter. Abbie was the spitting image of her mother. Everything she did reflected a piece of Annabelle that was gone. It took Henry a long time to see those pieces as parts of Annabelle that were still with them. Henry also had bouts of very real anger toward Annabelle for dying, especially when Abbie disobeyed him and screamed for her mother. His heart broke for Abbie in those moments because he had wanted the exact same thing. But then there were times where Abbie crawled onto her father's lap, kissed him on the cheek, and said, "I love you, Daddy."

Time passed, and soon the loss of Annabelle became manageable. He made a conscious decision to keep her memory alive. It was important to him that Abbie know her mother in a way that she would have wanted to have been remembered. So he told her stories. He told her stories about how Annabelle selflessly cared for her in the late-night hours when she was a baby. Abbie loved hearing how, when she cried, her mother was the only one that could calm her. Sharing memories of her with his daughter also helped Henry remember Annabelle when it became hard for him to recall every feature of her face, what her hair smelled like, or how her skin felt. Besides keeping her memory alive in Abbie, Henry taught her how to tie her shoes, ride a bike, throw a football, cook, and even how to dance. Abbie taught him how to smile. Together, they became strong.

Henry often thought that Abbie should have a mother figure in her life, but he never became comfortable with dating after Annabelle's passing. She had set the bar high, and although he had met a few nice women when Abbie was a teenager, nothing ever came of it. He knew it wouldn't have been fair to anyone if he was constantly comparing her to his wife.

Henry's mind made its way back to the present. He folded up his newspaper and put his coffee cup in the sink. Abbie, Henry decided, was the best thing that he had done with his life. He was proud of her for believing in herself and being brave enough to spread her wings in North Carolina. He smiled to himself and was thankful for each and every moment he spent being her father.

4

MICHAEL

SAM AND BULL RACED into the kitchen early Thursday morning at the sound of their breakfast being poured into their bowls. Michael prepared a thermos of coffee for the road and then threw on a long sleeved flannel shirt and jeans. After he laced up his work boots, he locked up the house, hopped into the truck, and headed toward Southport to meet Stephen and Paul at their first job site. It was 7:00 a.m., and the sun was already shining. The air was cooler and crisper than the previous day. He rolled both windows of the pickup down and breathed in the morning.

Stephen and Paul had arrived at the job site just before Michael. They were scheduled for routine maintenance on the grounds of an office park that morning. Later that day they would move on to an apartment complex, an outdoor shopping mall, and two residential properties. The three of them were in for a long day. Stephen and Paul were sitting on the curb of the parking lot as Michael pulled up, their tools and equipment already unloaded. Both were dressed in hooded sweatshirts and work boots. Michael nodded to them as he parked the truck.

"Mornin', guys," Michael called to them.

They waved back. "Morning," they said in unison.

The three of them got to work right away. Paul hopped on the lawnmower, Michael worked on weed whacking and edging, and Stephen trimmed hedges. Michael enjoyed working with his friends. They had met in high school, each in different grades, but were very close. Michael was the youngest, at twenty-nine. Stephen and Paul were thirty and thirty-one. At fifteen, Michael started mowing lawns for friends and family to earn extra money. A year later, he had more customers than he could handle, so Stephen and Paul began to help. Their work was top-notch. Word of mouth of their services traveled fast. By the time they graduated high school, they had established customers in three counties. The three of them had intentions of continuing to work full time once they entered college. Michael followed in his father's footsteps and studied engineering. Stephen was interested in biology, and Paul, computer science. Stephen ended up dropping out after his first year of school because he had been more interested in dating than studying. However, he continued to work for Michael. Like Stephen, Paul realized that school, work, and a social life were difficult to maintain. He continued to go to school full time and work for Michael part time. Unfortunately, Paul didn't graduate either.

Michael stayed the course. He took a full load of classes each semester, including summers, as well as worked between forty and sixty hours per week. He paid for each semester out of pocket, so he wouldn't have to bear the burden of student loans after graduation. He went on occasional dates, but he didn't have much time for a social life. He dated one girl steadily for six months about a year after he graduated, but that had been his most serious relationship to date.

Michael, Stephen, and Paul had been through everything together. Paul had gotten married when he was twenty-five but then was divorced two years later. Stephen and Michael had both stood up with him on his wedding day and took him out for drinks the day his divorce was final. Stephen's father was diagnosed with cancer the following year, and each of them pitched in to help his family, whether it was making a mortgage payment, helping with repairs around the house, or running errands. Stephen and Paul supported Michael by attending the funeral of his grandfather and later helped him move to the farm.

The sun grew hotter as the day progressed. Hooded sweatshirts were tossed in the back of the truck, and Michael tied his flannel shirt around his waist. They grabbed burgers and fries for lunch and sat on the back of Michael's tailgate. They talked as they ate.

Stephen asked Michael, "So are you excited for your big date tomorrow, lover boy?" Michael grinned, with food in his mouth, and jokingly punched Stephen in the arm.

Paul piped up, "Dude, I have never seen you so googly-eyed over a girl before."

Michael shrugged and continued to eat. It was very rare that he asked women out, so Stephen and Paul were both surprised when he left the note at the diner for Abbie. They were even more surprised when he went back inside to ask her out in person. Whether Michael knew it yet or not, his friends knew that he was already head over heels for Abbie.

"Where are you taking her?" Paul asked.

"I was thinking about maybe The Pier," Michael said. The Pier was a unique place for a date. The long boardwalk jutted out over the water and was lined with vendors and crowded with tourists. It was bustling with people, no matter the time of day, but scenic at the same time. There were several places to eat, depending on what they were in the mood for, from fancy restaurants to hot dog stands. The three of them agreed that it was a good place for a first date.

They finished up their lunch and got back to work. They were in a small neighborhood, digging up old stumps, cleaning up overgrown bushes, and cutting the grass. Michael was mowing while Paul tended to the stumps, and Stephen, the bushes. Paul fired up the chainsaw and cut away at a stump that was being particularly stubborn. Michael had his headphones in but could still hear the hum of the lawnmower and the buzz of the chainsaw. His back was to Stephen and Paul as he walked in neat rows across the lawn. He didn't think anything of it when he heard the chainsaw shut off. However, he instinctively whipped around when he heard a bloodcurdling scream coming from Paul's direction.

All Michael saw was the blood. He wasn't sure how it happened, but Paul was on the ground, screaming in agony as the lower half of his leg was drenched in blood. He had somehow sliced his calf wide open while working on the stump. Michael raced over to Paul.

"Call nine-one-one!" Michael shouted to Stephen. Stephen ran to the truck to grab a cell phone. Michael slid to the ground and grabbed Paul. "I gotcha," Michael said to him, trying to control the panic in his voice. Paul's face was turning pale. His eyes pleaded for Michael to help him. Michael quickly removed his belt and wrapped it around Paul's leg just below the knee. He yanked it tight, simulating a tourniquet. In doing so he saw muscle and bone beneath the tear in Paul's jeans. Michael quickly removed his flannel shirt and wrapped that around

Paul's wound and tried to stop the bleeding. He then propped it up on the stump near Paul.

"Is it bad?" Paul cried between gritted teeth.

"Nah," Michael lied. He looked Paul in the eyes and said as calmly as he could, "You're going to be fine, man." Despite Michael's best efforts to control the blood loss, it was everywhere. The flannel shirt was soaked through.

C'mon, Michael said to himself. *Where is Stephen? Hell, where is the damn ambulance?*

Just then Stephen came rushing over to them. "They are on their way!" he called out. "They will be here any—" Stephen stopped short. "Oh god," he said. He doubled over and vomited.

Paul shot a panicked looked at Michael.

"Hey," Michael said in a serious voice to Paul. "Don't look at him. Look at me. This is nothing." Michael pointed to the leg. Sirens blared in the distance. Paul became short of breath. Stephen sat with his head between his knees to keep from passing out. Although Michael was the youngest of the three, he felt like an older brother looking after his younger siblings, or like a captain of a ship, steering them to calm waters.

Paramedics raced to the scene, and within minutes Paul was given a proper tourniquet, an IV, pain meds, and some oxygen. The three of them piled into the ambulance and were rushed to the hospital. Neither of them said a word while in the back of the bus. Michael and Stephen were in a fog. Before they knew it, they were in the waiting room of the hospital while Paul was whisked away to surgery.

After Michael got over the shock of what happened not thirty minutes earlier, he sat forward in his chair and pulled out his cell phone. He called Paul's mother and asked her to come. He also called his customers for the rest of the day as well as the following day and explained that there had been a family emergency and that he would have to reschedule their services.

Paul's family arrived, and a few hours later they were able to see him. He was out of surgery and in stable condition. Michael and Stephen stayed in the waiting room while Paul's family went in to see him. Michael and Stephen were the only two in the waiting room at one point. Michael was distracting himself from reality by playing a game on his phone.

Stephen spoke for the first time in hours. "So, where did you learn that?"

Michael looked up at Stephen. "Learn what?" he asked.

"What to do with his leg," he stated, recalling Michael's quick response to the situation.

Michael stopped to think. Up until that point he hadn't thought about what had happened. He just acted on instinct. "I saw my grandpa do something similar to one of our horses that was injured when I was a kid," he remembered. "I think I responded the way anyone else would have in an emergency." As soon as he said it, he wished he hadn't, as he recalled Stephen's reaction to the injury.

Stephen chuckled, embarrassed. "Yeah. You don't have to act so modest. You were awesome. I think it's safe to say I can't handle these types of situations."

"Well I'm just glad I was there to help," Michael said humbly.

It was getting late, and Paul's family began filing out of his hospital room. Each and every one of them thanked Michael and Stephen for helping to save Paul. When his family had cleared out, Michael and Stephen went in to see him. They stood by his bed, unsure of what to say. He sat slightly propped up, his leg wrapped and elevated. Paul gave the two of them a medicated smirk and a thumbs- up. The three of them knew that Paul had been very lucky. Michael patted Paul on the shoulder. They both knew what the other was thinking, and they both knew their sentiments didn't need to be spoken aloud.

"Dang, Paul," Stephen said, breaking the silence. He reached for Paul's chart that was at the end of the bed, "A hundred and sixteen staples!"

Paul smiled groggily. His voice was hoarse from being intubated, but he managed to say, "Consider this my two-week notice."

5

ABBIE

IT WAS LATE WHEN Abbie got home Thursday evening. She had unexpectedly worked a double shift because Meghan had wanted the night off at the last minute. Abbie didn't mind, even though she knew she would be exhausted as soon as she agreed to stay late. She needed the extra money, and figured it would help the day pass quickly as well as take her mind off of her upcoming date with Michael.

Abbie had stopped at a consignment store on her way to work and managed to find an outfit to wear on her date the following evening. She picked out a white linen skirt that floated just above her knee, a form-fitting navy blue camisole, and a flowing, gray cardigan. She also bought a pair of brown strappy sandals and a matching brown purse with a skinny strap. She was even happier when her total only came to twenty-five dollars. She decided she should shop at consignment stores more often.

Abbie worked through lunch and dinner and stayed after hours to help clean up. It was past dark by the time she and Karl closed up the diner, so he offered to give her a ride home. She locked up her bike at the shop, and Karl assured her he would also pick her up the next morning for her breakfast shift at 6:00 a.m. They rode to her house in silence. Both of them were tired, and their eyes focused on the headlights shining on the stretch of road before them. The light bobbed up and down with every bump in the road, nearly hypnotizing the two of them. Abbie struggled to stay awake. She wondered if Karl was as tired as she was. Luckily, the trip to Abbie's house wasn't long, and Karl soon dropped her off in her driveway. She yawned and waved after him as he pulled away.

Once in the house, Abbie turned on the lights. She thought about making something to eat, but instead she wandered into the bedroom. She pulled a handful of dollar bills out of her pocket. She put half in the envelope in her dresser drawer and the other half in her purse. She yawned, rubbed her eyes, pulled back the covers on her bed, and lay down, still wearing her clothes. She only had intentions of relaxing for a short while, but she dozed off. When she woke it was the middle of the night. She changed out of her clothes and into pajamas and went to the kitchen to get a drink of water. She stood at the sink, gazing out the kitchen window and staring at the stars.

Her ears perked up when she thought she heard her cell phone ring from the bedroom. She was sure it was her imagination. After all, it was late, and she was half awake. But when she heard it ring a second time, she thought, *Who on earth would be calling at this hour?* Then she remembered her dad, hundreds of miles away. She dropped her glass into the sink and raced into the bedroom. She fumbled through her bag for her phone. She pulled it out and saw an unknown number on the screen.

She panicked. "Hello?" she answered frantically.

"Abbie?" an unfamiliar voice asked.

"Yes?" she asked, fearing the worst.

"It's Michael."

"Michael?" she asked, her head still foggy.

"Yeah," he stammered. "We met yesterday. At the diner?"

"Michael. Yes, of course I'm sorry. I thought my dad was calling." She blinked a few times and tried to shake her nerves. She couldn't believe that the most beautiful man she had ever met was on the other end of the phone call.

"I'm sorry to call so late," he apologized.

"Are you okay?" she asked.

"Yeah. I just wanted to call you. I'm so sorry, Abbie, but I have to break our date for tomorrow."

Now she was fully awake. Her heart rate sped up, and she wasn't sure about what to say. She felt a wave of nausea wash over her. In an instant she could see every chance she had with Michael vanishing into thin air.

"Oh," she said flatly.

"Wait. I want to explain."

Her ears perked up.

"There was a bad accident at work today. Paul was hurt, and I've been at the hospital all day and all night. I want to take you out, but I'm afraid I'll be too exhausted, and I don't want to come across as uninterested."

Abbie sat down on the edge of her bed. Her heart slowed, and she found her voice, "That's all right. What happened?"

He told her everything, sparing no details. He hadn't replayed it in his mind until then. As he talked, she shut off her bedroom light and got into bed. She was in awe at his ability to respond the way he had in an emergency. She knew he had saved Paul's life. Michael knew it as well, even though it scared him to admit he could have lost one of his best friends.

"Are you all right?" she asked him. He let out a deep sigh. She could tell he was just now coming to grips with what could have happened to Paul, and it was obvious Michael was having a hard time keeping it together. "If you want me to let you go, I can," she reassured him.

"No," he said. "I don't want you to let me go. Do you mind staying on the line a while longer? I'm driving home, and you are helping me stay awake," he chuckled. "Plus I enjoy talking to you."

Abbie smiled. She pulled the bedspread up around her chin and closed her eyes. She was exhausted but didn't want to pass up the chance for a conversation with Michael. They kept talking, long after Michael pulled in the driveway at his house, after his dogs met him at the door, and after he climbed into bed as well. He told her how he became friends with Stephen and Paul, about his landscaping business and about the farm. She loved hearing him talk about Sam and Bull, and he assured her she would meet them. Abbie told Michael about her dad. She explained how she lost her mom and how her dad raised her by himself. She told him about how she left Georgia, with just a bus ticket and a little bit of cash. She amazed him. He took her breath away, and they hadn't even gone out on a date yet.

They talked for hours. Abbie's shift started at 6:00 a.m., and the clock was nearing five. Michael had to head to work earlier than usual as well, to make up for the work that didn't get done the previous day because of the accident. Neither one had known about the others' morning shifts.

"So are you going in later tomorrow on account of how late you worked tonight?" he asked.

Abbie wasn't sure about how to answer. She was avoiding him asking about work because she had wanted to keep talking to him and did not want to make him feel guilty for keeping her on the phone. "Actually," she admitted, "Karl will be here in about forty-five minutes to pick me up."

"For work?" he asked, a bit shocked. "Abbie! Are you serious?"

"Yeah," she said, trying not to yawn. Instead she giggled and said, "My shift starts at 6:00 a.m."

"Oh, my goodness. I am so sorry to keep you on the phone all night."

"Don't be," she insisted. "It was my pleasure. Really."

He sighed. "Well, I guess it's a good thing we aren't going out tomorrow. I have to get up early too."

"Michael!" It was her turn to protest. "You should have said something!"

They both started laughing. Neither one knew how they were going to stay awake at work that day, but neither of them would have traded their conversation for a minute of sleep.

"Do you work this weekend?" Michael asked Abbie.

"No. I have Saturday and Sunday off."

"Can I take you out on Saturday?"

"You better," she flirted. They each wished each other a great day and then said their good-byes.

Abbie hung up the phone and quickly got ready for work. She jumped through the shower and towel dried her hair, throwing in a bit of product so that it wouldn't get frizzy. She pulled on a pair of jeans, a V-neck top, and a pair of flip-flops. Karl's headlights shone their way up the drive. It was still dark out, but the sun was trying to peer out from under the horizon. Abbie leaned her head against the car window as Karl drove them both into work. She closed her eyes and smiled to herself as she thought of Michael.

The morning dragged by as Abbie sucked down coffee and struggled to stay awake. She maintained a friendly demeanor, but Meghan and Tracey could tell she was exhausted. She was pleasant but quiet, and moving slower than usual. The breakfast rush had died down, and the three of them stood at the front counter, talking.

"Thanks for working last night," Meghan said. "What time did you guys get out of here? You look beat."

"Not too late," Abbie answered. "I just didn't sleep well."

"Well, you had better rest up before your date with Michael."

"Actually, he had to cancel."

Both girls looked shocked.

"Oh no! What happened?" Tracey asked.

"We rescheduled for Saturday. He called me late last night, and we were up even later talking." Abbie began to blush. She couldn't keep from grinning, and she told them about her conversation with Michael. Tracey and Meghan hung on every word Abbie said as she described Paul's accident and how Michael saved him. They all agreed that Michael was sweeter than any man they had ever met.

In the midst of their conversation, a delivery man walked into the diner with a bouquet of flowers. Tracey squealed and said, "Abbie, I'll bet those are for you." Sure enough, the man stated that the flowers were for Abbie Peterson. Abbie thanked him and took the flowers graciously. They were tulips, splashed with the colors of a sunrise. She held them to her nose and inhaled their fragrance. They smelled the way that summer felt, warm and inviting. She lifted the card, read it, and grinned as she held it to her chest. She had known that the conversation she had with Michael had gone well, but she had never expected flowers.

"What does it say?" Meghan begged to know as she reached for the card.

Abbie allowed Meghan to open it. She read it aloud. "'I can't wait to see you tomorrow.' Aw, Abbie, this is the sweetest thing ever."

Tracey nodded in agreement. The two of them couldn't hide the jealousy on their faces as they smelled her bouquet of flowers. Abbie set the flowers on the counter for everyone to enjoy and then got back to work.

Abbie had a difficult time focusing for the remainder of her shift. She was exhausted and excited at the same time. After the lunch rush, Tracey and Meghan insisted she go home to get some rest. Normally, Abbie would have stayed to help prep for dinner, but she was too tired to argue. She gathered her things but left her flowers. She knew it would be difficult to carry them home on her bike, and figured more people would enjoy them at the diner than at her house.

It was late afternoon by the time Abbie got home. She took her friends' advice and went straight to bed. She decided it had never felt so good to lay her head on a pillow, pull the covers up over her, and fall asleep.

Abbie dreamed of her mother. This happened from time to time. Abbie had little memory of Annabelle, and she often wondered if what few memories she had were fabricated from the stories her father told. In her dream, her mother was in a library wearing a long yellow dress. Her skin was tan, her hair long and dark. She was young, close to Abbie's age. Annabelle was walking quickly up and down the aisles of the library, scanning the shelves for a particular book. Abbie tried desperately to get her mother's attention. She tried to call out to her, but her throat barely let out a whisper. Finally, Annabelle whipped around and looked directly into Abbie's eyes. She held a finger to her lips, as her face and eyes issued a warning.

"Shh," Annabelle whispered to Abbie. As quickly as she appeared, her mother vanished, leaving Abbie alone in the library. Abbie woke up with a start. She was gasping for breath and sweating. She had never dreamed of her mother in that way. Her dreams were usually pleasant, almost whimsical. This one was startling.

Abbie wasn't sure how long she had slept, but it was nearly dark when she woke up. She got out of bed and went to the kitchen to get a drink of water. Her nerves started to calm as the cool water washed down her throat. She decided to call her father. She hadn't talked to him in a while, and she knew he would make her feel better.

"Hey, Dad," she said as he picked up on the other end.

"Hey, kiddo." Henry was happy to hear her voice.

She asked him how his day was and how things were going at home. He sounded lonely, and she made a mental note to try to call more often. She told him that work was going great and that she had enough money to take a class or two that fall. She told him about Michael. He made sure he gave his speech about being responsible. She rolled her eyes. She missed him.

"Dad, I'm thinking about trying to make a trip back home before classes start."

"Or I could always come see you," Henry offered. Abbie chuckled. She had never known her father to travel. She wasn't even sure if he had ever left Georgia.

"I miss you, so I wouldn't mind coming back for a weekend soon." She knew her father would like her to visit. She had hoped he was staying busy without her.

"Are you okay, Abbie?" he asked. He usually called her "kiddo," but with her calling so late, out of the blue, he had a sense that something was up.

She was silent for a moment. Then she said, "I had a dream about Mom."

"Oh," Henry said sweetly. "Well, tell me about it." He liked to hear about Abbie's dreams of her mother. He dreamed of Annabelle as well, but he felt a different sort of connection with his wife when she appeared in Abbie's dreams. Somehow it always made him feel as though they were still a family, as if Annabelle was in the next room, sharing secrets with his daughter.

"It was different this time." She described the dream to him. "It didn't seem like a dream, Dad. It was as if she was actually with me and that she was trying to tell me something. She didn't feel as if she were a memory or a story. She felt alive. Like I could reach out and touch her."

Henry knew just what Abbie meant. He often had those same types of dreams. Annabelle would come and sit with him for a while, then as quickly as she would come to him, she would go. Oftentimes they would talk, but sometimes no words were spoken. As he listened to Abbie, he closed his eyes and pictured Annabelle in his mind. He swore, as he inhaled, that he could smell her skin. When he exhaled, all he said was, "I know, kiddo. I know."

Abbie and Henry said their good-byes, and then she wandered back to her bedroom. Without much regard for the time, she decided to call Michael and thank him for the flowers. His phone rang several times before he picked up.

"Hello?" Michael answered, sounding a bit groggy.

"Michael?" she asked. "It's Abbie. I'm sorry. Did I wake you?"

"Hey," Michael said, happy to hear her voice. "No, you aren't waking me."

Abbie looked at the time. She knew he was lying but thought it was sweet. "I'm sorry to call so late. I don't want to keep you, but I wanted to thank you for the flowers. They are beautiful."

"You're welcome. It was the least I could do for canceling our first date."

"Our *first* date?" she teased. "You are making quite the assumption that there will be more than one."

Michael couldn't help but laugh. "Yeah, maybe I shouldn't assume such things. Just hope for them," he flirted back.

Abbie smiled to herself. She could tell he was smiling as well. They both chuckled, and then she said, "I'm looking forward to tomorrow. What time do you want to get together?"

He thought for a moment and said, "Will six o'clock work for you? We could go to dinner and then maybe walk The Pier after?"

"That sounds great. I've actually been wanting to go there since I moved here but haven't had the chance."

"Well, I'm happy I'm the one that gets to take you."

She blushed. "Sounds great." She enjoyed talking to Michael. It was easy. She asked about Paul. He said he was doing well and would most likely go home from the hospital in a day or two. They talked a while longer. When they both began yawning, they agreed to let the other go to sleep. She gave him directions to her house. He promised to be there right at six. "I can't wait," she said.

"Good night, Abbie."

"Good night, Michael."

6

MICHAEL

THE SUN WAS JUST peeking its way into view while the moon still hung in the backdrop of the sky when Michael stepped out on the front porch early Saturday morning. Sam and Bull played in the yard while Michael watched the fog roll back from the fields. He led the dogs to the back of the property to the pond and let them go for a swim. Sam and Bull raced each other, tails wagging, splashing their way into the water. They managed to scare away the ducks that peacefully floated on the pond. Michael sat in the shade of an oak tree and watched as the dogs played. The air was silent other than the paddling of the water and the buzz of the mosquitoes.

Michael picked a piece of tall grass and chewed on it a bit, pondering what the day would bring. He hadn't been out on a date in over a year. Naturally he had expected to be nervous, but he wasn't. Abbie gave him butterflies, but at the same time she calmed his nerves. He sat for a while, thinking of her and the conversations they shared the past two nights. Michael hoped for more conversations with her, beyond their date that evening.

The sun rose higher in the sky, and Michael figured he had better get the majority of the weekend chores out of the way before he picked up Abbie that evening. He stood up and whistled for the dogs to follow him to the house. Sam and Bull trudged out of the pond and trotted toward Michael, shaking the water off of their bodies. He headed toward the garage, where he kept the lawnmower. He planned on mowing as much as he could of the property that day as well as patch a leaky rain gutter and fix a broken window on the barn.

He got right to work. The dogs continued to wander around the yard as Michael made pass after pass with the mower. After the lawn was cut, in neat diagonal rows, it was early afternoon. Michael's body was drenched in sweat, and he cooled off with the hose by the house. He sprayed off bits of grass that had clung to the sweat on his skin as well as the grass on his boots. He went inside, fixed himself a sandwich for lunch, and then went back to work. He had just enough time to repair the gutter and the window before he got ready to go pick up Abbie for their date.

Clark Hammond pulled in the driveway just as Michael was about finished fixing the window on the barn. Michael waved to his dad.

"Hey, Dad!" Michael hollered as he climbed down from the ladder he was standing on and met his father near the house. Sam and Bull had also come to greet Clark.

"Hey, Son," said Clark, greeting him with a handshake and a hug. "I just stopped by to see how things were going out here." Clark made a point to come by the farm from time to time. Clark knew his son, and how he devoted his time to working, and it was often weeks before Michael realized he hadn't called or stopped by his parents' house, which was just up the road. Often, Elisabeth would send homemade baked goods or send food to fill their son's cabinets. This time it was both. Michael helped his dad haul three bags of groceries, two pies, and a loaf of homemade bread into the house and put them in the kitchen.

"Tell Mom I said thanks," Michael said, putting the groceries away.

"I will. She wanted to come but got called in to work."

Michael nodded. Most of his mother's time was spent working. Elisabeth devoted her entire life to caring for others. Elisabeth married Clark with the intention of having a large family, moving to the Hammond Farm, and raising all of her children there. However, there were complications with labor and delivery when she gave birth to Michael, and she was unable to have more children after he was born. Elisabeth was devastated. She loved Michael, but she went through a long period of mourning for the other children she would never have. Eugene and Pearl Hammond wanted Clark and Elisabeth to inherit the farm, but Michael's mother couldn't bear the thought of not filling the house with her own children. When Michael was a year old, Elisabeth went back to school to get her nursing degree. By the time Michael was school-aged, she was working nearly eighty hours a week. Michael could have resented his mother for working so much, but instead he thought of his mother as a saint. She often spoke of her patients as if they were her own family. Her patients saw her as a light in the darkness, a hand to hold, a friendly face full of laughter, a shoulder to cry on, and someone who listened to their fears and wishes about their conditions. To Michael, his mother was an example of love.

"Mom said she saw Paul yesterday," Clark told Michael. "She's very proud of you for how you responded in his situation."

Michael shrugged off his father's praise. "I did what anybody would have done." Michael did not want recognition for saving Paul. He was simply glad he had been there to help him.

Michael pulled two beers out of the refrigerator, opened them, and handed one to his father. Clark sat down at the kitchen table and changed the subject by casually looking around the room and saying, "So when are you going to find a young lady to fill this house with little ones?"

Nearly choking on his beer, Michael said, "What, these guys aren't enough for you?" He gestured toward Sam and Bull. The dogs were lying on the floor of the kitchen, enjoying the coolness of the hardwood as well as the warmth of the sunshine that streamed through the windows. Sam and Bull picked their heads up when Michael made reference to them. "Actually, Dad," he said, directing his attention back to Clark, "I am taking a girl out on a date tonight."

"Really?" Clark leaned forward, intrigued. "Tell me about her."

"Well I don't know too much yet. She's a waitress at Kate and Karl's. I met her when the guys and I went to lunch earlier this week."

"Ahh, Kate and Karl's ..." Clark's thoughts traveled back to when he had gone to school with the owners. However, he was more interested in hearing about Michael's date than affixing on memories. "Tell me about her."

A smile crept across Michael's face, and he sat down at the table, across from his father. He relaxed in the chair and told him about Abbie. "She's beautiful, Dad. Dark hair, dark eyes. And she's sweet. She's from Georgia. She moved here a few months ago by herself. I don't know much about her, but we've talked some, and we seem to have a real connection."

Clark sat back, nodding. He swallowed the last of his beer and said, "Well, I will get out of your hair so you can get to your date."

Michael finished his beer, stood up, and walked his father to the door. "Thanks, Dad. Thank Mom for me."

"I will."

Michael checked the time as his father pulled out of the driveway. He decided the repairs on the rain gutter would have to wait until the following day. He went upstairs, hopped in the shower, and got ready for his date with Abbie.

It was exactly six o'clock when Michael's old, blue truck pulled into Abbie's driveway. He shut off the engine, fixed his hair in the rearview mirror, opened the door to his truck, and got out. He had on blue jeans, a plain, gray, V-neck T-shirt, and sandals. He nervously smoothed his shirt as he walked up the driveway to Abbie's front porch.

Abbie walked out of the house just as Michael was walking up the steps to knock on the door. He stopped on the first step as she closed the door behind her. From the moment he first saw her in the diner, he thought she was beautiful. But now, standing there on the porch, she simply took his breath away. Their eyes locked as he burned the vision of her permanently into his memory. Her hair was down, flowing around her arms and shoulders. Her skirt and top flattered her figure, and he noticed she was wearing a small amount of makeup. His instinct was to take her in his arms, but instead he smiled and met her at the top of the steps.

"Hi," Abbie said, nervously tucking her hair behind her ears.

Michael found his voice and said, "Hi." They smiled at each other, still locking eyes, and he motioned toward the truck and said, "After you."

"Thank you."

He led her over to the passenger side of the truck and opened the door for her. He couldn't help but inhale the scent of her hair as she got into the truck. He closed the door behind her and got in on the other side. They both were quiet as he backed out of the driveway.

"How was your day?" Abbie asked, breaking the silence.

"It was great. I worked in the yard with the dogs, and my dad came over for a little while."

"Oh, that sounds nice." Abbie paused and then asked curiously, "What's your dad like?"

"Oh, he's great. I like it when he stops over. I don't visit my parents as often as I should."

"I can understand that."

"My mom is great too. She was working today, so she wasn't able to come." He chuckled a bit when he said, "She made up for her absence in baked goods." Abbie laughed as well. Michael continued, "I'm their only child, so I tend to be spoiled." His eyes focused on the road when he spoke, but he glanced at Abbie from time to time. He noticed she was facing him, completely engaged in the conversation.

"Oh, no kidding? I'm an only child too."

Michael smiled and said, "I think you may have mentioned that on the phone. It was just you and your dad, huh?"

"Yeah. Henry. He did a decent job of raising me by himself."

"He didn't remarry?"

"No. I don't think he will ever get over my mom. It's too bad, though. He's the greatest guy I know."

"He sounds great. How did he feel when you moved to North Carolina?"

"He was nervous at first, but he's also very supportive. I think we were both worried about the other being alone, but it seems to be working out. I promised him I would go back and visit soon." They continued making small talk as they neared their destination.

Michael had remembered that Abbie hadn't been to The Pier, and he was happy to be the one to take her. The Pier was an actual pier. It was a true tourist attraction, but even as a local, Michael had always enjoyed going, but hadn't been since he was a child. Michael parked the truck near the entrance, smiled at Abbie, and asked, "Are you ready for this?"

"Yes!" she clapped her hands together, gathered her purse, and got ready to get out of the truck.

"Wait, I'll get it," Michael said, referring to the door. Abbie hadn't realized he was going to open it for her, and she was a bit embarrassed. He quickly got out of the driver's side of the truck and jogged to the passenger side as she was opening her door. He opened it the rest of the way and he offered her his hand.

Abbie took his hand and said, "Thank you, Michael. Sorry, I'm not used to this." She laughed a little as he helped her out of the truck.

"Not used to what?" He wasn't sure if he should keep holding her hand once she was out of the truck, so he let go. They walked beside each other and headed toward the main entrance of The Pier. Music blared from the speakers that lined the length of the boardwalk, inviting the two of them to join the scene.

"The rules for going out on a date," she joked.

He put his hands in his pockets as he walked next to her, laughed, and said, "I don't know if there are rules. I just like to be nice. I hope that's what most people try to do on dates."

Abbie smiled at Michael. She hesitated but then said, "I actually wouldn't know." Michael wasn't sure if he heard her correctly, so he asked her what she meant. "I haven't been on any other dates," she admitted.

Michael stopped dead in his tracks. He wasn't sure if she was being serious until she turned and looked at him with a serious look on her face.

"I find that hard to believe," he said.

Her face did not change.

"Really?" he asked.

Abbie started to look a bit anxious and embarrassed and almost began to regret telling him she hadn't gone out on a date before.

"Abbie, I'm sorry. I don't mean to make you uncomfortable. I'm just shocked. I just assumed a girl like you had gone out on plenty of dates."

Abbie blushed a bit, smiled, shook off her insecurities, and said, "Nope. Guess not." She jabbed him in the arm and joked, "So the bar is set pretty low."

Michael laughed, winked at her, and said, "Well, maybe I can set it high for everyone else after me."

Although she hoped there wouldn't be dates with anyone else after him, Abbie agreed and said, "Deal."

They resumed walking toward The Pier. He placed his hand on the small of her back and led her through rows of cars until they reached the entrance. She naturally leaned in to him when he touched her. Abbie's eyes lit up with a childlike innocence when they started down the boardwalk. It was nearly dark outside by that time, so the flashing lights of the vendor signs stood out against the backdrop of the night.

"Are you hungry?" Michael asked Abbie.

"I'm always hungry," she joked.

Michael laughed, and they agreed to eat first. There were several nice restaurants along The Pier. Michael offered to take her to the one of her choosing.

"Actually," she said, "I was hoping we could get corndogs."

"Are you sure?" Michael asked. "Don't feel you have to pick something like that."

"No, I'm being honest. I haven't had food like that since I was a kid. Are we breaking date rules again?" She couldn't help but tease him and poke fun of herself.

"I think it's safe to say there are no rules." He winked at her, and they both laughed and allowed themselves to be swept up in the rush of the traffic of people. They stood in line for corndogs and french fries and watched the people pass by. They talked and laughed while they ate at a picnic table beside the food stand.

Michael thought Abbie was amazing. She was confident and funny and beautiful. He loved to hear her laugh. A few times she even tossed her head back, closed her eyes, and laughed so hard it brought tears to her eyes. Her happiness was contagious and made Michael's heart swell.

They continued on, stopping for elephant ears and souvenirs. Street musicians spread themselves out along the way and offered a variety of entertainment. At one point, they stood talking, facing each other, listening to a young college student play a few riffs on his guitar. A few people pushed past them, tripping Abbie and sending her body directly into Michael's. He instinctively grabbed her by the waist, and their faces were inches apart. He felt her breath on his neck. Abbie turned her face away, embarrassed, and she stepped back away from Michael. They both laughed and headed farther down the boardwalk.

Soon the crowds were thick with people, and Abbie struggled to stay next to Michael as they were separated by the rush of people. Michael reached for her, a few steps ahead of him, and grabbed her by the elbow. Abbie stopped in her tracks and let his hand slide down her arm and entwine her fingers with his.

"Is this okay?" he whispered in her ear through her hair. She nodded and smiled while biting her lip without saying a word. Michael smiled as well, and he led her through the crowd.

From that moment on, the rest of the date was a blur for Michael. The feeling of her hand in his was better than he could have imagined. He felt as though he could protect and care for her always. It felt so familiar, so right. Michael could tell that Abbie was soaking in everything there was to see and do on The Pier. And in a way, Michael was experiencing it for the first time, only from her perspective.

Fireworks lit up the sky over the water, and Michael and Abbie sat on a bench to watch. After talking most of the evening, they finished watching the fireworks in silence. Not an awkward silence, but a knowing silence, where words weren't needed. Abbie was the one that reached for Michael's hand then. He held her hand in both of his. Without thinking, he began tracing the edges of her fingertips with his. When he realized what he was doing, he stopped. Abbie looked over at him and smiled, giving him permission to continue. He shyly smiled back and resumed touching her fingers.

The fireworks faded, and the crowds died down. Michael and Abbie slowly walked back to the entrance of The Pier, neither wanting the night to end. Few words were spoken as they made their way back to Michael's truck. The stars were out, and she pointed out a few. Once they were at the truck, he opened the door for her. Again, he offered his hand to help her into the truck, and she took it. As she was about to climb into the truck she stopped, turned toward him, leaned her face in to his, and kissed him. Before Michael had a chance to take in what was happening, her lips pulled away from his, and she turned around and hopped into the truck.

Still in shock, Michael walked over to the driver's side and got in. Neither spoke of the kiss as they drove out of the parking lot; instead they laughed and discussed other things.

Michael mentioned the farm, which struck Abbie's curiosity.

"I've never been to a real farm," she said.

"Seriously?" Michael was a bit shocked. "A southern girl such as yourself has never been to a farm?"

She chuckled. "I grew up in a small town. There were farms nearby, but I've never actually been to one."

"I see." Michael took her statement as an opportunity, so he said, "Well, if you are interested, I can show you around the Hammond Farm."

"Really? I would love that."

"Are you busy tomorrow?" He hoped he wasn't being too forward, but her expression didn't indicate that the following day would be too soon to see him again.

"Not at all. What time should I come by?"

"I'm free all day. But how about I pick you up? I noticed you didn't have a car."

"I can ride my bike."

He chuckled. "It's quite a hike. I'll pick you up. How about ten o'clock?"

"That sounds great."

"Good. It's a date." Michael smiled at her, and she smiled back from the passenger seat.

"Yes, it's a date." Not long after that they pulled into Abbie's driveway. "Thank you so much for taking me out tonight, Michael."

He shifted the truck into park and said, "Not a problem. I had fun. Can I walk you to your door?"

Abbie agreed. This time she waited in the passenger seat for Michael to come around and open her door for her. She took his hand as she got out of the truck. Michael didn't let go of her hand as he closed the door and walked her up the steps of her front porch.

"I can't wait to see you tomorrow, Abbie," he said once they were in front of the door. This time he was prepared to kiss her. He placed his hands on her hips and turned her to face him. With her hands on his shoulders, she stood on her toes, and they leaned into each other and kissed. Her lips were soft and inviting. They closed their eyes and enjoyed the moment before pulling away. Michael wrapped his arms around her, and she laced her arms through his, and held him. With her head on his chest, Michael kissed Abbie's hair and said, "I'll see you in the morning."

Abbie picked up her head, gave him one more kiss, and said, "See you in the morning." She slowly let go of Michael, opened the door, and went inside. Michael turned and headed to his truck. His mind replayed every detail of the evening as he drove home.

7

ABBIE

IMAGES OF MICHAEL FLASHED through Abbie's mind that night, keeping her awake. She could still feel the touch of his skin as she hung onto the moments when Michael held her hand on The Pier and when he kissed her on the front porch. She had fallen asleep at some point because she woke up to the sun streaming through the open bedroom window. The curtains swayed as a warm breeze whispered its way into her room.

Still buried in the covers she rolled over to check the time on her phone, which was on the nightstand. It was just after eight o'clock. She also noticed she had a text message from Michael from two hours earlier. Abbie's heart leaped, and she wished she had been awake when he had sent it. *'Good Morning, Abbie. Hope you slept well. I enjoyed your company last night and can't wait to see you this morning.'* Abbie closed her eyes and smiled. She stretched her body across the bed, allowed her legs to dangle over the edge, and then let her feet fall to the floor.

The morning air had filled her cozy house along with the sounds of birds chirping in the open windows. Rising from her bed, Abbie walked down the hall, stepped into the bathroom, and turned on the shower. She looked in the mirror as it began to fog and wondered if she resembled her mother. The thought was fleeting, and she got into the shower. Once she was done, she wrapped her hair in a towel, put on her bathrobe, and then walked barefoot out to the kitchen to make herself a cup of coffee.

Coffee in hand, she went back to the bedroom to get her phone so she could text her father about her date with Michael. She smirked when she noticed her father had already texted her just a few minutes prior asking how the date went. Abbie wandered back out to the kitchen, where she sat sipping her coffee and texting her dad about the date. Without revealing too many details, she assured her father that Michael had been a perfect gentleman.

Abbie finished getting ready while she waited for Michael to arrive. She blew her hair dry and then tied it in a loose braid over one of her shoulders. Henry had shown her how to do her hair like that when she was just a girl. She pulled on a pair of jeans and a black scoop neck tank top. Abbie made a mental note that if she was going to keep seeing Michael, she wanted to wear nicer clothes.

She stood in front of the bathroom mirror, second-guessing her outfit when she heard Michael's truck roar its way into her driveway. Abbie quickly scooped up her purse and keys and threw on a pair of sandals. The back door to the kitchen was open, and she saw Michael walking up the drive through the screen door. Her heart raced a bit faster at the sight of him. He was dressed just as simply as she was, with jeans, a T-shirt, and boots. His shirt perfectly outlined the definition in his chest and shoulders. She couldn't help but stare.

Michael caught her gaze from inside behind the screen and smiled. "Sorry I'm a little late," he said from outside. She opened the door to invite him in, and he offered her a bouquet of fresh-picked wildflowers and a kiss on the cheek. His hair was still wet from his shower earlier that morning, and Abbie drank in the smell of soap when he leaned in to kiss her. He pointed toward the flowers that were now in her hands and said, "I saw those on the way in, and I just had to stop to pick them up."

Abbie held them to her nose. "They are beautiful. Thank you." She turned and started to look for a vase to put them in. She realized she didn't have one and settled on a drinking glass.

Michael smiled at her with his hands in his pockets. "You're welcome." He watched her glide over to the sink and fill the glass with water for her flowers.

"You were up early," Abbie said, teasing Michael about the text he sent that morning.

A bit embarrassed, he ran his hand through his hair, shrugged, and said, "I couldn't sleep." Abbie winked at him with a smile and turned back toward the sink to finish arranging the flowers in the glass. Michael made his way over to her and gently slipped his arms around her waist. Abbie's hands stopped what they were doing, and she closed her eyes and leaned into him. "Truth is," he said, lowering his face into her neck, "I missed you."

Eyes still closed, she exhaled, and said, "I missed you too." Abbie felt so safe in Michael's arms. She never wanted him to let her go. As instantly as she wished it, he slowly let go of her and suggested they get going.

"As much as I would love to hang out with you in your kitchen all day, I promised you a tour of the farm."

"Yes, I'm looking forward to it." She placed the flowers on the kitchen table and followed Michael out of the house to his truck. Abbie sat in the middle, next to Michael. The windows were rolled down, and wisps of her hair that fell out of her braid blew in the breeze. Michael rested his elbow on the window while he held the steering wheel with one hand and Abbie's hand with the other. The sun was shining, and it was one of the most gorgeous days they had had yet that year.

"Have you had breakfast?" Michael asked Abbie.

"I had coffee. Does that count?"

"Ha-ha. No. But that's good because I packed us breakfast." He motioned toward a picnic basket and a blanket on the floor of the passenger seat.

"That sounds perfect." They enjoyed the rest of the drive to the farm accompanied by the sound of the radio and the hum of the tires.

When they were still a fair distance from the farm, Michael pointed out the window and said, "Do you see those fields over that way?"

Abbie sat up straighter in the seat and said, "Yes."

"And those trees, beyond them, and the barns near the trees?"

"Yes?"

Michael looked at her and said with pride, "That's the place—Hammond Farm."

Abbie's eyes lit up. She hadn't expected the farm to be so beautiful. The trees swayed perfectly in the early-morning breeze. The sun spilled light through the branches and cast perfect shadows over the property. The truck led them closer to their destination. The sight of the farmhouse that stood under a canopy of mossy oaks and willow trees left her speechless. Even after Michael had parked the truck in the driveway, Abbie's eyes stayed fixed on her surroundings.

Michael opened the passenger side door, lifted the basket and blanket from the floor of the truck, offered his hand to her, and said, "Want to see the rest of it?"

"Absolutely," she said breathlessly, not taking her eyes off of the sight before her.

"Are you okay?" Michael chuckled.

"I've never seen anything like it. Everything is so beautiful."

"Thank you. I'll give you the full tour after breakfast."

"Ah, yes, breakfast." Abbie tore her eyes from her surroundings and looked at Michael. As they began walking back toward the pond, Sam and Bull came charging toward them. Abbie's face lit up when she saw them, and she and Michael both knelt down to greet them.

"Which one's which?" Abbie asked Michael.

"Bull is the smaller one," he said, as the dogs rolled onto their backs, begging them to rub their bellies.

Abbie sat right down on the ground and petted Sam and Bull. "I just love them!"

Michael chuckled and said, "Me too. They are good dogs, and they don't mind me for a roommate."

Abbie laughed, and Michael helped her stand up. She brushed off her jeans and took Michael's hand. Sam and Bull picked themselves up off the ground and wandered off through the trees. She and Michael walked hand in hand as he led her past the house and the barn and back to the pond. Her feet were wet with dew by the time they reached the pond. They spread the blanket by the water and sat down.

"So what's for breakfast?" Abbie asked as Michael opened up the picnic basket between them.

"Well, as you know, I couldn't sleep this morning, so I made hard-boiled eggs, blueberry muffins, and fresh squeezed orange juice," he said, pulling each one from the basket.

"You made all this?"

"Yeah."

"Wow. I'm impressed."

"Well, like I said, I couldn't sleep." Michael winked at her and poured her some orange juice from a thermos.

"Did your mom teach you how to cook and bake?"

"My grandma did mostly."

"That's sweet. This looks wonderful. Thank you." Abbie sat cross legged facing Michael and accepted a plate of food he had prepared for her. They ate quietly, enjoying the morning and the stillness of the pond and the warmth of the late-morning air. Dragonflies zipped along its surface without disturbing the reflection of the sky in the water.

"It's so peaceful out here," Abbie said after awhile. She had finished her food and sat with her knees bent, leaning back, and resting on her elbows.

"See those trees out that way?" Michael said, motioning toward the woods.

Abbie nodded.

"And those fields out there?"

Abbie sat up straighter as she followed the movements of his hands.

"That's about as far wide as the farm stretches. And my parents live on the other side of the woods."

"Wow." She was nearly speechless. After a few moments of silence, she said, "You're very fortunate, Michael."

"Thank you. I love it out here. I wish everyone could experience living out here."

"So you must want a family someday then? I can't imagine you want to stay at a place like this all by yourself."

Michael was quiet, thinking about how to answer her.

"I'm sorry," she apologized. "That's fairly personal."

"Oh, I don't mind you asking. Yes, I do want a family." He looked into her eyes, smiled, and said, "Someday." He leaned back on the blanket as well, next to Abbie, simulating her position on her elbows.

"What about you?" he asked, nudging her with his shoulder.

"Do I want a family?" she asked.

"Yes," he answered.

Abbie swallowed, then looked out at the water and smiled. "Absolutely." Her voice was nearly a whisper. She was quiet for a minute and said, "It was just my dad and I growing up, and I always missed my mom. I don't remember her, but I always felt that missing piece of our family. My dad and I are close, but I always wonder how great it would have been to have one more person to share all that love with, like my mom. So I want a big family." Michael could feel the happiness in her voice when she said, "I just think that the love between two people would only multiply with each new addition."

"I've never thought of it like that," Michael said. "I hope you have a big family one day, Abbie." He leaned over and kissed her temple. She leaned into him and accepted his kiss. He changed the subject and asked, "Well, where do you want to go first? We could go back to the woods; we could ride the tractor out to the fields; I could show you the barns, or we could tour the house."

"All of the above," she said, excited. She sprang to her feet and grabbed his hand to pull him up to her. She threw her arms around his neck and kissed him. "Thank you for bringing me here," she said as their lips parted.

"I'm glad you came." He kissed her again, softly, slowly, his hands on her cheeks, pulling her face into him. Abbie stood on her toes with her hands on Michael's back. She felt the ripple of his muscles beneath his T-shirt. She gently pulled her lips from his.

"Let's go see the house and then the barn," she suggested.

"Sounds good." Michael kissed her forehead as Abbie lowered her heels to the ground.

By the time they had finished breakfast and packed up the blanket and the picnic basket, the sun was high in the sky, and the early-summer air was scorching. Hand in hand, they walked back to the house. Beads of sweat formed on Michael's brow, and they were both exhausted by the time they reached the porch to the house.

Slightly out of breath, Michael asked, "Would you like some water?"

"I'd love some." Abbie followed Michael into the house. She immediately fell in love with her surroundings. Michael got each of them a glass of water and then led her through each room of the house. One side of the kitchen led to a large dining room through a set of pocket doors, the other to the living room, which used to be a great room used for entertaining. Both the living room and the kitchen led out to the front porch. Two staircases led upstairs, one from the living room, the other from the dining room.

Glasses of water in hand, they made their way upstairs to a large U-shaped hallway with four adjacent bedrooms. Michael's room, the master bedroom, led to an outdoor balcony. Another staircase led to a loft on the third floor. It was currently used for storage, but as he led

47

her up the second set of stairs, Michael explained that it was one of the many places his grandmother loved to paint.

"Everything is so beautiful," Abbie said, impressed. She noticed a piano in the corner of the room. She walked over to it and asked, "Do you mind if I play?"

"Sure," Michael said. "I'm not sure if it's tuned."

"Only one way to find out." Abbie winked and lifted the cover of the piano overtop the keys and blew a cloud of dust off of them and into the air. She crouched down and began to play a few chords.

"Sounds in tune to me." She continued to play, hesitant at first, as if she hadn't had the keys beneath her fingers in quite some time. Then, as if music was coming from inside herself and out through the piano, her fingers floated over the keys, playing one of the most beautiful songs Michael had ever heard. It sounded like rainy days and felt like happiness.

Michael reached for Abbie to take her into his arms, but they were interrupted by her phone ringing from two floors below.

"You should get that," he whispered.

"Is that my phone?" she asked, embarrassed.

"It's not my phone," he chuckled.

"It can wait." Abbie leaned into Michael and kissed him. Michael pulled her into him and kissed her back. Her phone however, kept ringing.

Michael pulled his lips away from Abbie and said, "It might be important."

Abbie giggled, pulled his face back into hers, and continued to kiss him, becoming more aggressive. "Nope," she smiled and said with her lips brushing his, "This is too good." Michael smiled, put his hands on her face, and gave in to her passionate kissing.

The phone continued to ring. They both started laughing and Michael stepped back from her, grabbed her hands, and said, "Someone must really need to talk to you."

"I knew I should have turned the ringer off," Abbie chuckled.

"Let's go. I want to show you the rest of the farm anyway."

They chased each other down the stairs, laughing the entire way. Abbie pulled her cell phone out of her purse while Michael stood behind her with his arms around her waist, smelling her hair.

"Oh, it was my dad," she said after looking at the list of missed calls. "I should probably call him back." She faced Michael and said, "Sorry. I won't be long."

"No problem at all. Take your time."

Abbie smiled at him and then went outside to the front porch to return her father's phone call. "Hi, Dad," she said when he answered.

"Hey, kiddo!"

"Well, you sound happy. Everything all right? I'm sorry I didn't pick up right away."

"Everything is fine."

There was a bit of interference on the line, and Abbie asked, "Are you driving?"

"Yeah. Hey, kiddo, I was wondering, where is a good place to grab a bite to eat around here?"

"Um, what? Dad? Eat around where?" Her heart skipped a beat, and she asked, "Where exactly are you?"

"I am *exactly* twenty miles outside of Wilmington."

Abbie squealed with delight. "Are you serious? Dad! Are you coming to see me?"

"Yes. Can you meet for lunch?"

"Ha-ha, of course! Can I bring a friend?"

"Sure! The more the merrier."

Abbie gave her father directions to 'Kate and Karl's' diner and then opened the door to the house and peeked her head inside.

"Hey, Michael," she called out. "Do you want to go meet my dad?"

8

HENRY

THE DRIVE FROM GEORGIA to North Carolina was prompted by
a vision of Annabelle the evening prior. Henry had been thinking of
Abbie since their conversation late Friday. On Saturday, he spent the
day missing Abbie, which led to missing Annabelle. That night, Henry
dreamt of his wife. It was as if she knew he needed to hear her voice
and see her face. Annabelle snuck into his room while he was sleeping
and sat on the bed they used to share.

"Henry, wake up," Annabelle said to him, stirring him awake. Her
voice was sweet and quiet. Henry opened his eyes and saw his wife
smiling at him. She didn't look a day over twenty-five.

"Annabelle," he said with a sigh.

She was playful but direct, "Just go to her, Henry."

"Huh?"

"Abbie. Go to her. She's young. Has a lot going on. It could be
months before she has a chance to come home."

Henry was silent. She knew he was thinking of all the reasons why
he shouldn't go, or couldn't go. She also knew that Henry knew his
excuses didn't hold much merit, and that was why he stayed silent.

She laughed quietly and said, "Henry, I know what you are thinking.
I've been married to you for twenty-three years. Get out of the house."

"She doesn't need her old dad bothering her," he argued.

"Henry." This time she was serious. "She needs to see you more
than you need to see her. Go to her."

He woke up. The bedroom was dark, and a chill blew in from outside through the window. Unable to fall back asleep, Henry got out of bed and shut the window, and the curtains collapsed as the air went still. Henry could feel the emptiness of the room that Annabelle had left once he awoke. He sat on the edge of the bed with his head in his hands, wondering if he would ever stop missing her.

Annabelle's words rang through his thoughts, *"Go to her."*

Henry had no interest in traveling. Ever since his wife had passed, Henry clung to the familiarity and predictability of his surroundings. Sadly, the farthest he had ever taken Abbie on vacation was Tybee Island. He was not at all surprised when his daughter decided she needed to spread her wings. And now, Annabelle was urging him to do the same.

Henry didn't spend much time questioning Annabelle's request for him to go see Abbie. Her words rang true; they had been married for longer than twenty years, and she knew him. And in a way, he still knew her, trusted her, and chose to listen to her. He stood up from the bed, turned the bedroom light on, went to his closet, and dug out a suitcase. Henry and Annabelle had received the luggage as a wedding gift, and Henry could count on one hand the number of times it had actually been used. Unsure of how long he would be away, Henry put faith in the fact that Annabelle knew he wouldn't want to be gone long. He hoped whatever it was she needed him to do could be accomplished in a matter of a few days.

Dawn was breaking as Henry slipped on his shoes and jacket. He prepared a thermos of coffee for the road and switched the lights off in the house. His keys jangled in his hand as he locked the back door. Stones crunched beneath the tires of his car as Henry slowly pulled out of the driveway.

As the car accelerated onto US 17, he felt the layers of twenty years worth of insecurities peel back and fall away. He settled into the scent of the sea and the taste of salt in his mouth as he drove up the coast, windows down. The drive was more pleasant than he had anticipated and he began to regret the years he spent confining himself to what he was accustomed to.

When Henry heard the excitement in Abbie's voice on the other end of the line, he knew he had made the right decision to see her. Abbie sounded just as surprised as Henry was that he was making the trip. He reread the directions Abbie gave him to 'Kate and Karl's' that he had scribbled on a piece of paper while driving.

As he neared the destination, the road seemed to wind aimlessly without much civilization in sight. Henry thought for sure he was lost, but a small town gradually came to life before him. Trees lined the streets, and people strolled the sidewalks, some walking dogs, others pushing strollers. He passed a barbershop, a bookstore, and several other locally owned businesses until he reached the diner. Kate and Karl's was located at the end of the main road.

Henry parked on the far end of the lot. As soon as he got out of his car, he saw Abbie jump out of the cab of an old blue pickup and come racing toward him.

"Dad!" she squealed and ran into his arms.

"Hey, kiddo." He said with a smile and hugged her tight. Henry noticed a handsome gentleman with dark hair come sauntering toward them, his hands in his pockets.

"Dad, this is Michael," Abbie said when Michael approached. She turned to Michael and said, "Michael, this in Henry, my dad." The two of them exchanged greetings and shook hands. The three of them walked toward the diner. "I can't believe you're here, Dad."

Henry, looking a little embarrassed, said, "Me either."

"How was your drive?" Michael asked.

"Beautiful. I had never been up the eastern shoreline."

"He's never been out of *Georgia*," Abbie joked.

Michael turned toward Henry. "Is that so? Well, I'm glad you could make it."

"I'm glad I could come."

Once inside, Tracey and Meghan approached them, both excited to meet Henry and Michael.

"Abbie, who are these good-looking gentlemen?" Meghan asked with a flirtatious smile.

Abbie formalized the introductions, once again. "Henry, Michael, this is Tracey and Meghan. Tracey, Megan, this is my dad, Henry, and well, I've told you about Michael." Abbie winked, and Michael blushed slightly.

Tracey led the three of them to their seats, and Meghan followed.

"Abbie has told us so much about the both of you," Meghan said as Tracey took their drink orders. Once their order was taken, Tracey and Meghan bustled back to the kitchen.

The young waitresses swooned over Michael, but he didn't seem to notice. Instead, he held Abbie's hand under the table.

"So sorry about that," Abbie apologized to both of them. "They tend to get a little excited when new people come into the diner. They're used to the locals."

"They seem nice," Henry noted. He was happy that Abbie had found a nice community to call home. "They are. I love working here."

Henry realized that his daughter may never come back to Georgia. Surprisingly, this did not upset him. Instead, he welcomed an overwhelming acceptance into his heart for Abbie's new life. He looked into his daughter's eyes, and he could see that Abbie saw his approval. They exchanged knowing smiles.

"How long are you in town for?" Michael asked Henry.

Henry switched his focus from Abbie to Michael. "I'm not sure yet." He chuckled a bit and said, "I didn't have a plan when I set out this morning. I just knew I had to come and see how Abbie was getting along out here."

Abbie could tell her father wasn't telling the entire truth. "Is everything okay, Dad?"

They were interrupted by Meghan as she approached their booth with their drinks. "Food will be right up, guys," she said, chomping on a wad of gum. She winked at them and moved on to her other tables.

"What do you mean?" Henry asked. "Of course everything is okay."

Abbie lowered her voice and questioned her father. "Dad, I know you. You just decided this morning to come here? We hardly made it to the other side of Savannah when I was a kid. Something is up."

Deflecting, Henry took a sip of his water and joked, "Can't a father come visit his daughter?"

Abbie was silent and stared at him. She was giving him a look that he knew all too well. Annabelle used to give him the exact same look when she sensed he was holding back his thoughts or feelings from her.

"It was Mom, wasn't it?" she asked, her voice still lowered. Michael looked back and forth between Abbie and Henry, confused. Abbie narrowed her eyes at her father and asked again, "Dad? Wasn't it?"

Henry rolled his eyes and admitted with a smirk, "You are just like her. I have to give you credit, kiddo. I can't keep anything from you."

A smile spread across Abbie's face, and her eyes lit up. She clasped both hands on top of the table, leaned forward, and said, "What did she say?"

Henry looked nervously at Michael, afraid of what he was thinking. How could the two of them possibly explain to Michael that their dead wife and mother visited them in their dreams? Henry shot a look at his daughter, hoping she could read his mind. She did.

Abbie looked at Michael and began to explain. "Dad and I both dream about my mother. Sometimes she talks to us. It may seem strange. In fact, most people think it's strange, so we tend to keep it between us. But you should hear this, Michael. See, before today I figured it would take a miracle to get my dad to come out here. And here he is. So my mom must have said something to rattle him enough to get him to come." Abbie turned back to Henry. "So what did she say?"

Meghan came by with their food, but neither one of the three of them looked up at her. "Let me know if you guys need anything," she said to them, oblivious to the question that hung in the air at their table.

Once Meghan walked away, Henry spoke. "She said I had to come."

"I knew it!" she exclaimed, relaxing back into her seat. "What else?" Abbie was nonchalant about her question as she took a bite of her food.

Henry and Michael also reached for their food. "There wasn't much to it. I tried to get out of the trip. I told her you were coming home when you had the time. She told me to come anyway."

"So that's it?" Abbie asked.

Henry chewed his food without answering her. His eyes avoided hers, but he could tell Abbie knew there was more. He swallowed his food, took a drink of his water, and said, "She said that you needed to see me more than I needed to see you."

Abbie had a puzzled look on her face. "What does that mean?" she asked.

Henry laughed. "I was hoping you could answer that one, kiddo."

"Did she make it sound like I was unhappy?"

Henry shrugged. "I don't know what she meant by that. She sounded concerned."

"Hmm," was all Abbie could manage to say.

Henry was just as confused as his daughter was.

"Maybe she didn't need you to know the reasons just yet," Michael offered. It was the first time he had spoken since they started the conversation about Henry's dream, and both Henry and Abbie were surprised at his response. They weren't expecting such an acceptance of what the two of them were discussing.

Abbie laughed and said, "We know it sounds crazy."

"I don't think it sounds crazy at all," Michael said in a serious voice. "I wish I was able to communicate with my grandfather that passed away. He was my role model when I was a kid, and I miss him a lot." He nodded toward Henry and said, "And I know for a fact that if he told me in a dream to drive across the country, I would do it, without question."

"Thank you," Henry responded.

The three of them continued to eat, talk, and laugh. Henry shared stories from Abbie's childhood. He could tell that Michael enjoyed learning about Abbie from a different perspective. Looking at Abbie, he couldn't remember the last time she had looked so happy. That only made him question further why Annabelle would claim that Abbie needed him more than he needed her. She seemed happy and comfortable in her surroundings.

They finished their food, and Meghan cleared away their plates. "On the house, guys," she said, referring to their bill. "Karl said so." Meghan pointed a finger at Karl, who stood back and saluted them from the front counter.

Abbie smiled and waved as Henry and Michael nodded in appreciation.

"Dad, I'm assuming you are staying with me? I don't have much space, but there is a couch in the living room."

"Oh nonsense," Henry said, batting a hand at her. "I planned on finding a motel in Wilmington or near there."

Michael spoke up, "You can just stay at my place. No need to get a motel. I have plenty of room, if you are interested."

Abbie agreed. "Oh, Dad, you will love it. Michael has a beautiful home on a farm."

"Nah. I don't want to impose."

"I insist," Michael said. "In fact, I still owe Abbie a tour of the rest of the farm. We could all go check it out, grill some steaks for dinner, have a bonfire. I've got extra bedrooms for everyone."

"That's a great idea," Abbie chimed in.

Henry was still unsure. It was not his intention to take up all of Abbie's time while he was there. However, the look on both of their faces told him he had better take them up on their offer.

"Well, all right, but just for tonight," Henry agreed.

A smile spread across Abbie's face. The three of them got up from the booth to leave, waving good-bye to Meghan, Tracey, and Karl. Once they were in the parking lot, Henry shook Michael's hand and agreed to follow him and Abbie to the farm.

Abbie gave her father a hug and whispered in his ear, "Love you, Dad. Thanks for listening to Mom."

He hugged her a bit tighter before letting her go. As Henry followed the blue truck to the farm, he wondered why Annabelle had said what she had about Abbie. She seemed fine. Happy, even. Maybe Michael had been right. The answers weren't apparent upon his arrival, but maybe they would be by the time he left. For the time being, he simply smiled as he watched Abbie put her head on Michael's shoulder in the truck in front of him.

9

ABBIE

STICKS AND LEAVES SNAPPED beneath Abbie and Michael's feet as they gathered wood for a bonfire they had started near the house. Michael had treated Abbie and Henry to a steak dinner and gave them a tour of the farm, as promised. The three of them planned to relax by the fire for the remainder of the evening. The sky grew dark, and the stars were out just in time to drape the sky in flecks of light for the three of them to enjoy around the warmth and glow of a fire in Michael's backyard. Michael and Abbie had driven his truck out to the woods to gather a few fallen branches, stealing kisses from each other along the way. Once the truck was loaded up, they headed back to the house. Abbie sat close to Michael, both of her arms curled up around one of his.

"Are you happy your dad came?" he asked her.

"Absolutely," she answered.

"You can tell he sincerely loves you."

Abbie smiled. "He's the best. Thank you again for letting him stay here."

"Are you comfortable staying?" he asked Abbie.

"Yes." Abbie paused and then said to him, "I know it's only our second date, but I feel as though I've known you my entire life. I really like you a lot, Michael."

Michael slowed the truck to a stop. They were only halfway to the house. Abbie wondered what he was doing, but he didn't give her much time to think. He turned his body toward hers and took her face in his hands. She put her hands on his arms.

"Abbie, I know exactly what you mean." He looked her directly in her eyes and said, "You are exactly the girl I've been looking for." His words nearly melted Abbie. He continued by saying, "You're beautiful, so sure of yourself, funny, and you simply love life." His eyes searched hers for hesitation or doubt. When he didn't see any, he closed his eyes and wrapped his lips around hers.

Abbie gave in to him, and she kissed him slowly, moving her hands from his arms to his shoulders and down his back. Her heart raced as he kissed her, and she knew for sure she was falling in love. She was simply hoping he would catch her.

"We should get back to the bonfire," he said, eyes still closed.

Abbie let out a long sigh, and then she laughed and said, "Yes, we should. I don't want my dad to get lonely." They both laughed as Michael put the truck in drive and headed back to the house.

Henry was sitting in a lawn chair next to a small fire with Sam and Bull curled up at his feet when Abbie and Michael drove up. The three of them put more wood on the fire, and before long, it was roaring. Abbie sat quietly as Michael and Henry did most of the talking while the fire blazed. The conversations carried late into the night and the fire eventually became a pile of burning coals. Michael stood up and offered to show Abbie and Henry their bedrooms.

"Thanks again, Michael," Abbie said to him as they all walked into the house, followed by Sam and Bull.

"Yes, thank you," Henry chimed in.

"Well, it's no problem at all. I have all of this room, and I might as well put it to good use." Michael led Henry to a room upstairs down the hall from his own. He offered Abbie the master bedroom, but she declined, taking a smaller room next to it.

Henry quickly said good night to Abbie, went to his room, and shut the door. Henry was not at all old-fashioned, and wouldn't mind if she and Michael decided to share a room, but he didn't want to make things awkward for either of them by lingering.

Michael and Abbie stood in the hallway, both unsure of what to say to the other. She had not expected to be staying the night at his house, and the thought of it gave her butterflies in her stomach. She wondered if he had ever had any overnight female guests.

Michael interrupted her thoughts by saying, "Do you want some different clothes to sleep in?"

"Yeah, that would be great."

"I'll be right back." Michael kissed her on the forehead and ducked into his room to find her something to wear to bed. Sam and Bull followed after him and got comfortable on the floor by Michael's bed.

Abbie went into her room and began turning down the bed. She turned around when she felt Michael standing in the doorway.

He held out an oversized T-shirt and said, "Will this work?"

"Yes," she said, taking the shirt from him.

They both tried not to let an awkward silence hang in the air, so Michael asked, "When do you have to work tomorrow?"

"Not until after lunch. I can have my dad take me so you can go to work in the morning."

"I don't mind taking you home. We don't have too many jobs tomorrow, so Stephen is going to cover them so I can go see Paul."

"Oh, that's great." Abbie's eyes fixed on Michael's. They were the kindest eyes she had ever known. She could tell that he saw her for who she was and who she wanted to become. Michael stood in front of her, his eyes searching hers for answers to the questions in his heart.

"What?" he asked, flirtatiously.

"Nothing," she answered, smiling at him. Then she whispered, "I just like looking at you."

"I like looking at you too." He stepped toward her, put his hand on the small of her back, and pulled her waist to his. She put her hand on his chest and kissed him. The warmth of his mouth overtook her as she melted into him as he moved his hand to her hair and ran it down the length of her braid, untying her hair band that held it together. Michael unlaced her hair and let it fall around her face and shoulders.

Abbie knew she was in love with Michael. When she pulled away from him, she could see in his eyes that he felt the same way. Words didn't need to be exchanged. As they stood there, Abbie wanted more from Michael, and she could tell he did as well.

"I should go," Michael whispered and kissed her on the cheek.

Abbie nodded, eyes closed, "Good night, Michael."

"Night, Abbie." He kept his eyes on her as he walked backward out of her bedroom.

After he had pulled the door shut, Abbie stood still, unable to move, sure the spell she was under would break if she did. Instead, she lifted Michael's shirt to her face and inhaled its scent. When she finally slipped into it, she felt her flesh come alive knowing that same shirt had once draped his body.

To her surprise, she fell asleep rather quickly once she had crawled into bed. It was unclear to her when her thoughts drifted into dreaming, but she soon found herself chasing her mother's ghost throughout the night. Annabelle was wearing the same yellow dress that she had been in Abbie's previous dream. Abbie focused on her mother's face and features. She was older, by twenty years, but still beautiful. Tiny lines had formed near her eyes and mouth, and her hair was sprinkled with bits of silver. Her hands also appeared older and showed signs of age.

Annabelle began to vanish, and Abbie chased her down dark hallways in a place with which she was unfamiliar, trying desperately to catch her. Her voice shouted silent pleas to gain Annabelle's attention, but to no avail. Flashes of light lit up the darkness in her dream, and yet she was still unable to recognize the location. At one point, Annabelle had disappeared. Abbie found herself bent over, catching her breath on what felt like concrete. She placed her hand on the cold, damp ground, still trying to make sense of where she was. Her eyes had just began to focus when she caught a glimpse of Annabelle.

Abbie sprang to her feet and ran after her. Although she was dreaming, she could feel her lungs burn as she raced to catch up with her. Annabelle's yellow dress sailed behind her, and she dipped in and out of empty corridors, leaving her daughter behind. The flashing light was nearly blinding Abbie. She stopped running, caught her breath, and rubbed her eyes with her hands several times, trying to focus.

Suddenly, Annabelle's face came into view, and with wide eyes she inhaled sharply and cried out, "Abbie, run! *Run!*" Abbie froze, completely caught off guard by the panic in her mother's eyes. Annabelle disappeared, and Abbie somehow managed to get her feet to move, but not before being pulled to the ground.

Sweating and out of breath, Abbie woke up, terrified. She saw a figure moving toward her in the dark. She instinctively threw the covers off of her and scurried to the other side of the bed, trying to get away, confused about where she was, and what was happening. The figure lunged at her, trying to grab her. She tried to let out a scream, but a hand covered her mouth.

"Abbie," she heard the figure whisper. "Abbie, shh, it's okay. It's me, Michael." Now she was wide awake and began to recall where she was and why she was there. Once she calmed down and her body relaxed, he let go of her and released his hand from her mouth. "I'm so sorry I scared you, Abbie. I didn't want you to wake up your dad. I heard you talking in here, and I wanted to make sure you were all right."

"Talking?" she asked in a confused whisper.

"Yeah I couldn't make out what you were saying."

Her breathing returned to normal, and she quickly became aware of how indecently she was dressed, wearing only Michael's T-shirt. She grabbed a blanket from the bed and pulled it over her.

"I'm sorry. I was dreaming."

"You sounded upset, so I wanted to see if you were all right. Are you okay, Abbie?" She nodded but didn't convince Michael, so he said, "I can stay right here with you if you need me to."

Embarrassed, she struggled with what to say. However, she was shaken up by the dream, and Michael could clearly tell. Desperately wanting to feel the safety of his arms she asked, "You don't mind?"

"Not at all," he assured her. He helped her up off of the floor and into the bed. He slid under the covers next to her and wrapped his arms around her and held her. "Do you want to talk about it?" he asked.

"Not tonight. Stay with me until I fall asleep?"

"I promise I won't leave until you do."

Abbie nestled herself into Michael's chest and she let out a long sigh. He held her close, whispering words of comfort while lightly stroking her hair. Their breathing synced together as they drifted off to sleep.

She wasn't sure when Michael left her room, but she was alone when she awoke the next morning. The house was silent as she slid out from under the covers and slipped on her jeans from the previous day, not bothering to change out of Michael's T-shirt. It was still fairly early, so she tiptoed down the stairs so as not to wake anyone else. When she entered the kitchen, she found her father lacing up his shoes at the kitchen table.

"Hey, kiddo," he said, looking up at her.

"Taking off?" Abbie asked.

"Yeah, I think I'll go wander around the neighborhood a bit. Maybe catch up with you later tonight?"

"Sounds great, Dad." Abbie hugged her father and said, "I'm so glad you came."

"Me too."

The screen door creaked open and closed as Henry left the house. Abbie watched him pull out of the driveway as she pondered her dream from the night before. She tried to shake the image of her mother's panicked face from memory, but it was nearly impossible.

Why does she want me to run? she wondered. *Where to? And from what?* Her dreams of Annabelle had never been like the ones she was currently experiencing. And for her father to drive hundreds of miles at her mother's urging was enough for Abbie to take them very seriously.

In order to distract herself, Abbie searched through Michael's kitchen cupboards in hopes of finding something to make for breakfast. Instead she found the ingredients for chocolate chip cookies.

The upstairs shower turned on and not long after it turned off, Michael and the dogs came downstairs. Abbie turned when she saw him standing in the doorway wearing nothing but blue jeans, with bare feet. Michael rapped a knuckle on the doorway as if requesting permission to enter the kitchen. Unable to take her eyes from his toned figure, still damp from the shower, she wiped her brow with the back of her hand.

"Oh, hey," she managed to say, feeling breathless as his body moved toward her. She was suddenly aware of her messy hair and the fact that she was covered in flour. "Sorry about the mess," she laughed, referring to the kitchen as well as herself. "I thought it might be nice for you to take some cookies to Paul."

"Thanks, Abbie. That's sweet of you."

"And I needed something to occupy my thoughts," she admitted. She continued to move about the kitchen, mixing and pouring ingredients and checking the temperature of the oven. She avoided looking at him as she apologized for her behavior in the night. "I'm so sorry you had to see that."

Michael leaned his elbows on the counter and watched her work. "No need to apologize. Do you want to talk about it at all?" He sensed that she was still shaken up.

"I'm not quite sure what to say. I don't want to bother you with it."

Michael stool up straight and said, "You certainly aren't bothering me."

She was silent for a while but then decided to share what was on her mind. "I've never talked to anyone about this besides my dad. I know the conversation from yesterday about my mother was a bit heavy. I don't expect you to understand or to even want to understand—"

Michael interrupted her by holding up his hand and saying, "Let me just stop you before you get ahead of yourself, Abbie. Let me assure you that I'm very interested in you. All of you. Even the parts that you think might not be something that the average person would want to know about. I want to know about them. I want to know all there is to know about you, including the stuff that might not be easy to hear or understand. So, please, tell me about what happened to you last night. Don't be embarrassed or feel as though you need to hold anything back. I'm here to listen, not to judge you."

Surprised at his response, she was unsure of where to start. Once she began describing the dream she had the previous evening, the words flowed freely. She watched as Michael listened intently as she talked. Abbie continued to float around the kitchen, finishing up the cookies, all the while questioning out loud her mother's behavior in both she and her father's dreams. Michael didn't offer up suggestions or try to help her make sense of the dreams. He simply listened, which was exactly what she needed.

10

MICHAEL

FROM THE TIME IT took Michael to drop off Abbie at Kate and Karl's and drive to Paul's house, he was already missing her. The past two days were by far the best he had ever had. He was falling head over heels for a girl from Georgia whom he had just met in a diner.

"Hey, man!" Michael said to Paul as he walked into his friend's living room.

"Hey, Michael." Paul was sitting propped up in a recliner watching television. His injured leg was wrapped in bandages. A set of crutches lay next to Paul on the floor. "What's in there?" Paul asked, referring to the plastic container in Michael's hands.

"Ah, cookies," Michael said handing the container to Paul.

"Your mom make these?" Paul asked nonchalantly as he opened the container, pulled out a cookie, and bit into it.

"Uh, no actually," Michael said, taking a seat on the couch. "Abbie made them."

Paul's ears perked up, and he looked at Michael. "Abbie?" he asked, with a mouthful of cookie. "From the diner?"

Michael chuckled and said, "Yeah, Abbie from the diner." Michael sat back on the couch and couldn't help but smile.

Paul laughed as well, pointing a cookie in Michael's direction, and said, "Aww, man, you're in love."

"What? Ha-ha, nah." Michael tried to play off his feelings for Abbie in front of his friend. He rubbed a hand over his face and then through his hair. He leaned back on the couch, put both hands behind his head, looked at Paul and said, "Maybe." A smile formed in the corner of his mouth, and he said, "She's pretty great."

"Well you should keep her around." Paul shoved another cookie in his mouth. "She makes a damn good cookie."

Michael laughed out loud and sat thinking to himself about Abbie. He finally said, "I definitely want to be with her. I realize I just met her, but from what I can tell, she has all of the qualities I am looking for."

"Yeah. Like cookie-making abilities," Paul joked, eating another one.

"I'll be sure to tell her you like them."

"So tell me about Abbie." Paul put the lid on the container, put the cookies down, and focused his attention on Michael. "What's got you so smitten?"

"Well she loves the farm, so that's a good thing. She wants to go to school, so she's saving money for that. Family is important to her, and she wants a lot of kids. She moved here by herself without any money or a plan. No car, no job, but she's making it work. She's not like most girls around here. She loves life and is not afraid to go after what she wants."

"Including you," Paul joked.

"Including me." Michael went on to tell Paul that Abbie made the first move for their first kiss. He explained how down to earth and real she was.

"Plus, she's gorgeous," Paul added.

"She's beautiful,' Michael agreed. "But she has no idea. She's confident about who she is and who she wants to be, but is completely shy about her looks. It's an endearing quality."

"Well that's great, man. I'm really happy for you."

"Thank you. I just hope she feels the same way. Anyway, enough about me. How are you? How's the leg?"

"It's all right I guess. Hurts like hell, but the drugs they gave me are good." Paul chuckled and said, "I never thought I'd damn near cut my own leg off."

"Well, I'm just glad you're doing well. Stephen and I already talked, and we are going to make sure everything is taken care of around here for you."

It went without saying, but Paul knew Michael was talking about taking care of Paul financially while he couldn't work. The three of them could always count on each other, and they never took advantage of one another. Paul and Stephen were the brothers he never had.

Michael stayed for a while with Paul. At one point, Paul had taken a dose of his medications and eventually fell asleep. Michael turned the volume down on the television and left without waking him.

As Michael drove home from Paul's house, he couldn't help but think about Abbie. An idea started to form in his mind, and he pulled out his cell phone and gave Stephen a call.

"Are you busy tonight?" Michael asked.

"Nope," Stephen said on the other end of the line.

"Can you meet me at my house in about half an hour?"

"Sure thing. What do you need?"

"I've got something in mind that I want to do for Abbie, but I need your help."

"No problem. I'll head right over."

"Great. See you soon."

Three hours later, Michael and Stephen plopped down on the couch in Michael's living room. Exhausted, Stephen asked Michael, "Well? Do you think she will like it?"

"I hope so. That was a lot of work. Thanks for your help."

"Anytime."

The two of them wandered out onto the porch and shared a couple of beers as night began to fall on the farm. As Stephen pulled out of the driveway awhile later, Michael gathered up the dogs and headed inside.

Just as he was climbing into bed, Michael's phone rang. It was Abbie. She had just gotten home from her shift at the diner, and she, too, was headed to bed.

"I won't keep you long," she said. "I just wanted to hear your voice and ask you when I could see you again."

"I'm glad you called," Michael assured her. "I've been missing you since I dropped you off earlier."

"Really?" she asked, delighted.

"As a matter of fact, I have a surprise for you."

"A surprise?" she inquired. "For me?"

"Yeah, a surprise for you," he chuckled. "But you will have to come over and see it."

"I can do that." Abbie was excited. "When can I see you again?"

"How about this weekend? I'd love to cook dinner for you at my house."

"That sounds perfect, Michael."

"Great. It's a date."

They shared a few more words and then hung up, wishing the other a good night. As Michael drifted off to sleep, his thoughts of Abbie turned into dreams. He pursued Abbie as she laughed and danced her way through his thoughts while he slept. Stunning and glowing with pure joy and life, Abbie was as beautiful as ever. At one point she looked a bit older, yet still breathtaking. She kept whispering in his ear, but he couldn't understand what she was saying. He tried to reach out to her as she floated away in a beautiful dress but couldn't seem to catch her. Her whispers grew louder, and before he woke up, he heard her say, "Find her."

It was hours later when he awoke from the dream, but to him it felt like minutes. He tossed and turned a bit, trying to get back to sleep, but was unsuccessful. He decided to call Abbie, but as he noticed the time, he hoped she wouldn't answer.

She picked up on the second ring.

"Hello?" Given the hour, she sounded very much awake.

"Abbie? Did I wake you?" Michael asked.

"No, actually. My dad and I are up talking. We meant to go to bed hours ago, but we've been too busy catching up. Shouldn't you be sleeping? It's late."

"Yeah, I guess so. I actually couldn't sleep, so I was hoping I might talk to you again. Even if it was just for a little while."

"Oh, that's so sweet. I can't wait to see you again, Michael."

"I can't wait to see you." Then he joked with her by saying, "If only I could just get you out of my head long enough to go back to sleep. But then there you are as well."

"Oh yeah?" she asked, encouraging him to explain.

He laughed, somewhat embarrassed, and said, "I was just dreaming about you, actually."

"Really? Tell me about it."

Michael's voice indicated that his mind was traveling to a place of tranquility as he recalled the dream. "You looked amazing. You were dancing and wearing a beautiful dress. You were a little bit older than you are now. Still very pretty, though. You kept whispering to me to come find you. Well, Abbie, I have definitely found you." Michael finished talking and then waited for Abbie to respond to his openness. Instead, there was silence.

"Abbie?" he asked. "Are you there?"

"I'm here," she stated. "Michael, I have to ask. What color was the dress?"

"Hmmm?" he asked, unsure of what she meant.

"The dress, Michael. The one I was wearing in the dream. What color was it?"

He had to stop and think. He hadn't paid attention to the dress. He was simply delighted he was dreaming of her. He thought for another moment and finally said, "I guess it might have been yellow."

There was another silence, and then Abbie finally said, "Michael?"

"Yes?"

"I think you were dreaming of my mother."

11

ABBIE

IT WAS ONE OF those days where Abbie couldn't shake the feeling that something wasn't quite right. The sensation began to rise inside of her not long after she woke up, and carried on into the day. She figured it would subside as she rode her bicycle into work, and even as she started her shift at the diner, but it didn't. Unable to pinpoint from where her uneasiness was stemming, she decided to tell herself it was simply because her father had left the day prior to go back to Georgia. She hadn't realized how much she missed him until he came to see her, and now that he was gone, she felt an emptiness that wasn't there before. She seemed to understand Annabelle's urging Henry to come to North Carolina. It was, in fact, possible that she was missing him more than she had realized. Even still, she couldn't help but feel that her world had somehow shifted.

To occupy her thoughts, she thought of Michael. His sparkling blue eyes and perfect smile came to mind, and she recalled the sensation of his mouth on hers. She could hardly stand the last few days they had been apart and longed to be in his arms again.

Abbie swept a broom across the floor of the diner while she quietly hummed to herself. It was near closing time, and most all of the customers had cleared out. Meghan happened to be working with her that evening, and she sat, propped up on a stool at the counter, thumbing through a magazine.

"When are you going out with Michael again?" Meghan asked, interrupting Abbie's thoughts.

"Tomorrow," Abbie said dreamily as she twirled herself around the broom. "He's making me dinner at his house. He also said he has a surprise for me."

Meghan swiveled around on the stool in order to face Abbie and asked, intrigued, "Oh I wonder what it is? I'll bet it's a key to his house. Or sexy lingerie."

Abbie laughed out loud. "I doubt it is either one of those."

The last few customers filed out of the diner, and Abbie walked over to clear away the dishes and wipe down the table.

Meghan continued by rolling her eyes and saying with a sarcastic laugh, "Well, whatever it is, I'll bet it will be perfect. I mean, he is perfect; you are perfect; you guys are the perfect couple, so it would only make sense that the surprise be perfect."

Meghan's comments made Abbie blush. "Neither of us is perfect," Abbie said, smiling. "And we aren't a couple."

"Well, not yet, maybe," Meghan offered, "but I'm sure you will be soon."

Abbie made her way back to the kitchen with the broom in one hand and a stack of dirty dishes in the other. Meghan trailed behind her.

"I sure hope so," Abbie admitted. She plopped the dishes in the sink, looked at Meghan, and said with a faraway look on her face, "He is amazing. Everything about him is irresistible."

Meghan leaned against the sink and said, "You guys are made for each other. Do you think you are in love with him?" she asked, her eyes wide.

Abbie bit her lip, afraid to admit out loud that she was, indeed, falling in love with Michael. "I think so," was all she managed to say.

Meghan threw her arms around Abbie in excitement and squealed with delight.

Before either of them could continue talking, they heard the front door open, which meant that they had customers. They giggled their way to the front of the diner but grew quiet by the time they had reached the front counter.

Two men in dark suits and ties had walked in. They weren't locals; that much was certain. They each were wearing sunglasses, which Abbie thought was a little odd, considering it was near dark. Both were very tall, slightly heavyset, with broad shoulders—near replicas of each other. The uneasy feeling that she had worked so hard to ignore that day, suddenly began to resurface. She happened to glance outside at a newer model black Suburban they had parked right outside the entrance to the diner.

Meghan interrupted Abbie's thoughts. "Seriously? We close in fifteen minutes," she whispered, annoyed.

Abbie started to grab a notepad from her apron.

"I got it," Meghan said to Abbie. Abbie watched as Meghan strolled over to their table and took their order. She couldn't quite hear the conversation, but Abbie could tell Meghan was flirting with them by how she had her hip cocked to the side and by the way she threw her head back to laugh at something that most likely wasn't funny.

That's so Meghan, Abbie said to herself, shaking her head and chuckling as she made her way back to the kitchen. For the moment, she couldn't remember what had made her feel so uncomfortable.

Abbie found Karl in the back of the kitchen and said, "Don't close down the kitchen just yet. Meghan is taking an order."

Annoyed, Karl checked his watch. "Fifteen minutes before we close ..." he mumbled under his breath. "Would you mind turning the sign around on the front door, Abbie?" Karl was normally delighted to have the extra business, regardless if it was after hours, but that night he, too, was a bit unnerved, for no particular reason.

"No problem," she said, and made her way back up front. Meghan was filling drinks at the soda machine as Abbie walked to the front door. She locked it and flipped around the Open sign to read Closed. Two sets of eyes watched her as she walked to and from the door. Abbie shot Meghan a look as if to ask her if she was also getting a strange vibe from their customers.

"At least they took their sunglasses off," Meghan whispered, reading Abbie's thoughts once they were standing next to each other.

"I know, right?" Abbie whispered back, laughing slightly, rolling her eyes. Meghan passed Abbie their food order to take back to Karl as Meghan went back to the table with their drinks.

"Thanks," Karl said sarcastically once Abbie gave him the slip of paper. He fired up the burners on the stoves and grabbed several pots and pans from the racks above.

Abbie made her way back to the front of the diner. Meghan was wiping down tables, and Abbie tidied up around the counter. The two men sitting at the booth talked quietly with serious looks on their faces and their hands folded on top of the table.

Meghan shot Abbie a look from across the dining room and mouthed the word "jerks," referring to their customers. Abbie tried not to crack a smile. Meghan began imitating their sober facial expressions, and Abbie turned away so she wouldn't laugh. She couldn't help but agree. These guests in particular were by far the most unfriendly that she had seen come into the diner. They definitely didn't seem to have any regard for the fact that at that point, the diner was closed for the evening.

Karl hollered from the kitchen once the food was ready. Abbie held a hand up at Meghan, who was just about finished wiping down the tables, indicating that she would bring the food out for her. Meghan nodded a thank-you her way.

Abbie brought the food tray out on one hand and placed the plates of food in front of each of them. "Hey, guys! I'm Abbie. You've already met Meghan," she said, motioning to her friend. Each of their faces remained stoic, so Abbie pushed even further for a response. "Haven't seen you folks in before. Are you in town for business?"

"No," one of them said sternly, avoiding eye contact and further conversation.

"Just passing through," the other said, looking directly at Abbie. His eyes were steely, gray, vapid holes that made her very uneasy.

Abbie felt her face get hot but managed to smile at both of them and politely said, "Well, just let us know if you need anything." She tucked the tray under her arm, turned on her heel, and walked away.

"I hope they leave soon," Meghan whispered. "Tracey and I are supposed to go out tonight."

"You can just go," Abbie offered. "I'm sure Karl won't mind." Both girls walked back to the kitchen, where Karl was finishing up the last bit of dishes. "You don't mind if Meghan takes off, right, Karl?" she asked him.

"Nah, get out of here," he said, waving a hand in their direction.

After Meghan left, Karl and Abbie wandered to the front of the diner to check on their guests. As Abbie approached, the two men hushed their conversation as she refilled their drinks. They didn't thank her, simply resumed talking in whispers as she walked away. She couldn't shake how uneasy the two of them were making her feel. She was certain it was only because it was uncommon that she met unfriendly people at Kate and Karl's.

A half an hour after closing time, the men finished their meals, and Abbie went to clear their dishes and leave them their individual checks. "Thanks for comin' in, fellas," she said pleasantly. "We hope you enjoyed your meal. Come again if you ever pass through again."

Just then the man with the gray eyes grabbed her by her wrist as she reached for the last of their dishes. She gasped, startled, and her eyes caught his. "We will," he said and gave her a leering smile as he shoved several twenty dollar bills into her hand.

"That should cover it," the other man said.

Abbie nodded, without words, and the other man let go of her wrist. "Take care," she said, trying not to sound intimidated as they stood up to leave. Both men adjusted their suits and marched out of the diner.

Karl had seen the entire scene unfold and asked Abbie how she was as she scurried past him toward the kitchen.

"I'm fine," she said, trying to laugh it off.

"Toss those dishes in the sink, and then we will head out," Karl offered. "We can clean those up in the morning. I'm sure you want to get home as much as I do."

"If not more," she mumbled under her breath.

Karl shut the lights off in the diner, and then held the door open for Abbie as they walked out. The black Suburban had just left the parking lot, its taillights still visible on the road, cigarette butts still glowing on the pavement.

12

MICHAEL

"KEEP YOUR EYES CLOSED."

"I am." Abbie was laughing at Michael. He had picked her up that afternoon and was now leading her blindly from his kitchen into the living room.

"Are they still closed?" Michael teased.

"Yes," she laughed. "Michael, come on. I don't like surprises. Show me already!"

He was laughing as well. He took a step back from her so he could see her reaction when he said, "Okay. Open them."

Abbie opened her eyes. Her smile fell, but her face lit up, and she drew her hands to her cheeks in astonishment. "Michael," she whispered. Her eyes fell upon the piano that she had played for Michael just days earlier in the attic.

"Stephen helped me bring it down the other day. We cleaned it up, and I had it tuned. For you."

"For me?" She looked at Michael as she stepped toward it, gently placing her hands on the keys.

"I just thought that now that I know someone who can play it, it should be played. I'd like to think that now it will be used on a more regular basis." He stood with his legs shoulder-width apart, hands in his pockets. He started to blush, hoping he wasn't being too forward.

"Wow, Michael. I'm so flattered." Abbie knew that Michael's gesture meant that he wanted her to be somewhat of a permanent fixture in his home. She sat down on the piano bench and began to play. The melody flowed naturally from her fingertips, playing from notes etched deep into her soul.

Michael stared in awe at Abbie as she filled the house with music. She was beautiful. As she sat at the piano, he couldn't help but notice the curve of her spine and the way her hair swayed as she moved, ever so slightly, with the music. As her hands floated across the keys, Michael walked over to her, leaned down, and whispered in her ear, "Keep playing. I'll start dinner." He kissed her on the cheek and headed to the kitchen.

Once in the kitchen, Michael began chopping vegetables, grilling chicken, and boiling water for pasta. He couldn't help but think he could get used to cooking for Abbie. He secretly hoped that one day she would fulfill his dreams of having a wife and raising children in that house with him.

As the dinner simmered on the stove, Michael opened a bottle of wine and poured two glasses. He was just about to carry the glasses into the living room where Abbie was playing when he heard the music stop.

Abbie entered the kitchen a moment later and said while inhaling the kitchen's aroma, "Wow. It smells delicious in here."

"Thank you," Michael said. "It should be ready soon. Would you like some wine?"

"I would love some." She took a glass from his hand, brushing her fingers on his. The sensation was nearly electrifying. As she took a sip of her wine, her eyes met Michael's. She wondered if she would ever get used to the way his eyes made her heart race.

Michael took a sip of his wine as well, without taking his eyes off of Abbie. He set his glass down on the island and moved closer to her. He took her glass from her and placed it next to his. Responding to his cue, Abbie slipped her hands around his waist and lifted her chin to meet his lips. Michael was nearly certain Abbie felt his heart leaping from his chest. To be fair, her heart was racing just as fast. He wanted her, more than ever, as they stood kissing in the kitchen. Sensing the same longing in her kiss, he pulled her closer. They were interrupted by a hiss coming from the top of the stove. Droplets of sauce sputtered from the pan and landed on the stove.

"I suppose you better keep an eye on dinner," Abbie said flirtatiously.

"I guess so," Michael said as they both laughed. He tended to the food while Abbie resumed drinking her wine. His movements suggested he was focused on dinner, but his mind was completely occupied with thoughts of Abbie. He could feel her eyes on him, watching as he lit the candles on the dining room table, as she swirled the wine in her glass.

"Anything I can do to help?" she called from the kitchen.

"Nope. It's almost ready. You just relax," Michael called back. Once the meal was prepared and on the dining room table, he led her to her seat.

"Thank you," she said as he pulled out her chair.

Michael poured them each more wine as she helped herself to the cuisine.

"This looks great, Michael. Is this one of your grandmother's recipes?"

"Actually, this one is my own."

"It's delicious," she said, taking a bite.

"Thank you."

"Tell me about your mom."

"My mom?"

"Yeah I want to know about her—from your point of view."

"She's a good woman. A hard worker." Michael went on to tell Abbie about what happened when Michael was born, her reasons for not moving to the farm, and her dedication to her career.

"Sounds like that may have been a little bit tough on you?" Abbie inquired.

Michael sort of shrugged, but then he said, "I think it would have been nice to have her around a little more than she was. I think she has regrets about that as well. But she always made sure I was surrounded by love."

"Well that's all that really matters," Abbie decided. She held up her glass, "Cheers to your mom."

"And to your mom as well," Michael added, raising his glass.

Abbie gave him a knowing smile, and their glasses clanked together. "That's sweet," she said. "Thank you."

Abbie was incredibly easy to talk to, Michael decided. She was intelligent, and they had a great deal in common. Her laugh was contagious, and he was consumed by her genuineness. She was the type of person that was herself in anyone's company, and he loved that about her.

Once they were done eating, they migrated to the living room, where they continued their conversation, legs pulled up on the couch, facing each other. Sam and Bull curled up on the floor in front of them.

Several hours had gone by before either of them realized what time it was. "Wow, it's getting late. I didn't mean to keep you out for as long as I did," Michael said. "Was there a particular time you wanted me to take you home tonight?"

Abbie sat quietly, staring at Michael intently. He was a bit taken aback by the look in her eyes. Abbie crawled toward him on the couch and said playfully, "How about tomorrow?" She kissed him on the mouth, and Michael allowed her to climb onto his lap. Abbie's mouth was eager and warm on his lips. It was impossible to resist her.

Michael pulled away from her, slightly breathless, and said, "Wait. I want to make sure I understand what you mean."

"Michael," Abbie said, attempting to clarify, "I'm in love with you. I'd like to stay here with you tonight. I want to be with you." She gazed into his eyes and searched for any underlying doubt.

Fully understanding what she meant, Michael pulled her face into his and kissed her. He pulled her legs around his waist, put his arms underneath her legs and stood up, her body wrapped around his.

"I love you too, Abbie," he whispered, his lips opening just for a moment to breathe those words.

Michael carried Abbie upstairs and into the master bedroom. He laid her down gently on the bed, and he lay down beside her. They stared at each other, their faces illuminated by the glow of the moon that peeked in through the windows. He repeated the words he had just spoken. "I love you, Abbie. I'm so glad we found each other."

"Me too," she said. "I couldn't have asked for anyone better to be in my life."

"I'm not going anywhere. I'm here for always."

Michael took Abbie in his arms. They made love slowly, passionately, as if neither one of them wanted it to end. His fingers traced over every inch of her skin, memorizing each detail. He deliberately took his time, kissing her eyelids, her fingertips, elbows, hips, toes. Every part of her was beautiful, and he wanted to make sure she felt that way. Whispers of love and promises were spoken throughout the night, underneath bedsheets and blankets.

They fell asleep just before dawn, their bodies intertwined and exhausted, each dreaming of the other. When they awoke the next morning, they made love again. Only this time, it was more playful than before. By then, their bodies greeted each other like old friends.

Michael left Abbie to sleep while he threw on a pair of jeans and headed to the kitchen to make coffee for the two of them. When he came back upstairs with two piping hot cups, Abbie had pulled on one of his clean T-shirts and was seated out on the balcony outside the master bedroom. Seated in a wicker chair with her feet propped up on the railing of the balcony, she breathed in the morning.

"Hi," he said, joining her, handing her a coffee cup. He couldn't help but notice her bare legs, stretched out before him.

"Well, hi," she said, accepting the cup with both hands.

Abbie reached for Michael's hand, and they sat in a comforting silence as they enjoyed the warm, summer air and the sound of the trees, quietly rustling in the breeze.

Michael fixed his eyes on Abbie, who was gazing out over the property. She was simply stunning, even when she wasn't trying to be. Her hair was disheveled from the previous evening, and any bit of makeup she may have had on the day before was long since gone. Michael couldn't help but picture the two of them, holding hands like they were, forty, or even fifty years into the future. He didn't want to spend another day without her. He decided that from then on he would do whatever he could to keep her in his life. He never imagined it would be the last day he would ever spend with her.

13

ABBIE

"**Damnit.**"

Meghan had just spilled soda down the front of her apron and was cursing under her breath. It was Friday night, and Abbie had never seen the diner so busy. Meghan had explained to Abbie earlier that week that the town's peak summer tourist season was upon them and to expect floods of people leaving or heading into Wilmington. Abbie had been working double shifts all week. She was happy to be making extra money, but she was exhausted and hadn't seen Michael in days. She tried to stay focused as she rushed around, taking orders and clearing tables.

"You okay?" Abbie asked Meghan as she rushed by her with a tray of food. She looked back at Meghan to see if she had heard her.

Annoyed, Meghan nodded and raised a hand in Abbie's direction, indicating for her not to worry. Abbie didn't have time to worry, even if she had wanted to. She had been on her feet since early that morning, dying for a break. Yet, there was a thirty-minute wait for a table, and customers continued to arrive in droves.

Kate and Karl were both in the kitchen, cooking and washing dishes as fast as they could. They lived for the busy season and were in good spirits. Abbie had rushed back with a load of dirty dishes only to find the both of them singing and laughing.

"Hello, Abbie, darling!" Kate called to her from behind a mountain of suds at the sink. "How's it look up front?"

"Same as it has been all day," she said, forcing a smile. Abbie loved working for such an enthusiastic couple, but she was drained of energy.

"Chin up, my dear!" Kate attempted to encourage Abbie. "Just think, we close in an hour, and you will have a fistful of money to take home."

Kate did have a point, Abbie thought to herself. Within the last week she had made enough money to pay for the classes she was hoping to take that fall, plus extra. Gathering up some motivation, Abbie slapped a smile on her face and headed back out to the dining room to help Meghan finish up for the night.

The last customers of the evening finally left an hour after closing. Abbie and Meghan plopped down at a booth, completely worn out. After a few exaggerated sighs, they both started laughing.

"I smell like soda," Meghan said, pointing to her apron, still laughing. "Good thing I brought a change of clothes for tonight."

"You're going out tonight?" Abbie asked, shocked. "After the day we've had? All I want to do is sleep."

"I had planned on it. Hey, you should come, Abbie! A few of us girls are going to have some drinks in Wilmington. It'll be a blast."

"I don't know," Abbie said, yawning. "I'm beat."

"Oh, come on. It will be fun. I've got an extra outfit in my car you can wear."

"What's wrong with what I've got on?" Abbie asked, looking down at her clothes. Abbie knew Meghan was referring to the way she was modestly dressed.

"Oh, nothing," Meghan said, trying to recover. "I was just saying, if you are interested in changing, I have extra clothes."

"Thanks."

"Does that mean you will come out?" Meghan's eyes got wide with excitement, and she clasped her hands together.

Abbie cracked a smile and said, "Oh, sure, why not?"

The two of them looked around the diner and figured they had an hour of cleaning ahead of them. Gaining a second wind, they stood up and got to work.

Just then, Kate appeared from the kitchen and said to the both of them, "You ladies can head out if you'd like. You've busted your tails all day; go ahead and get out of here."

Meghan stripped off her apron without hesitation.

"Thank you, Kate," Abbie said graciously.

"Let's go," Meghan said hurriedly, grabbing Abbie's hand, "before she changes her mind."

Kate laughed and waved them off as Abbie and Meghan headed out of the diner. Abbie mouthed a *thank you* at Kate as Meghan rushed them out to her car. The parking lot was nearly empty as they trudged across it to Meghan's car.

"I'm going to change my clothes," Meghan said to Abbie, rummaging through her backseat for a change of clothes.

"That's fine," Abbie said. It was nearly dark, but the summer heat was still unrelenting. Abbie checked her reflection in the window of Meghan's car, fixing her hair and adjusting her shorts. Abbie did a double take and watched Meghan changed her clothes, out in the open, stripping down to her bra and underwear in the parking lot, and then changing into a dress that she had in her car.

"What?" Meghan asked Abbie, as if her behavior was perfectly normal. "No one saw. And I don't care if they did. Come on. Let's go."

Abbie laughed and got into the car. Her friend's behavior never failed to surprise her. Meghan checked her makeup in the rearview mirror, strapped on her seatbelt, and pulled the car out of the parking lot. Abbie turned up the music on the radio, and they sang the entire way to Wilmington. Abbie had nearly forgotten how tired she was at that point. She pulled her cell phone out of her purse and texted Michael. *'Going out for drinks with Meghan. Call you later. I miss you so much. I love you.'*

Michael texted her back and said, *'Have a great time. Love and miss you too.'*

Twenty minutes later, Abbie and Meghan were parked on a side street in downtown Wilmington. Once they had stepped out of Meghan's car, the streetlights beamed down on both of them.

Abbie caught her breath as she saw what Meghan was wearing. It was an all too familiar yellow dress. She stopped in her tracks as she immediately realized it was the exact dress that Annabelle was wearing in Abbie's recent dreams.

Meghan turned around when she realized Abbie wasn't beside her. "Is something wrong?" Meghan asked.

Abbie's face went white. "Where did you get that dress?"

"Oh, I got it at that consignment shop near the diner," Meghan boasted, looking down, admiring the dress, and swaying from side to side a bit. "Isn't it great?"

Abbie couldn't move. She could barely speak, or take her eyes off of the dress, but she managed to say, "It looks great."

Meghan took a step closer to Abbie, attempted to get her to look at her by saying, "Seriously, Abbie. You look like you've seen a ghost."

Abbie couldn't help but laugh out loud at Meghan's accusation. Meghan didn't know why she was laughing but laughed right along with Abbie, linking her arm with hers, and led her up the street to the nearest bar.

"Tracey is meeting us," Meghan said. "I think she might be bringing a few other girls."

"Great," Abbie recited, keeping her pace in line with Meghan's. The moment felt a bit surreal as she stared at the dress, wondering how it materialized from her dreams. She wasn't sure if she would be able to shake the anxiety that washed over her, but she followed Meghan to the bar anyway.

The girls walked straight to the bartender once they stepped inside, and Meghan ordered them each a cocktail. Abbie hoped that a few drinks would help her relax and have a good time. She thanked Meghan but had to nearly shout over the music that blared overhead. Tracey joined them not long after their first drink. By that time, Abbie began to loosen up a little.

"Tell us what's going on with you and Michael," Tracey begged Abbie after she had ordered herself a drink.

Abbie began to blush.

"Have you guys done it yet?" Meghan asked, nonchalantly, sipping her drink.

"Oh my goodness," Abbie said, turning a deeper shade of red.

"Holy smokes, you did, didn't you?" Tracey asked, intrigued. "How was it? I'll bet it was hot. Michael is so gorgeous. Abbie, you are so lucky."

Abbie laughed at her friends' comments and without revealing too much she said, "He's amazing."

"Did you tell him you love him?" Meghan gasped, clutching Abbie's arm.

"Who said it first? Was it him? He said it first, didn't he?" Tracey persisted.

"Shh, you guys!" Abbie was a bit overwhelmed by Tracey and Meghan's interest in her relationship with Michael. Attempting to quiet the two of them, she leaned in close to them and said, "Keep your voices down."

"Oh, come on, tell us *something*," Meghan begged.

After a few moments, Abbie said with a sly smile, "I said it first."

Tracey and Meghan could hardly contain themselves as they waited for Abbie to give them more details. Before Abbie could get a word out, a waitress had brought over a round of drinks to them.

"These are from the guys over there," the waitress said, pointing to a group of gentlemen across the bar.

"Oh, hell yeah," Tracey said under her breath, checking out the guys that were now waving at the three of them.

"Definitely not my type," Meghan said, "but thanks for the free drinks." She laughed and raised her glass to the gentlemen.

"I'm going over there," Tracey said. And with that, she gave them a wink and strutted across the bar. Abbie was shocked at Tracey's boldness, but Meghan didn't seem to notice. She was too busy waiting for Abbie to give her more details about Michael.

"He seems so smooth and romantic," Meghan said. "Is he like that when you guys are together?"

"Yes, actually," Abbie gushed. She told Meghan about the meal Michael had cooked and about the piano he had put in his living room for her.

"Do you think that means he wants you to move in?" Meghan asked.

Before Abbie could answer, Tracey poked her head into their conversation. She mentioned she was going on to a different bar with the guys that had just purchased their drinks.

"Text us when you want to leave," Meghan told Tracey as she walked away.

Abbie and Meghan continued their conversation about Michael while sipping their drinks. By that time, the bar was packed, and it was becoming difficult to hold a conversation. Out of the corner of Abbie's eye, she thought she saw someone that looked familiar. Meghan whipped her head around to try to catch a glimpse of who had caught Abbie's eye.

"Hey," Meghan said, "Isn't that—?"

Standing directly in Abbie's line of sight was a set of steely gray eyes. Her blood immediately went cold. She would have recognized those eyes anywhere. An all-too-familiar feeling of anxiety she had recently been experiencing flooded over her. In an instant, she began to panic. Her mother's warnings resonated in her ears as she recognized the two men that drove the black Suburban to the diner just days before. This time, they weren't wearing suits and ties. They blended in with everyone else, making it a bit harder for Abbie to track them in the crowd.

"Let's go," Abbie said, "Now." She wasn't even sure why she said it, but she knew they needed to act, right then.

"What?" Meghan protested.

"Now!" Abbie urged. She grabbed Meghan's arm and pulled her to the exit. Once they got outside, Abbie confirmed with Meghan who she had seen in the bar.

"So what?" Meghan said. "They probably didn't even seen us, and even if they did, why the hell are we running from them?"

"You need to trust me," Abbie insisted, grabbing Meghan by the hand as she began running down the street toward the car.

"Abbie, wait!" Meghan called out, jerking her back toward her.

Abbie turned back, not only to see Meghan's face covered in confusion, but she also spotted the two men they were trying to get away from. Abbie locked eyes with them, and they began to walk faster and push through the crowd on the sidewalk toward Abbie and Meghan.

"Meghan, run! They are following us!" Abbie was whispering to Meghan, but her voice echoed an urgency that Meghan didn't argue with.

"Abbie, I don't have my keys!" Meghan said, trying to keep up with Abbie.

"What do you mean you don't have them?" Abbie stopped dead in her tracks. They were feet away from Meghan's car.

"They're gone. I must have dropped them."

"Meghan, look at me," Abbie said, stressing the seriousness of the situation. "We have to go. Now."

Scared, Meghan nodded, trusting Abbie completely as they both began to run. They both could clearly see that they were being chased. They pushed their way through crowds of people, and after they had run a few blocks, Abbie pulled Meghan down a less busy side street. It was dark, desolate, and eerily familiar. Meghan wasn't running nearly as fast as Abbie, and when she looked back at her, encouraging her to run fast, Abbie could clearly see Meghan's dress flowing about her, just as it had when her mother had worn it in the dream.

Abbie felt sick as the pieces of her dreams were falling into place. She now understood what her mother was warning her about. She cursed herself at her inability to see it beforehand.

"Abbie!" Meghan shrieked.

She turned around to see that the man with the steely gray eyes had nearly caught up to them by running at full speed in their direction.

"Come *on*!" Abbie screamed, trying not to cry. She was completely terrified and wasn't sure how much longer she and Meghan could keep running. She had noticed that Meghan had lost her shoes at some point. Despite her bare feet, Meghan kept running. Abbie still had sandals on her feet; however, she had lost her purse somehow while rushing through the crowds.

"We have to hide," Meghan said, panicking.

Hiding seemed like their best option, so Abbie and Meghan began trying the doors on the storefronts on the street. They weren't having any luck, and their predators were gaining on them. They cut down several more side streets, and just when Abbie was about to give up hope, she spotted an open window. Meghan saw it too, and they raced toward it.

Upon their arrival, they realized the window wasn't open nearly as far as it needed to be for them to squeeze through. They both grabbed the edge of the window and heaved it upward, breaking the hinge and sending the window crashing to the ground. They pushed in the screen, and Abbie shoved Meghan through the window before she climbed in after her. Just as Abbie was pulling herself through, one of the men rounded the corner, spotting them.

"They saw us," Abbie told her calmly. Meghan became hysterical. Abbie grabbed her and covered her mouth to keep her quiet. "You have to keep it together. Come on. We have to hide."

Their eyes focused on their surroundings. Abbie broke out into a cold sweat when she realized they were in a library.

"Damnit," Abbie said under her breath as she realized she was colliding with yet another piece of her mother's prophecy. The halls that they began to race down, which were once unfamiliar, Abbie clearly recognized as the ones from her dream. Shadows stalked Abbie and Meghan, and they could feel themselves being hunted by the men from whom they were fleeing.

Soon, they were in the main part of the library and were surrounded by shelves of books. Out of breath, Abbie wasn't sure how much longer she could continue to run. Her eyes were drawn to a dark corner of the library, and she led Meghan to it. They both crouched down underneath a desk and pulled a chair in front of them, hiding them from view. She desperately wished that either of them had a cell phone to call for help.

Abbie recalled her mother's warnings. In the first dream she had urged her to be silent; in the second, to run. As she and Meghan sat silently panting from underneath the desk, sweat rolling down their backs, it dawned on Abbie that her mother never told her to hide. Her mouth went dry as she realized she had made a terrible mistake. She knew she had just put both of them in serious danger.

As soon as her mistake had registered in her mind, a pair of steel-toed boots appeared before them. Meghan screamed as the man yanked the chair away from the desk, sending it crashing to the other side of the room. He grabbed both Meghan and Abbie by the hair and pulled them out from under the desk. Their trembling bodies spilled out onto the floor, and they clung to each other as the man pointed a gun at them.

"Please," Meghan begged, "don't hurt us."

Abbie remained silent, in shock at the events that were unfolding, regretting ignoring every single sign that was given to her up until that point. She couldn't help but think she could have prevented the entire situation.

"Get up," the man demanded.

The girls scurried to their feet.

"Walk," he said, shoving them in front of him. "If you try to run, I will shoot you," he warned. His voice was flat but serious, almost as if he had said the words countless times before.

He led them to the back entrance of the library. He opened the door to meet the black Suburban that had once parked in the lot at the diner. The vehicle was running, and the quieter gentleman, the one that had avoided Abbie's eyes at the diner, was in the driver's seat.

Before Abbie and Meghan had a chance to even think about escaping, the back door to the Suburban opened, and they were pushed inside. The first thing Abbie noticed was that the backseat had been removed as well as the inside handles on the doors. Meghan also noticed and started hyperventilating. Abbie had no idea what was about to happen to them, but she was sure nothing good could come of the situation. Her heart began to race, but she attempted to stay calm and quiet her friend. They scurried to the far back corner of the Suburban and huddled together.

As the Suburban sped off, the men began arguing in the front seat. Abbie couldn't quite make out what they were saying, but in their hushed conversation she gathered that the driver called the man with the steely gray eyes, Griffin. Certain she wasn't supposed to hear it, and most likely wouldn't hear them mention each other by name again, Abbie locked the name in her memory.

Abbie scanned the vehicle for an escape plan. Griffin must have known what she was thinking because he sprang into the back seat to bind their hands and feet with duct tape. Meghan became hysterical and combative, kicking and shrieking as hard and as loud as she could. Griffin immediately slammed her head into the side of the vehicle, knocking her unconscious. Instinctively, Abbie screamed.

"Shut up," Griffin said, covering her mouth with his hand. Her terrified eyes locked with his, and she agreed by frantically nodding her head. He shoved her mouth away from his hand.

Once he finished wrapping duct tape around Meghan's limp hands and feet, he started on Abbie's. Abbie knew she had to stay conscious in order to come up with a plan to escape, so she didn't fight him as she held her hands out in front of her, allowing him to tie her up. She refused to cry or appear weak so she gritted her teeth to keep the tears in her eyes from spilling. She looked over at Meghan. Blood was trickling from a gash in the back of her head, but she appeared to be breathing. Griffin returned to the front of the Suburban and appeared to be giving directions to the driver.

Abbie tried to look out the window to see if she could make out where they were. The sky was pitch black, but she gauged by the speed of the Suburban that they were on the freeway. She wiggled her hands and feet to see if it was possible for her to break free. Her attempt was noticed by the driver, and her skin began to crawl as he called her by name.

"Abbie!" he snapped from the front seat. "Don't bother with that," he said, referring to her trying to loosen the duct tape.

Speechless, Abbie couldn't recall how he would know her name. It suddenly dawned on her that she had introduced herself to them at the diner. Afraid to move, she felt the color leave her face.

Griffin turned around in his seat and said, "We've been following you and Meghan for over a week. We knew you would be perfect."

Abbie swallowed hard. "Perfect for what?" she asked hesitantly.

"You'll see." The driver answered that time, looking at her through the rearview mirror. His words were matter-of-fact and were laced with an eeriness that made Abbie believe that the situation was hopeless.

Meghan started to regain consciousness, and Abbie tried to warn her with her eyes to be quiet. When Meghan started to sob, Abbie scooted closer to her and tried to shush her.

"She's going to be a problem," the driver said to Griffin. Nodding in agreement, Griffin climbed into the backseat. He grabbed Meghan by the arm, pulling her away from Abbie. Meghan screamed, and in an instant, Griffin twisted her head, snapping her neck. Meghan slumped to the floor, her eyes still open.

It had all happened so fast. Abbie couldn't keep from crying, and she covered her mouth with her hands, trying to stay quiet. She stared into Meghan's lifeless eyes as Griffin made his way back to the front seat.

"I'm so sorry," Abbie whispered, tears streaming down her face, as she reached out and touched her friend's hair. Meghan lay there, lifeless in her yellow dress, a haunting reminder that she had failed to heed Annabelle's warnings. She squinted her eyes shut and prayed for Michael to rescue her. The thought of never seeing him again made her stomach churn.

Hours and many miles later, the Suburban came to a stop. Abbie was exhausted but determined to keep her eyes open. Griffin had crawled into the backseat, pushing Meghan's body out of the way as if it was any other object that just so happened to be in his way. He cut Abbie's duct table from her arms and legs.

"We are switching vehicles," he explained to her. "You can get out to pee, but you've got three minutes. Don't even think about running." He pulled up the front of his shirt and showed her the pistol he was carrying. "I will have no problem shooting you."

Abbie believed him. Griffin grabbed hold of her arm as she exited the Suburban. She squinted as her eyes adjusted to the light. Her eyes were swollen from crying and lack of sleep. As she focused, she realized they were in a secluded, wooded area. She knew that even if she did run, she had little chance of coming across anyone that could help her. Griffin allowed Abbie to go to the bathroom behind a tree as he stood waiting for her. When she had finished, he led her to an identical vehicle and put her in the backseat. Certain they were taking the other vehicle to get rid of Meghan's body, she whispered a prayer that her friend rest in peace.

Once inside the other Suburban, Abbie's eyes quickly darted around to look for a way to escape. This time, the seats were intact as well as the handles on the doors, giving Abbie a glimmer of hope. Griffin was in the driver's seat this time, allowing the previous driver to sleep in the passenger seat. As they started to drive away, Abbie realized they forgot to tape up her hands and feet. She knew she had a very small window of opportunity if she was going to make it out alive.

The Suburban rambled its way out of the woods, and Abbie peered out the window and watched as the trees slipped past, faster and faster as the vehicle gained speed. She shut her eyes, inhaled all of the strength she could gather, and when she exhaled she jerked the door handle open, slamming the weight of her body into the door with her shoulder, and leaped out of the Suburban. She tumbled out onto the shoulder of the road, gravel driving its way into her flesh as she skidded across the pavement. Tires from the Suburban screeched to a halt, and she heard car doors slam as she gained her footing and darted back into the woods.

Part
2

14

JACKSON

THE HEELS AND TOES of Jackson Wells's shoes clicked and clacked as he walked down the linoleum hallway of the Richmond Police Department in Virginia, carrying a Styrofoam cup of coffee and a pad of paper attached to a clipboard. Jackson was tall and handsome, in his midthirties, with chestnut eyes and straw-colored hair. He was dressed in slacks and a shirt and tie. His hands were manicured, his hair well-groomed, and his face clean-shaven. A pistol hung holstered at his hip. He had just driven in from Washington, DC, on a special assignment. At the end of the hallway, he pushed open a steel door to an interrogation room.

Curled up in the corner of the room on a small cot was a frail figure, covered in scrapes and bruises. Her hair was matted to her neck and shoulders, her eyes bloodshot, and lips, cracked. Her clothes were muddy, a bit torn, and bloodstained. A glass of water sat on the floor beside her, untouched. Detectives had spoken with her hours earlier and, based on her testimony, made the decision to call the US Marshals Service.

"Abbie Peterson?" he asked gently, crouching down next to her. "Jackson Wells, Department of Justice," he said, extending a hand. He got word that patrolmen brought her to the station that morning after they spotted her on the side of the freeway, crawling out of the woods.

Abbie lifted her head but did not shake Jackson's hand. Instead she drew her knees in to her chest, looked down at the floor, and said, "I want to call my dad."

"I'm afraid we can't do that just yet," he said calmly. "We need to discuss a few more things before we can let anyone know where you are."

Abbie began to cry.

"I know that sounds unfair, Miss Peterson, but we just want to keep you safe." Jackson continued to talk, staying by her side as she cried. "Police officers along the East Coast have been instructed to contact the US Department of Justice if victims such as yourself are taken into custody. Currently, there is a large human trafficking operation under way along the East Coast. The conversation we are about to have is going to be very difficult, but I need you to help me, Abbie. Can you do that?"

As soon as he spoke her name, Abbie lifted her eyes to meet his. She nodded silently, wiping her tears away.

"I'd like to piece together a timeline of events, and then I'm going to ask you to look at a few photos. Can you help me do that, Abbie?" He deliberately said her name once more to better establish her trust and build a connection with her.

Jackson continued by saying, "My notes say that officers picked you up on the side of the road near Interstate 95. They also said you refused medical treatment after they called an ambulance."

"Yes. I'm not going to a hospital." Abbie shifted on the cot and said in a hoarse whisper, "I don't have any broken bones, and I don't need stitches. So if it's all right with you, I'd rather not go."

Jackson nodded and confirmed, "That's not a problem. Let's talk about the timeline. From what I understand, the abduction took place in downtown Wilmington, North Carolina, around eleven yesterday evening."

"Yes, I think so," Abbie said quietly. "Meghan and I left work around ten. We drove to Wilmington, had a few drinks, tried to leave, and were chased through downtown by two men that eventually abducted us. We ended up in a library, and that's where they caught us."

"Two men, correct?" Jackson asked, scribbling down notes on the notepad.

"Yes. I don't remember mentioning it earlier, but we had seen them prior to last night. They came into the diner where we work."

Jackson looked up from his notes. He had met other victims of human trafficking, but none of them had been stalked prior to their abductions. He didn't say it out loud, but he knew Abbie was in more danger than he had originally believed.

"When was that?" he asked.

"A little over a week ago."

Still scribbling, Jackson continued to note the details of Abbie's story. She described what happened in the Suburban once they were caught, the injuries Meghan sustained, and the events leading up to her death.

"I think I'm going to be sick," Abbie whispered after she finished reliving the details of what happened to Meghan. She tumbled off of the cot and hobbled over to a wastebasket that was nearby, and dry heaved into it. Jackson left his clipboard and coffee on the floor by the cot and placed a hand on Abbie's back as she keeled over the wastebasket. Jackson knew it wasn't protocol to touch the victims, but he couldn't help but show Abbie compassion.

Abbie started to shake uncontrollably as she stood up, and she attempted to walk back to the cot.

"Easy does it," Jackson said quietly as he guided her steps and helped her sit down. He picked up a blanket from the cot and draped it over her shoulders and offered her the glass of water that was still on the floor. They were silent for a few minutes, and then Abbie decided to speak.

"They didn't hurt me, if that's what you are wondering," she told him. "They tried to, when I ran away."

"I was told you jumped from a moving vehicle," Jackson said, impressed, gathering his items from the floor and taking a seat in a folding chair next to a table in the middle of the room. "You must have run like hell."

"Yes, I did." Abbie's voice stayed steady and serious. It was as if she was telling Jackson a story that had happened to someone else. "I didn't look back once," she explained. "Not even when they were shooting at me."

"There were guns?" he asked. Jackson clicked his pen and resumed writing.

"Yes."

"How many?"

"I'm not sure." Abbie rubbed her eyes and sipped her water. "At least one."

Jackson jotted down a few more notes and asked, "After you fled the vehicle, about how far or long did you run until you reached the road where the patrol car was parked?"

Abbie pondered the question and said, "I'm not really sure. They followed me for a long time. I just kept running." She closed her eyes and continued telling the story. "I knew they wouldn't be able to keep up, and someone would have seen their car parked by the road eventually, so I figured it was only a matter of time before they turned back and left me alone. Once I knew they were gone I was completely lost in the woods, so I tried to listen for cars and looked for houses. It was so quiet for a while. After a few hours or so, I saw the police car through the trees, so I started running again. The road was quiet, in the middle of nowhere. And they were just parked there, with the car running, as if they were waiting for me. On our way here they told me they were looking for a dog, but it was a miracle, I swear."

Jackson was unsure of how to respond, so he remained focused on the timeline. "Based on when these officers found you, or when you found them, rather, it sounds like you were in the woods for about five hours or so."

Abbie nodded and agreed that that was most likely the case.

"I've got some photos I would like you to take a look at," Jackson said, pulling a manila envelope from his clipboard. If you could simply tell me if you recognize any of these men, I would appreciate that." He drew a stack of photos from the envelope and passed them over to Abbie.

With the blanket still wrapped around her, she reached for the photos with an unsteady hand. Jackson couldn't help but feel a bit of empathy for her. She was young, and most likely had her whole life ahead of her until the previous evening. Witnessing a murder changes a person—hardens them. He was hoping it wouldn't be impossible for her to move on with her life. She rifled through the photos, quickly discarding the ones with faces she didn't recognize. She selected two photos and then handed them back to Jackson.

Jackson rubbed a hand over his face as he looked at the photos. Out of all of the photos Abbie could have chosen, he prayed she would not have picked either one of them.

"Would you excuse me?" Jackson said to Abbie.

Abbie nodded and slowly lay down on the cot. Jackson had a strong urge to tuck the blanket around her delicate body, but he resisted. Instead he stepped out of the room and made a call on his cell phone.

"Harper?" he asked when the other line picked up. "Wells, here. I've got a bit of a situation." He paused in between sentences as his immediate supervisor, Glenn Harper, responded on the other line. "I've got a key witness to a murder that took place last night. She was abducted last night by Griffin Ford and Alex McCain ... Yes, sir ... if we can find them, and she testifies, we may be able to shut down the entire operation ... Yes, she is still here ... No, we won't let her leave ... No phone calls? Okay, I can do that ... So what are you thinking is the best way to ensure her safety? I was afraid you were going to say that ... all right ... Let's put it into action ... I will tell her ... Thank you, Harper."

Jackson hung up the phone and walked back into the room. He took a seat across from her and rested his elbows on his knees, placed his hands together, and touched his fingertips to his chin. Abbie sat up on the cot. She looked exhausted, and Jackson was dreading what he was about to tell her.

"When can I go home?" she asked. "Or even make a phone call? My boyfriend is probably worried sick."

Jackson's eyes rested on hers as he began to talk. "Abbie, my job at the Department of Justice is to keep victims, such as yourself, safe during a murder investigation as well as during the trial. In a situation like this, we would house you in a remote location until the trial is over, and the perpetrators are incarcerated."

"So you are saying that I have to wait until after a trial until I can go home?" she asked, beginning to get upset.

"However," Jackson's eyes fell to the floor as he continued, "your situation is a bit unique. Based on the photos of the men that you have identified for me, your life would still be in danger, even after these particular criminals are behind bars."

Abbie shot straight up and moved to the edge of the cot. "What are you saying?"

"What I'm saying is, we are now obligated to ensure your safety, as well as the safety of your loved ones, indefinitely."

Abbie was still confused. "Like some sort of witness protection?"

"Witness protection, exactly," he stated.

"So my loved ones would be protected? They have to go into witness protection as well?"

"Not exactly," Jackson said, starting in on the tough part of the conversation. "Here is how it will work. After our conversation today, you will be transported in an unmarked vehicle to a hotel, where you will stay for approximately forty-eight to seventy-two hours. During that time, our job is to organize and provide documentation for a new identity for you, a vehicle, some cash, and a place to live. From this point on, you will not be able to contact anyone that you currently know or have known in the past."

Abbie stood up, and began pacing around the room. "You can't be serious," she protested.

"I know this is difficult. But to be honest, this is what is best for everyone involved. Let me explain why this has to happen," Jackson said, rising to his feet. "As of right now, the last time you were seen alive was this morning when you fled from that Suburban. The last people on earth to see you alive were the men that killed Meghan. Those men are the key leaders in the largest human trafficking operation in the nation. If they know you are alive and you helped to lock them up, they wouldn't hesitate to have one of their comrades harm you and your family in their honor. And they would most likely get paid to do it. If they assume that you died in those woods, the odds of harm coming to you or your loved ones drop significantly."

The room was silent. Jackson let Abbie pace around the room as the reality of what was about to happen settled with her.

"There will be missing persons reports for us," she said as she continued to pace. "Your plan isn't going to work. I know my father, and I know Michael, and they will both do whatever it takes to find me."

Jackson nodded. "We are prepared for families to take these actions. What will end up happening is there will be an investigation for both of your disappearances. Search parties will form. Meghan's body will hopefully be found. Yours, I'm afraid, will not. Your actions will be monitored to ensure that you are not leaving a trail of bread crumbs, so to speak, for anyone to follow. It's my job to make sure that any trail leading to you results in a dead end."

Abbie began to cry.

Jackson could count on one hand the number of times he had ever had to put a victim into witness protection, and Abbie was, by far, the youngest. He knew that she was wishing she could go back in time and change the course of events that led her to that exact moment. She was headed down a path that left her with no choice other than to cause pain, suffering, and loss to herself and her loved ones. She also knew that if she didn't move in that direction, the pain, suffering, and losses could be far greater than what they were already about to endure.

"I know this is hard to hear," Jackson attempted to say.

"You don't know anything," Abbie scoffed, tears streaming down her face.

Jackson remained silent. He decided to leave her alone to process what he had just told her. He needed to make several phone calls anyway to start the witness protection process for Abbie. He stepped out of the room and pulled out his cell phone.

"Harper. Wells, again. She's all set. One more thing ... I'm assigning myself to this case."

15

MICHAEL

STORM CLOUDS ROLLED IN over the treetops of Hammond Farm and thunder rumbled off in the distance. Despite the imminent rain showers, the heat of the day was scorching. Michael had just finished mowing the grass as rain began to sputter. He whistled to Sam and Bull, signaling them to head toward the house. They obeyed as Michael checked his cell phone for the hundredth time that morning, waiting to hear from Abbie. He hadn't heard from her since the previous evening, and he was beginning to grow concerned. It seemed unlike Abbie to not text or call him, especially after mentioning that she would.

Once he was inside, Michael peeled off his sweat-soaked clothes and took a shower. After he washed up, he busied himself with chores inside his house, trying to keep his mind off of Abbie. He had to admit, it was moving a lot faster than he had expected it to, but he was in love with her. Now, after not hearing from her, he was beginning to second-guess whether or not Abbie felt the same way about him.

In an attempt to calm his nerves, he walked into the living room, sat down on the couch, and turned on the television. Uninterested, he shut it back off after only a few minutes. He lay down on the couch and attempted to take a nap. Normally he would have found the sound of the rain hitting the porch to be soothing, but it only agitated him that much more.

Michael got up from the couch and checked his phone once more while he paced between the kitchen and the living room. Still, he hadn't heard from her. He tried calling her again, and instead of ringing, her voice mail immediately picked up. He had already left two messages for her, so he decided against leaving another one. He grabbed his keys from the kitchen counter, and Sam and Bull came scurrying into the kitchen.

"Come on," he said to the dogs, and the three of them ran out into the pouring rain. He opened the driver's side door to his truck, and Sam and Bull leaped into the front seat. Michael hopped in after them and fired up the engine. Stretching one arm across the back of the seat, he turned his head, peered out the back window, and guided the truck out of the driveway. The dogs sat up straight and watched out the window as the rain came down.

The windshield wipers on the truck splashed back and forth, barely keeping up with the steady downpour. At the risk of appearing too overprotective, Michael drove to Abbie's house. He hoped that the worst that could happen is that he would have to apologize for stopping by unannounced. The truth was, he couldn't shake the feeling that something had happened to her.

Abbie's bicycle was parked by the back porch when Michael pulled into her driveway. He left the engine running while the dogs stayed in the truck. He sprinted up the porch steps and knocked on the door. Minutes passed, and the door went unanswered. Michael put his hands in his pockets and glanced through a window near the door. When he didn't see any indication that she was home, he went back to his truck. He sat there for a few minutes, soaked from the rain, unsure of what to do. Michael leaned over, opened the glove compartment, and rifled through it until he found a scrap piece of paper and a pen. He quickly scribbled a note for Abbie that said:

> *'Missing you. Just thought I'd drop by. Call me.*
> *—Michael'*

He ran back up to Abbie's front porch and tucked the folded note in the front door. Concern quickly turned into worry as Michael drove away from Abbie's house. He told himself to remain calm as he drove the few miles into town to see if maybe she had gone into work on her day off. That didn't seem unlike her, he told himself. He rested his elbow on the door and chewed on one of his knuckles. The rain was relentless, and the sound of it grew louder on the hood of the truck.

Once he reached the diner, mud splashed onto his windows as the truck wallowed through puddles in the parking lot. Tracey greeted Michael when he walked through the entrance.

"Hey, Michael," she said to him as he wiped his boots on a rug just inside the door.

"Hi, Tracey?" he asked, hoping he remembered her name correctly.

"That's me. Do you need a table?"

"No, I'm actually wondering if Abbie is working. Is she here today?" He was slightly embarrassed.

"No, she isn't," Tracey said, slightly annoyed. She had just finished refilling drinks at one of her tables and walked over to Michael. "Meghan was supposed to work today, but she didn't show up. I called Abbie to see if she could cover for her, but she didn't answer. I figured she was with you."

"No, she wasn't with me …" his voice trailed off. Michael didn't know what to think at that point, and he could tell Tracey was just as confused.

Tracey gave Michael a strange look and said, "Well, if you happen to see them, tell them I'm not happy with them."

"Why is that?" he asked, concerned.

"I was supposed to ride home with them last night. I left the bar without them, but texted them when I was ready to leave so we could meet up. Neither one of them texted back. I waited by Meghan's car for almost an hour before I decided to call a cab. Cost me twenty-five bucks to get home."

"So they just never showed up?"

"Nope. I don't know where they ran off to, but they totally ditched me."

Michael wasn't sure Tracey was grasping the fact that neither one of them had any idea where both Abbie and Meghan were.

"Where do you think they are?" Michael asked Tracey.

"I don't know," she shrugged as she grabbed a tray of food from behind the counter. Michael waited by the door as Tracey delivered the food to the designated table.

"That seems a bit concerning," Michael said once Tracey walked back over to him with the empty tray down by her side.

A look of realization began to creep across Tracey's face, and she said, "Oh. Yeah. I guess you are right. I wonder where else they could be?" she asked as her voice trailed off.

"Well, if you happen to see either one of them, could you let me know?"

"Sure thing, Michael." Tracey pulled her notepad from her apron, and they exchanged phone numbers.

He thanked her and walked back out to his truck. Sam and Bull were impatiently waiting for him, their noses pressed to the glass on the window. Michael tried not to allow panic to set in as he sat in the parking lot, petting the dogs. A knot formed in the pit of his stomach as he contemplated where else he should look for not only Abbie, but Meghan as well. The fact that both of them hadn't been seen since the night before made him wonder if he should contact the police. Brushing off the idea, as it was a bit premature, he put his truck in drive and left the diner.

Lightning lit up the sky, which had grown dark gray. Sam and Bull whimpered some when the thunder clapped. Michael attempted to calm them, although, deep inside, he was starting to panic. He couldn't help but think that something bad had happened to Abbie and Meghan. He held out hope that Abbie would be at his house when he returned. As Michael pulled back into his driveway, and he and the dogs entered the house, his heart sank. The house was just as he left it, with no sign that Abbie had been there.

The storm raged over the farm, and there was little for Michael to do inside the house to keep busy. He paced the house, continuing to check his phone. He dialed Abbie's number several more times; each time her voice mail picked up. Time seemed to stand still that afternoon, and by evening Michael was positive something was wrong.

In his desperation, Michael looked up Henry's contact information in an online Georgia directory. Once he found an address and phone number he called. Henry picked up on the second ring.

"Hello," Henry said.

"Henry?" Michael asked.

"Yes?"

"This is Michael."

"What can I do for you, Michael?"

103

"Well, I was actually wondering if you have heard from Abbie recently. Since yesterday, perhaps?"

Henry stopped to think for a moment, and then he said, "I don't think I heard from her yesterday. It may have been the day before. Is something wrong?"

"I haven't heard from her since last night. I know that doesn't sound all that strange, but she went out with friends last night and said she would call once she made it home safe. She never called. I have tried calling her several times today, but she hasn't answered. I've stopped by the diner and her house, and she wasn't at either place. I was hoping you had heard from her."

"No, Michael. I'm sorry; I have not."

"Do you have any idea where she might be?"

Henry thought for a minute and said, "To be honest, I don't think she has much time to wander anywhere else besides work and home, and the rest of the time I figure she is with you."

Michael chuckled half-heartedly. "I think you might be right, sir."

"I'm sure she will turn up. She might still be with her friends from last night."

"I asked one of her coworkers when I stopped into the diner if they had heard anything from Meghan, the other girl who she was with, but she hadn't." The panic was starting to rise in his voice, and Michael was having a hard time toning it down.

Henry was silent. "I'm not really sure," he said finally.

Neither one of them knew what to say. They had run out of reassuring words for each other. Michael broke the silence by saying, "I will make a few more phone calls. I will let you know if I hear from her."

"Thank you, Michael. I will do the same."

Michael's nerves were in no better shape after he hung up with Henry than before the phone call. He called Tracey to see if perhaps Abbie and Meghan had stopped by the diner or had called. Tracey stated she still had yet to see or hear from them. He asked her to call if they turned up.

Fearing the worst, Michael found a list of hospitals in Wilmington as well as a phone number for the Wilmington Police Department. He figured at that point it wouldn't hurt to rule out that she had been in some sort of accident. Each hospital confirmed that she had not been brought in, and, instead of feeling relieved, it only caused him to worry. Feeling a bit irrational, he called the police.

"Hi, my name is Michael Hammond," he said when an operator picked up. "I know this sounds a bit odd, but I think I may need to report two missing people."

16

ABBIE

LARGE GRAY CLOUDS FORMED in the distance as Abbie followed Jackson out to a navy blue sedan parked behind the police department. Rain soon followed, mixing with the tears that rolled silently down her cheeks. Each step she took was heavier than the previous one, as if she was wearing shoes made of concrete. She had never felt so empty, broken, or lost in her life.

Jackson opened the car door for her, closing it carefully and quietly after she was inside. Words weren't exchanged during the car ride from the police station to the hotel where she would stay temporarily.

Once they were parked behind the building, Jackson said, "I need to brief you on what is going to happen over the next few days."

Abbie remained silent, looking straight ahead. Her eyes were on a pair of sparrows, building a nest in the eaves of the hotel. Each bird took turns flying to and from the nest, each putting forth an effort to build a home they would share.

"I will escort you inside, do a sweep of your room, and make sure it's secure, then I will go to my room, directly across the hall. Security cameras have already been set up in your room, and I will surveillance the doors and windows from my room. Also, a patrol car will be canvassing the parking lot around the clock. A night shift officer will take over for me this evening. I will be back in the morning. We will stay until your documentation and the details of your relocation are arranged. It should take about two or three days."

Abbie wasn't listening to Jackson. "Do you know what kind of birds those are?" she asked Jackson, pointing to the pair, working diligently on their nest.

"What?" Jackson asked, a bit caught off guard. His eyes followed the direction she was pointing and said, "No, I'm afraid not."

Attempting to direct her attention back to him, he said, "We should have new clothes for you in about an hour. Those will be delivered."

"They're sparrows." Her eyes remained fixed on the birds.

Jackson wasn't sure how to respond, so he allowed her to finish her thoughts.

"Sparrows aren't anything special, not particularly beautiful, sort of small ..." Abbie's voice trailed off.

"We had quite a few sparrows in our barn when I was a child. Despite our best efforts, we couldn't seem to get rid of them," he added, still unsure of the point she was trying to make.

She turned her face toward his. "No one notices them until they build a nest someplace like your barn, as you mentioned, or those eaves up there. They have to fight like hell to keep the home they worked so hard to create because someone will most likely come along and try to destroy it." She looked back at the birds. This time she wasn't talking to Jackson in particular. She simply wanted to say the words that came next. "I hope they stay there, tucked in under the eaves, safe from anyone who tries to take everything they have away from them."

Her words hung in the air like the thick, dark clouds that were now directly overhead. Jackson didn't know how to respond to her interpretation of the sparrows. Abbie didn't wait for a response, and she opened the car door and got out.

"You coming?" she asked as she shut the car door.

"Hey!" Jackson called after her as she headed toward the hotel. He quickened his pace to catch up with her. "I need you to stay next to me," he said quietly to her once he caught up. "You aren't safe. Not yet."

Again, Abbie didn't seem to hear him, and if she did, she didn't care.

Jackson grabbed a key card from his pocket, swiped it through the key reader, and then opened the door once the indicator light flashed. He led Abbie down a hallway to her hotel room and, using the same key, opened her door. Once they were inside, he drew the pistol from his waist, motioning Abbie to be quiet and to stay by the door. She remained still as Jackson inspected Abbie's hotel room, making certain there were no signs of intruders. When he was sure there was no one else in the room, he checked hidden surveillance cameras on the windows and doors. Jackson tucked his gun back into his holster and motioned for Abbie to step farther into the room.

"I'll bring your clothes by when they arrive." Jackson's words were firm yet gentle as he spoke to her. "I will be right across the hall if you need anything. I'm going to have to ask you to not leave your room. I know, it's going to feel a lot like house arrest, maybe even prison at first. My job is to make sure that you are safe. Please don't make my job difficult by making any poor decisions."

"I see you already took the phone," Abbie motioned to an empty bedside table where a phone would have been. The cables splayed out of the jack in the wall.

"Unfortunately, we can't take any chances."

As Abbie nodded, she could feel the tears welling up once more. The weight of what had happened in the last twenty-four hours had not fully set in. She hadn't slept or had anything to eat since the previous day, and her ability to think was inhibited. She avoided looking at Jackson, who was standing there, hands in his pockets, chewing on his bottom lip, looking at her with sympathetic eyes. Instead she walked into the bathroom, turned on the water in the tub, and closed the door behind her.

Steam filled the room as she blindly stripped off her clothes. She wiped the moisture that began to form on the mirror with her hand and barely recognized her own reflection. Staring back at her was a woman that would never be able to see her father or Michael or Meghan ever again. She stepped into the shower and began to sob uncontrollably. Dirt and blood that had been caked to her skin pooled in the bottom of the tub and circled the drain.

Abbie cried for Meghan. She began dry heaving again when she pictured her friend's lifeless eyes staring back at her. If only she could have done something to keep Griffin from killing her.

She felt as if her life was slipping down the drain along with the dirt, blood, and filth of the last twenty-four hours. It killed her to think of the worry that Michael must have been experiencing. If only she could tell him she was alive, that she loved him and missed him, and that if she could have done anything to change what happened, she would have.

It suddenly dawned on Abbie why Annabelle sent Henry to see her. Her mother knew that Abbie needed her father more than he had in those final days. It angered Abbie to know that her mother was aware of what would happen and had allowed the events to unfold. Feeling hopeless and angry, Abbie continued to cry, and fell into a heap in the shower. She allowed the water to beat down on her and drown out her cries for all that she had lost.

After the water began to run cold, Abbie took a few deep breaths and gathered the strength to get out of the tub. She tossed her dirty clothes into the trash. She didn't want to hang on to them as a reminder of a night of inexplicable terror. She pulled on a bathrobe that was on the back of the door and then walked out of the bathroom.

Jackson had left the room. She looked over at the entrance and noticed a paper bag that Jackson must have left just inside the door while she was in the shower. She walked over and picked up the bag. Attached was a note that said:

> *'Hope these are the right size. I'll bring you some*
> *food in a bit. You should eat something. —J'*

She dumped the bag onto the bed, and two pair of jeans, two T-shirts, and a sweatshirt, as well as several undergarments, fell out.

Abbie jumped when she heard a knock at the door. She tiptoed to the door, peered into the eyehole, and saw Jackson. She turned the knob and opened the door a crack.

"I brought food," Jackson said, holding up a grocery bag.

Abbie held the door open a bit wider, forgetting that all she was wearing was a bathrobe, and accepted the food.

Jackson's eyes looked down at the floor, caught off guard by what she was wearing. "I also have this," Jackson said, pulling a walkie-talkie from his back pocket. "In case you are in trouble or feel like you are in any danger."

Abbie took the device from him, looking it over.

"You'll turn this knob on and then just push this button if you need me," he explained while showing her how it worked. "I will keep mine on at all times. Once my night shift replacement arrives, I will make sure he has this and will leave it on to listen for you."

"Thank you," she said quietly, forcing a half smile.

"I'll be just across the hall, Abbie," Jackson said. He smiled and nodded in her direction as he walked out the door.

Abbie could tell that he felt a bit of sympathy for her. He had kind eyes and a friendly smile that she hadn't noticed earlier that day. She decided to do her best not to hate him for not allowing her to go back home.

Her mind was still in a fog as she slipped her robe off and threw on a few articles of clothing that were strewn about the bed. She opened the grocery bag and found a box of granola bars, a sandwich, some chips, and a banana, as well as a bottle of water. Her stomach turned at the thought of food, so she closed the bag and walked over to the only window that was in the room.

Rain was falling at a steady pace, and droplets streamed down the windowpane. Street lights flickered on as dusk faded into night. She closed the drapes and crawled into one of the queen-sized beds.

Sleep was one of the many things Abbie wished for in that moment. The other was that the bed would engulf her body, and she would disappear. The loss of Meghan weighed heavy on her heart, and she couldn't bear the thought that her friend's body was lying somewhere like a piece of trash, tossed aside, hidden from the rest of the world. She also wished for Michael. She would have given anything for him to sweep into her room and whisk her away to a place where they could hide, together. Her heart had been ripped from her chest, and a gaping hole remained, bleeding with a hopelessness that left her empty and broken.

Every time Abbie drifted off to sleep, she was startled awake by the click of other hotel room doors, ice machines, elevators, and her own imagination, creating nightmares that replayed in her mind. Desperate for sleep, she grabbed the walkie-talkie and signaled Jackson to answer.

Instead of answering, she heard Jackson leave his room, scurry across the hall, and knock loudly on her door. Abbie leaped out of bed and reached the door as he banged on it once more. Her head pounded at the sound of Jackson hammering on the door, so she flung it open, in an attempt to put a stop to the noise as quickly as possible. The light from the hallway beamed into her dark hotel room, and Abbie shielded her eyes from the glare.

Jackson flew into Abbie's room, gun drawn, pushing past her. Abbie gasped and nearly fell into the bathroom.

"What are you doing?" she called out to Jackson.

"Are you okay?" Jackson asked her, a panicked look in his eye.

"What? Yes, I'm okay," Abbie said, slightly annoyed with all of the racket. Her head pounded louder, and she held onto the wall to brace herself from the pain.

"You signaled me on the walkie-talkie, so I assumed something was wrong," Jackson said, holstering his gun.

"I'm sorry," Abbie said, slightly embarrassed. "I just ..." she began to stammer and attempted to recover by saying, "I couldn't sleep."

Jackson looked at her sympathetically. His eyes told her that he wanted to protect her not only because it was his job but also as a friend.

"Would it be too much to ask if you stayed in my room with me?"

Jackson was caught off guard. Abbie could tell that he wasn't expecting her to say that and that he wasn't sure how to respond.

"If you prefer I stay with you, I can accommodate that," Jackson said.

Abbie's tired eyes pleaded with Jackson's to stay with her. She was afraid that if she closed her eyes, the darkness of the night and the loneliness of the room would consume her, and she would disappear.

"Please," was all that she managed to say.

Jackson nodded, confirming that he would stay. He pulled a chair into the center of the room near the walkway, acting as a shield between Abbie and the door to the hotel room.

Abbie switched on a lamp that sat on a stand in between the two queen-sized beds. She then groggily crawled into the bed farthest from Jackson, and pulled up the covers around her. Her eyes wept for the last time that day as she drifted off to sleep.

17

JACKSON

ABBIE'S BODY ROSE AND fell ever so slightly while she lay sleeping in the bed in her hotel room. Jackson had been gazing at her, watching her breathe, for over an hour. He noticed that the grocery bag went untouched on the table in the corner of the room. Certain that she had no appetite but convinced she was dehydrated and hadn't eaten at all that day, he made a mental note to encourage her to eat and drink when she woke up.

Matthew Sloan, Jackson's night shift replacement, arrived for duty shortly after Abbie had fallen asleep. Jackson slipped out of the room, just in time to meet Sloan at his hotel room door. Sloan was in his early forties, a bit heavyset, and very outspoken.

"Hey, Wells," Sloan said, acknowledging Jackson as they headed inside the room.

"The witness is requesting additional protection in her room this evening," Jackson explained to Sloan.

"Is that so?" Sloan was a bit surprised by Jackson's willingness to accommodate such a request but didn't question it further. Instead, Sloan set his briefcase and luggage down near the laptop that was set up to monitor the surveillance cameras from inside that room.

"I'd like to try to establish this witness's trust," Jackson explained. "That way there is less of a chance of her becoming a flight risk."

Sloan knew there was a chance that Jackson was embellishing the reason he insisted on being the one to stay in Abbie's room with her, but he didn't question it further. He simply winked at Jackson and said, "None of my business. Just here to do my job. Enjoy your sleepover."

Jackson rolled his eyes at Sloan, tossed him the walkie-talkie, and said, "Let me know if you need anything."

Sloan nodded after him.

Jackson quietly snuck back into Abbie's room and took a seat in the chair without disturbing her sleep. The room was silent except for the hum of the air conditioner that occasionally clicked on and off. The lamp that was dimly switched on by the bed was the only source of light in the darkened room. Abbie was curled into the far corner of the bed, underneath a shadow the light had cast over her.

Hours felt like minutes as Jackson watched her sleep. Technically, he was off duty, but for some reason, he felt indebted to her. He felt a pang of guilt for taking such a young girl away from her life and loved ones, forcing her to start over alone.

Jackson wasn't sure that at her age he would have been strong enough to endure such a task. When he was twenty-two, he was a spoiled army brat that had eaten from a silver spoon his entire life. With little regard for anyone but himself, he lived recklessly. After a night of drinking too much alcohol and driving too fast, Jackson and his best friend, Travis, were in a terrible car accident. Travis had been driving, and the vehicle ultimately smashed through a guardrail and rolled down the embankment into a ravine. Travis was killed instantly. Jackson sustained life-threatening injuries and spent six weeks in the hospital. He spent six months after that in physical therapy recovering from his injuries.

The loss of Travis changed Jackson's life. He quit drinking altogether and also made the decision to pursue a career in law enforcement. Ten years later, he was granted his current position in the United States Department of Justice after serving a number of years for the Baltimore Police Department.

Now, at thirty-five, Travis's death still haunted Jackson. He buried himself in his work, allowing his career to be his main priority, leaving little time for family or friends. He dated every now and again but had always managed to keep himself from becoming too vulnerable or attached.

Abbie tossed and turned in her sleep, and Jackson found himself wondering what she was dreaming about. His heart ached at the thought of her reliving her friend's death in her dreams. He had only spent a few hours with Abbie, but for some reason he was drawn to her. It wasn't because she was gorgeous, Jackson decided. It was more than that. Both she and Jackson had experienced tragedy and suffering, but Jackson sensed that she would rise above it, despite how bleak her situation appeared to be. He sensed how genuine she was, and her graciousness would allow her to move past what happened to her in a way that Jackson never could. Even in her current state of weakness, Abbie's strength was apparent to him.

Jackson loosened his tie, propped his feet up on the bed that Abbie wasn't sleeping in, and rested a hand on his gun. His intention wasn't to close his eyes for too long. Each time he heard footsteps in the hallway, and every time Abbie stirred in her sleep, Jackson's eyes popped open, ready to take action if need be.

At one point, Jackson looked over at Abbie as she slowly pulled the covers back and swung her legs out over the side of the bed. Her back was facing him. She let out a heavy sigh as she got up and walked past Jackson to the bathroom. Her face was expressionless. His eyes were on her the entire time, but she didn't seem to notice he was even in the room. Abbie walked back out of the bathroom and started rifling through the grocery bag. She pulled out the bottle of water and the sandwich. She sat on the edge of the bed and carefully unwrapped the sandwich and began to nibble at it. She still hadn't acknowledged Jackson, but his eyes stayed fixed on her.

After a long silence, she slowly turned her head toward him and asked, "Could you have someone bring me a toothbrush and some toothpaste tomorrow?"

Jackson sat up straight, a little shocked that she said anything to him, and answered her back by saying, "Do you need anything else?"

Abbie focused her attention back to her sandwich, took another bite, and silently shook her head. She took another sip of her water and then placed them both on the nightstand before crawling back into bed. She reached for the remote control and switched on the TV.

"You can sleep in the bed," Abbie said to Jackson, pointing to the bed next to hers.

"The chair is fine with me," Jackson said, knowing full well he was going to have a kink in his neck the following morning.

Abbie was silent as she flipped through the channels but eventually said, "You're the only person I have contact with right now, Mr. Wells. I can either hate you for it, or try to be your friend. Until I decide which one of those I have the energy for, it would be rude of me to not offer you to sleep in a perfectly available bed."

"Don't worry about me," Jackson said. "Try to sleep." He would have been much more comfortable in the bed; however, he didn't want to make Abbie uncomfortable in any way.

Abbie turned the lamp off on the nightstand so that only the glow of the television illuminated the room.

Soon, both of them drifted off to sleep.

Jackson woke early the next morning while Abbie was still sleeping. As he stood up from the chair, the stiffness in his legs, back, and neck was a bit more intense than he had anticipated. He quietly opened the drawer of the bedside table, found a pad of paper and a pen, and left her a note.

'I'll be back later this morning. I'll bring breakfast. Stay put.'

Jackson quietly slipped out of the room without waking her. He let himself into the room across the hall. Sloan was sitting at a table near the window, reading a book and eyeing the surveillance videos that streamed in on several monitors on the table.

"Wells," Sloan said to Jackson, acknowledging him with a bit of a curious look on his face.

Jackson ignored the look and said, "I'll be back at 8:00 a.m."

"How was your slumber party?" Sloan asked, jokingly.

Jackson knew his coworker's comments wouldn't be avoided. "C'mon, Sloan, you know it wasn't like that. You watched the cameras all night. Nothing happened."

"I'm just messing with you, man. It's just not like you to go beyond the call of duty in that sort of way."

"I feel bad for her. She's way too young to have gone through what she did. And now she's all alone. She's terrified. That's why I stayed last night. No harm done."

"I'm sure the fact that she's attractive had nothing to do with your decision to stay," Sloan joked.

115

Jackson smirked and rolled his eyes but didn't answer. "I'll be back at eight," Jackson repeated, and left the hotel room.

His eyes instinctively surveyed the exterior of the building as well as the parking lot as Jackson exited the building. He walked quickly but cautiously to the blue sedan, scanning around, under, and inside the vehicle before letting himself inside. Not far from the hotel was a gas station, where he purchased coffee and three bags of doughnuts for himself, Abbie, and Sloan. He also remembered to pick up a toothbrush and toothpaste for Abbie as she requested.

Jackson made it back to the hotel at exactly 8:00 a.m. He stopped by Abbie's room first and knocked on the door. When she didn't answer, he unlocked the door, bent down, and placed a cup of coffee, one of the bags of doughnuts, and her toothbrush and toothpaste on the floor inside the door, just as he had done the previous day. Sloan opened the door to his room across the hall and poked his head out as Jackson was rising to his feet.

"I thought I smelled coffee," Sloan said to Jackson as he held the door open for him to step inside. As Jackson walked through the door, Sloan plucked a bag of doughnuts and a cup of coffee from the drink carrier in Jackson's hand.

"Help yourself," Jackson said sarcastically.

"These came for you," Sloan said, taking a large bite of his doughnut and motioning toward the bed. A stack of neatly pressed shirts and slacks inside several garment bags lay across the bed. Next to it was a piece of luggage with other clothing items. Jackson had had his secretary overnight him some personal belongings once he assigned himself to Abbie's case.

"Keep an eye on her. I'm going to take a shower," Jackson said, motioning to the monitors where Sloan sat.

"I sure will," Sloan said with a smirk under his breath.

Jackson shut the bathroom door without reacting to Sloan's comments. As Jackson showered and shaved, he wrestled with his thoughts about Abbie. It was only natural that he wanted to protect her. After all, that was his job. Abbie was attractive, he readily admitted, but it wasn't the main reason he wanted to be assigned to her case. At least, that's what he was trying to tell himself. After running a dab of gel through his hair and tucking in his shirt, Jackson stepped out of the bathroom.

"Damnit," he heard Sloan mutter under his breath from across the room.

Jackson shot a look in Sloan's direction.

"What?" Jackson asked, his voice rising with concern.

"She's gone," Sloan said, reaching for his gun that lay on the table.

"What the hell, Sloan?" Jackson shouted, reaching for his gun as well, which was already holstered to his hip. You were supposed to watch her!"

"I took my eye off the monitor for a second," Sloan insisted.

"Grab the walkie-talkie and see if she will respond," Jackson ordered as he rushed out of the room. "Check her room; I'm going outside. She couldn't have gotten far," Jackson shouted to Sloan as he raced down the hall toward the exit.

18

ABBIE

A WAVE OF REALITY washed over Abbie as soon as she woke up from her first night in the hotel room. As soon as she remembered where she was, and why she was there, her nausea returned.

Abbie wasn't sure how she was able to sleep during her first night at the hotel. She figured it had something to do with Jackson's presence, allowing her to feel somewhat safe. She thought for sure that if she was left alone for too long, too many memories, good and bad, would haunt her to the point of insanity.

The thought of staying inside the hotel room all day seemed a bit daunting. Slipping on her sandals, she prepared to go outside, but then she noticed the items that Jackson had left for her by the door. She quickly brushed her teeth, grabbed the coffee, and headed out the door.

It was colder than she had anticipated, so she flipped the hood of her sweatshirt up over her head. She had taken a seat on the walkway and, after a few moments, had a lapse of déjà vu. She felt as if she had sat on that same slab of pavement before. She suddenly realized that it was the unfamiliar concrete she had sat on in her last dream of Annabelle. Abbie shivered as she took a sip of her coffee.

Just as she was curling her knees into her chest, Jackson came bursting through the door, nearly running her over. His gun was drawn, and Abbie leaped to her feet, frightened. Jackson whipped around, surprised to see her sitting there.

"Good grief, Abbie!" he said, exasperated.

"What?" she asked, a bit taken by surprise. Just then, another man came running out, also wielding a gun, whom she hadn't seen before. Startled, she dropped her coffee and instinctively turned to run. Before she could get far, Jackson called out to her.

"Abbie! Abbie, it's okay!" Jackson headed toward her. She turned around, her eyes darting between Jackson and the other man. Both men quickly put their guns away and lifted their hands out to their sides, showing her they weren't going to hurt her.

Abbie took a deep breath and said, "What is going on?"

"Abbie, this is Matthew Sloan," Jackson said, pointing to him. "He works with me. He was my night shift replacement."

Sloan nodded at Abbie and gave her a half smile.

"Abbie, we need to go back inside," Jackson urged as he held the door open for her.

Without a word, Abbie walked back into the hotel. She heard Jackson and Sloan exchange a few words before Sloan left for the day, and Jackson followed her inside.

"I'm sorry," Abbie said to Jackson as they walked back to her room.

"You can't leave like that," Jackson said, followed by a heavy sigh of relief. "I thought the worst had happened." He unlocked Abbie's room, and again, checked to make sure it was safe before letting her inside.

Abbie started to cry. She couldn't help it. Feeling as though she was losing control, she started to hyperventilate.

"Abbie? Please don't cry," Jackson said, taking a step toward her.

She only cried harder. She slid down to the floor, head in her hands, and let out a scream. Jackson immediately fell to her side, took her in his arms, and held her tight. He spoke in a soft voice next to her ear to try to calm her.

"Abbie. I need you to calm down. Listen to me, Abbie. It's going to be fine." Jackson held her tight, trying to get her to relax.

Abbie buried her head into Jackson's shoulder, soaking his shirt with her tears. She felt as though her heart was going to physically shatter to pieces. She missed Michael. Her heart broke for Meghan and her family. And she would have given anything to see her father again. She continued to sob and shake uncontrollably in Jackson's arms.

"Abbie. Hey. Shh." Jackson continued to try to calm her down. He lifted her head in his hands so he could look into her eyes. Abbie pressed her lips together to try to keep quiet. Her eyes wouldn't focus on his.

Jackson kept saying her name in an attempt to connect with her, as he had done the previous day at the police station. "Abbie, look at me. I think you may be experiencing a panic attack. I can get you a sedative to calm you down. Abbie, would you like me to get you something to help you relax?"

"I don't want anything," she said as she gulped in air between each syllable. "I just want to go home."

"I know," Jackson said sympathetically. "But it's just not safe. Do you think your dad or your boyfriend would want you to risk your safety for them? Also, would you want to risk theirs?"

Abbie looked into Jackson's eyes. She hadn't taken his questions into consideration before. All along she had been focusing on what had happened to her, her inability to accept it, and how she would have given anything to change it. Jackson was forcing her to realize that she simply couldn't change what happened, and now she had to focus on keeping herself and her family safe. Her breathing began to slow as she sat back and put his questions into perspective.

"Abbie, listen to me," Jackson continued once he realized his words had her attention. "These men that killed Meghan wouldn't think twice about killing you or your family in order to keep themselves out of jail. Once we find Griffin and Alex, they are going away for life. But it won't stop there. Too many people rely on them for money. A lot of money. So if those people aren't getting paid, they will be ready to kill for it."

"It's just not fair," Abbie whispered.

"Trust me, Abbie, I know more than anyone how unfair this is." Jackson thought of Travis when he made that statement but decided not to disclose any further information. "Think of it like this, if you can. Meghan's death was horribly tragic. Your eyewitness account of her murder can save the lives of countless others. However, if they ever find out you are alive, even after Griffin and Alex are in jail, others just like them will have plenty of opportunity to harm you or your family. We need Meghan's death to have not been in vain. So, please, Abbie, you have to do this for them—for Meghan, for the other victims, for your family. You have to be strong. You have to be their hero."

Abbie's breathing returned to normal by the time Jackson was done with his speech. She wiped the tears from her cheeks with her shirtsleeves and then reluctantly nodded her head, acknowledging that he was right. Jackson stood up and then offered her his hand to help her up. Abbie accepted it. Jackson's cell phone began to ring as she rose to her feet.

"I'm going to step out and take this," Jackson said when he looked to see who was calling. "Can I get you some coffee while I'm out?"

"Yes, please," Abbie said quietly.

"Wells," Jackson said, answering his phone on the third ring. "Stay here," he said to Abbie as he walked backward toward the door.

Abbie mouthed an *I will* in his direction as she sat on the bed she had slept in the night before. She turned on the television in an attempt to distract herself from thinking of Michael. It was useless. His sparkling blue eyes and amazing smile were all she could picture in her mind. Her skin could still feel the strength of his hands, and her lips still felt his kiss. The past few weeks with Michael were more than she could have asked for, and she was head over heels in love with him. Had she known that would have been all the time they would have shared, she still would have agreed to go out with him the day he asked her at the diner. Losing herself in memories of Michael only made it that much harder for her to travel back to reality.

The door to the hotel room opened, and Jackson walked in. Coffee in hand, he walked over to the bed and handed it to her. Abbie graciously accepted the coffee with both hands and brought it to her lips. As she sipped it, Jackson sat down in the chair he had occupied the night before and began to speak.

"The phone call was regarding your relocation," he said.

Abbie looked up at Jackson but didn't say a word. She simply continued sipping her coffee, waiting for him to continue.

"The documents should be arriving within the hour. I will look them over, review them with you, and form a plan of action at that point. We will most likely leave this afternoon, a little sooner than we had originally thought."

There was a long silence between the two of them. Abbie looked around the room, as if she was ignoring what Jackson was telling her.

When Abbie finally spoke, she asked, with the coffee cup still by her mouth, "Did they find Meghan?"

Jackson paused. He leaned back in the chair and said, "Not yet. But we have dozens of people out looking. The chances of finding her are still relatively high, so don't give up hope."

Abbie nodded. "Are there missing persons reports for her and me yet?"

"Not yet. Again, that's only a matter of time as well."

Abbie's shoulders sagged as she stood up. "Well, I guess that's it then," she said as she let out a long sigh. She walked over to the window and opened the curtain, letting in some light. She sipped her coffee as she gazed out at the parking lot.

"I'd really like to go outside," she said after a long silence.

Jackson was hesitant. "Abbie, I would love to have you go outside. However, we just really aren't sure who could be watching. I promise you, once you are in a safer location, you will have quite a bit more freedom."

Abbie didn't answer. Instead she slowly closed the drapes, flopped down on the bed, and stared at the ceiling.

Jackson stood up from the chair and said, "I'm going to be across the hall. I will let you know when your documentation arrives."

Abbie remained silent. She closed her eyes, drew in a deep breath, and let it out slowly.

Jackson realized she wasn't going to respond to him, so he simply said, "If you need anything at all, Abbie, just let me know."

Abbie rolled over on the bed so that she was facing away from Jackson. He turned and walked out of the room. The silence in the room once she was alone was deafening, and Abbie was reminded how truly lost she was. A numbness slowly covered her, from the inside out. Drained of energy, she lay perfectly still, longing for tears to spill or for her heart to ache, but neither happened. She was certain that her emotions were shutting down to keep her from losing her mind.

The nausea, however, was overwhelming. Abbie had barely eaten a thing in the last few days, and knew she had better, but the thought of bringing food to her lips made her stomach churn. She got up from the bed, went into the bathroom, filled a cup with water from the faucet, and drank it slowly. It didn't help. She doubled over and heaved into the trash can. Her eyes watered as her stomach lurched in agony. The cool tile floor was her only comfort, so she lay down and allowed it to keep her calm.

Abbie drifted in and out of sleep on the bathroom floor. After what seemed like an hour, maybe more, there was a knock at the door. She opened her eyes but didn't speak.

"It's Jackson," Abbie heard him say as he opened the door a crack. Abbie's mouth was dry, but she managed to say, "Come on in."

Jackson entered her room and was caught off guard by the sight of her on the bathroom floor. Instinctively, he went to her.

"I'm okay," she reassured him, keeping her eyes closed.

"Actually, you're severely dehydrated and need to eat something. If you want to keep yourself out of the hospital, you need to drink some water and eat some food. Please."

Abbie tried to sit up. She most definitely didn't want to go to the hospital. Jackson assisted her in getting a drink of water after he helped her into a seated position.

"What's that?" Abbie asked Jackson as she pointed to a large manila envelope that Jackson had brought in with him.

"That is your new driver's license, birth certificate, registration to a vehicle, $1,500 cash, and a name and number of a woman who is offering you a job and a place to stay," he said.

"Oh," Abbie said flatly.

"I came by to tell you that we will be leaving in an hour." Jackson stood up and reached his hand down to help Abbie up. She looked away from him, and reluctantly put her hand in his, allowing him to pull her to her feet.

"Where are we going?" she asked as they both walked out of the bathroom.

"Omaha," Jackson said as he opened up the envelope, removed the documents, and passed them to Abbie to review. "I spoke personally with the woman you will be working for. In order to keep your situation 100 percent confidential, she is under the impression that we are relocating you from a battered women's shelter. It was the best explanation to guarantee that she would keep your anonymity should someone ask any questions."

Abbie sat down in the chair, taking it all in as she looked at her new ID cards. "Sarah Walker," Abbie said aloud as she read the name on her driver's license.

"That's who you need to be from now on," Jackson said firmly. "No one can know that you are really Abigail Peterson."

Abbie raised her eyebrows and scratched her head, trying to accept her new reality and wondering if she could even pull it off.

Jackson continued. "The cash in the envelope should allow you enough for other expenses until you get on your feet. Like I said, we've got a vehicle for you once we reach the relocation checkpoint."

"Do you really think this is going to work?" Abbie asked as she tucked the documents back into the envelope.

"It's really up to you," Jackson explained. "Everything on our end is secure. I'm assigned to your case from here on out. Once I'm back in DC, I'll make sure no one finds you, as I explained before. It's your job to make people believe that you are actually Sarah Walker. You can't bring any part of your past with you; you can't share stories about where you grew up. Don't even tell people what your dog's name was when you were a kid."

"I didn't have a dog."

"Well, then tell people you did."

Abbie rolled her eyes but then realized Jackson was being serious.

"It's a twenty-hour drive from Virginia to Nebraska. I'll coach you on what to say, what not to say, how to respond in certain situations; we can practice your new name—anything to prepare you for being someone completely different."

Abbie looked straight into Jackson's eyes and said, "I hate this."

"I know. But you have to remember how many people you are protecting by doing this. If you keep that in the back of your mind, I think it will be easier for you to deal with."

Abbie nodded.

"You need to eat something before we leave." Jackson found the bag of food he brought the previous day. He brought it to Abbie, and she selected a few items from it. Jackson got her a large glass of water from the bathroom and said, "I'm going to gather my things and prepare for us to leave. I'll come back and get you within the hour. Please be ready."

Abbie nodded. As Jackson opened the door to leave she said, "Jackson?"

With his hand on the doorknob he turned to look at her.

"Thank you," she said.

"Of course." He then left the room.

An hour later, Jackson returned to Abbie's room. She had eaten most of the food that Jackson had offered her, and she was beginning to feel better. By the time she had packed her things to leave, her nausea had subsided. Jackson quickly removed all of the surveillance equipment from her room and packed it away with his things. He left Abbie in the room while he pulled the car up to the back entrance. After loading their belongings into the trunk, he escorted her to the car.

As they began to drive out of the parking lot to begin their journey to Omaha, Abbie looked up at the eaves, where she had seen the birds when they first arrived. The sparrows were gone, and the nest they worked so hard to build was nowhere in sight.

19

MICHAEL

"I JUST DON'T GET it."

Michael and Stephen were at Paul's house, and the three of them were sitting in the kitchen, having a few drinks. Michael was pacing about while Stephen and Paul sat on a pair of bar stools at one end of the kitchen counter. The two of them were silent as Michael darted from one end of the kitchen to the other, pondering the reasons why no one had heard from Abbie or Meghan in over a week. Meghan's car had been found the morning after she and Abbie disappeared, but there was no sign of either one of them.

"Something is wrong, I just know it," Michael continued. "Abbie would never do this. Especially not after what happened between us the last time we were together."

"Have you heard anything back from the police?" Stephen asked, taking a sip of his drink.

"No," Michael said, rubbing his head as he stared out the window, facing away from his friends. The hot summer sun blazed in the late-afternoon sky, beating down through the kitchen window, causing Michael to shield his eyes. His hands were shaking, and his vision was slightly blurry. Michael had hardly slept since Abbie had disappeared. Each hour that passed without hearing from her only caused the knot in his stomach to grow that much larger. Alcohol wasn't helping. He was too agitated to even touch his drink.

Both Paul and Stephen were unsure of the words to say to console Michael. The three of them, as well as several others in the community, formed a network of people to search for the girls. Pictures of Abbie and Meghan were circulated throughout Wilmington and neighboring towns, but no one had seen them since the night they had disappeared.

Stephen polished off his drink and began to clear his throat. Michael turned to look at him. Stephen stared intently at his empty glass, narrowing his eyebrows and biting his lower lip, as if he were contemplating saying something that perhaps he shouldn't.

"Stephen?" Paul asked.

Michael spun around from the window as Paul interrupted his thoughts by drawing attention to Stephen. Michael also noticed that it looked as though something was on Stephen's mind.

Stephen kept his eyes low and didn't speak.

"Yeah, what is it?" Michael asked him.

"Nothing," he said innocently as he poured himself another drink.

"You look like something is on your mind," Paul suggested as he, too, finished his drink and poured another.

"It's nothing," Stephen said as he stood up from the counter and wandered about the kitchen.

Michael leaned against the counter next to Paul, and the two of them stared intently at Stephen, both of them knowing something was gnawing at him.

"All right, fine," he said, tossing a hand in the air, already regretting the words he hadn't yet spoken. Stephen took a deep breath and a big gulp of his drink, clenched his jaw as it burned going down his throat, and asked, "What if they don't want to be found?"

The silence that followed the question hung in the air like stale cigarette smoke at a barroom at the end of the night, thick enough to choke on. The few seconds that followed ticked by in slow motion.

Michael could hardly interpret what Stephen was suggesting. His brow furrowed as he cocked his head to the side and asked, "I'm sorry. What?"

Paul stayed silent. He was nearly shocked at what Stephen was suggesting but didn't push the idea out of his mind. He grabbed his crutches from beside the barstool and hobbled over to the other side of the room, leaving plenty of space between his friends.

Taking a step back, Stephen tried to recover. "I'm not saying that is what happened, but it might be a possibility."

Michael tried to stay calm. "I disagree," he managed to say. Stephen knew the details of Abbie and Michael's relationship, so for him to suggest that she would leave without telling him felt like betrayal.

"I'm just throwing ideas out there. I hate the thought that something bad has happened to them. Abbie hopped on a bus and moved here out of the blue one day. Who is to say that that isn't what happened last week? Maybe Meghan wanted to have an adventure of her own. You never know."

Michael put his hands in his pockets. "She wouldn't leave without saying good-bye. There is no way."

Stephen shrugged. "I know you don't see it this way, Michael, but I'm just trying to be optimistic. I don't want to think that anything bad has happened to them."

"Guys," Paul signaled a hand at them from the doorway of the kitchen, directing Stephen and Michael's attention to the living room, where a special news report was broadcasting from the television. Paul reached for the remote control to turn up the volume. Photographs of two men flashed across the screen.

> "...wanted in connection to a large-scale human
> trafficking operation. If you have seen either of these
> men, please contact the local police. These men
> are considered to be armed and dangerous. We are
> asking women of all ages to please use caution when
> approached by strangers..."

The special broadcast ended, and the three of them were silent. Paul and Stephen turned to Michael, only to see the color drain from his face. Stephen and Paul exchanged glances, unsure of what to say to Michael to keep his thoughts from running wild.

Michael sat down in a chair that was in the living room. He put his head in his hands and tried desperately to choke back tears. The very thought of Abbie being involved in something as horrible as what the news report had described left him feeling ill.

"Hey," Paul said to Michael. "I'm sure that has nothing to do with Abbie or Meghan," he added, motioning toward the television.

"It makes too much sense," Michael whispered under his breath.

Stephen didn't know what to say. He knew he had hurt Michael by suggesting that Abbie and Meghan had left on their own free will. At that point, if he were to recant, it would only suggest that maybe the two girls had been kidnapped and were, in fact, part of the horror to which the news report was referring.

Something in Michael snapped. He could no longer sit back and wait for Abbie to call or come home. He had to do something, though he wasn't completely sure as to what it was. Stephen and Paul were both offering up words to comfort Michael, but his mind was racing so quickly that he was unable to process them. He got up from the chair and headed to leave.

"Wait, Michael. Where are you going?" Paul asked.

Michael didn't say anything as he walked out the door.

Stephen followed after him and raced down the front steps once they were outside in order to catch up.

Paul hobbled after them and held the door open, watching as Michael quickly got into his truck and fired up the engine.

"I'm going to find her!" Michael hollered out to them. His tires kicked up gravel as he sped out of the driveway. He wasn't sure where he was headed, but he knew it was up to him if the search for Abbie and Meghan was going to be taken seriously.

Michael sped home, forming a plan. Once he was in the driveway, he could hear Sam and Bull barking from inside the house. He leaped out of the truck once it was in park, and raced up the back steps, two at a time, and flung the door open. The dogs nearly knocked Michael over when he walked inside. Giving them each a quick pat on the head, he raced past them, and darted up the stairs to his bedroom. As he began yanking clothes out of his dresser and closet and throwing them in a pile on his bed, he pulled his cell phone out of his pocket and called his father.

"Dad?" he said, trying to keep his voice steady.

"Yes?" he heard Clark say on the other end of the line.

"I need a favor."

"Yes?"

"I need you to watch the dogs and keep an eye on the farm for a while."

"Sure," Clark said, a bit taken aback. "What's going on?"

"No one is trying to find her, Dad!" Michael nearly shouted, his voice cracking.

Clark did his best to calm Michael. "Aww, Son. The police are doing everything they can."

"I can't wait on everyone else." Michael grabbed a duffel bag from under the bed and stuffed his clothes inside. He gathered it up, and then made his way to the bathroom, scooping up several toiletry items and adding them to the bag.

Clark knew that his son's determination could not be bargained with. "Stay safe," was all he said.

"I will," Michael said hurriedly as he ran back down the steps.

"Michael?"

"Yeah, Dad?" Michael asked as he held the phone with his shoulder, allowing himself to quickly feed the dogs before leaving.

"Bring her home."

"I will."

Michael left a light on over the stove, then locked up the back door as he exited the house. He threw his duffel bag in the passenger side of the truck, then ran over to the driver's side and climbed in. As he backed down the driveway and headed down the road, his heart was racing faster than he ever thought it could. A single tear slipped down his cheek, and he clenched his jaw, determined to hold back the flood that he could feel coming. Michael knew that wherever Abbie was, she needed him.

Picturing her alone and afraid made him sink the gas pedal into the floorboards. He felt a bit out of his mind, leaving like he was, but his only regret was not doing it sooner.

20

JACKSON

ABBIE SLEPT MOST OF the way to Omaha. Jackson did his best to keep himself from gazing over at her, wishing there was something he could do to mend her brokenness back together. He stayed focused by reminding himself that he had a job to do, and Abbie was simply a victim that needed protection, like all of the others that had come before her.

He kept his mind sharp as well as a constant eye on the rearview mirror for any vehicles that seemed suspicious. A few times, when he thought they were being followed, he exited the freeway and circled through a few neighborhoods, just to be certain they weren't being tailed.

They stopped for gasoline and food at a truck stop off of Interstate 64 that first night after a long day of driving. Jackson parked the car near the entrance, and the glow of the flickering Open sign in the diner window roused Abbie awake.

"Are you hungry?" Jackson asked her.

"Not really," Abbie said, yawning.

Jackson noticed she looked weaker since the last time they stopped. He was going to make sure she ate something while they were there. Stepping out of the driver's seat and tucking his shirt into the waist of his pants, he made his way over to the passenger side of the car. Abbie was getting out of the vehicle, steadying herself on the door frame, and she pulled herself upright.

"Easy," Jackson said softly as he offered his hand to help steady her.

"I'm fine," she said, forcing a half smile. She didn't take his hand.

Jackson stepped aside and allowed Abbie to walk ahead of him to the diner. He followed her inside, and they took a seat at a nearby table. The lights were dim at that hour, and only a handful of people occupied the tables in the diner.

"I'm going to need you to eat something," Jackson said to Abbie, lowering his eyes at her, speaking in soft tones.

Abbie looked at Jackson with agreeable eyes. They ordered beverages and food when their waitress came. Music played quietly on the jukebox. Jackson thought he recognized a Journey song make its way out of the speakers, one that he and Travis had often listened to back in their teenage years. He felt his face fall as the memory unexpectedly crossed his mind.

"Are you all right?" Abbie asked.

Jackson's snapped his attention back to Abbie. "Hmm?" he asked.

"You seemed like you were somewhere else for a second."

"Oh, um, no. I just haven't heard this song in a while."

Jackson avoided Abbie's eyes until he got his thoughts under control. He could tell that a woman like her could see right through him if he let her.

Their food arrived, and they ate quietly. Jackson noticed a little bit of color return to Abbie's cheeks.

"When do you think we will be there?" Abbie asked after awhile.

Jackson was surprised that she was making conversation.

"Probably tomorrow evening, depending on how early we head out," he said casually, his elbows on the table, holding a sandwich to his lips. Chewing his food, he thought for a bit about where they should stay that night. It was late, and he was getting tired.

As if she was reading his thoughts, Abbie yawned and asked, "Think we will stop soon?"

Jackson nodded, "Maybe in another hour or so." He put his uneaten sandwich on his plate and pushed it to the center of the table. He wiped his mouth and hands on a napkin and then tossed it on the plate as well.

The waitress walked by and slipped the check facedown on their table. Jackson picked it up, and when he did, his cell phone rang from his shirt pocket. He knew of only one person that would be calling him at that hour. The caller ID confirmed that his boss, Glenn Harper, was calling.

"I'll be right back," Jackson mouthed to Abbie as he took the check to the front counter to pay for their meal. "Don't go anywhere."

Abbie nodded and then curled up in the booth to gaze out the window while she waited for Jackson.

"Yeah?" Jackson said to Harper as he put the phone up to his ear.

"What in the *hell* is going on out there?" Harper said angrily on the other end of the line.

Jackson knew the lecture was coming. His behavior was less than professional toward Abbie, and he knew that Sloan would report back that he had stayed overnight, off duty, in Abbie's hotel room.

"Mom! Hey! How are you?" Jackson asked in a cheery voice, attempting to conceal the seriousness of the conversation to any bystanders, and not draw attention to himself.

"You could very well be jeopardizing this entire operation by your actions, Wells. Are you out of your damn mind?"

"We are doing great, thank you for asking," Jackson said as he handed a few twenty-dollar bills to the cashier with a wink and a smile, again, trying to relay to Harper that he had the situation under control without anyone picking up on what they were actually talking about.

Harper was furious. "You have completely violated protocol. You cannot get your emotions involved in this, Wells. You need to stay focused and certain that no one is following you. One misstep, and you could both be in danger."

"Not, to worry, Mom, we will be there tomorrow night."

"Damnit, Wells—"

"Love you too."

Jackson hung up his phone and walked back to the table where Abbie was sitting. He dropped a few dollar bills on the table as she stood up.

"Everything all right?" she asked.

"Yes," Jackson answered and then led the way to the exit. He knew that when he got back to Washington, DC, he would be faced with some fairly heavy consequences for his actions. He had never been emotionally attached to a case before, but for some reason, he knew he needed to spend as much time as he could with Abbie before he left her, all alone and afraid.

Once they were outside, Jackson opened Abbie's door for her while he kept his head up and an eye out for anyone that may have been watching them. The truck stop was nearly desolate, but Jackson remained cautious.

As they drove out of the parking lot and headed toward the interstate, Jackson's cell phone rang once more. With one hand on the steering wheel, he lifted his cell phone out of his pocket. Seeing that it was Harper, and knowing that he didn't want to deal with the conversation his boss was trying to have with him, he silenced the ringer and tucked the phone back into his pocket.

"Popular guy tonight," Abbie pointed out, jokingly.

Jackson's head jerked in Abbie's direction, struck by her attempt to be humorous. When he looked over at her she had a slight smile on her face, and he thought he heard her laugh. He realized that it was the first time since he met her that he had seen her smile. His heart swelled when he saw that at least a small amount of pain and sorrow had left her eyes, even if it was just for a moment. Jackson laughed but didn't comment in response to Abbie's joke. He looked over at her several more times and searched for any other signs that indicated she was beginning to feel a little less miserable and afraid.

Abbie reclined her chair a bit and curled her small frame up in to it as best as she could. Jackson relaxed a little and was no longer thinking about the impending repercussions of his actions on the assignment. His career was on the line, but that was the last thing on his mind as he watched Abbie drift off to sleep.

Since Travis's death, Jackson sought redemption for the part he played in the accident. In some ways, he felt that protecting Abbie and getting her to safety would help to heal years of guilt he had endured. In other ways, he was drawn to Abbie, and he would have taken away her pain sooner than he would his own.

An hour later, they were checking into a hotel near St. Louis. They were both exhausted after a long day in the car, and still had another long day ahead of them. Jackson walked Abbie to her room, quickly checked that the windows were locked, and then checked to make sure the locks on the inside of her door could be secured. He left a paper bag with her things in it on the bed. Just before he left, he pulled the phone out of the wall and tucked it under his arm.

"Sorry," he said to her. "Can't take any chances."

"I can still run away," Abbie said, half joking, half serious.

"I know," Jackson stated. "But I don't think you want to run. I think you know you are safer in here than anywhere out there." He motioned a hand toward the window, referencing the great big world she would be lost in if she were to leave.

Abbie's face grew serious as Jackson spoke to her.

"I also know that you would do anything to protect your family. So I am not worried that you will leave. However, I don't want you to be tempted to contact anyone, so I'm taking this," he said as he shifted the phone from one arm to the other.

Abbie agreed with what he was saying, but Jackson could tell that she was trying hard not to break down. Her eyes welled up with tears, and she swallowed hard as she crossed her arms over her chest and turned away from Jackson.

He instinctively wanted to take her in his arms.

"Thanks," she said as she walked to the other side of the room, keeping her back toward him.

Jackson paused for a moment and said, "If you need anything, I'm just next door."

Abbie didn't respond. He could see her shoulders start to shake as she tried not to cry in front of him. Knowing she wanted to be alone, Jackson quietly left.

The hours before dawn crept by slowly for the both of them. Jackson contemplated the fate of his career and, at the same time, wondered how he was going to feel about leaving Abbie the following day. Abbie sobbed for hours. She missed Michael. The thought of never seeing him again was physically making her ill. Her heart ached for what her father was going through. Meghan haunted her dreams, making it impossible to sleep.

When Jackson knocked on her door at 6:00 a.m., Abbie's eyes were nearly swollen shut from crying. Her hair was down, a bit unkempt from a night of broken sleep and tormented dreams.

"Let me grab my stuff," Abbie said in a voice just above a whisper. She put on a hooded sweatshirt and then wrapped her hair up in a quick, neat bun. She tucked a few stray hairs behind her ears, grabbed the crumpled-up paper bag that had her belongings in it, and they walked out together.

It took all morning and most of the afternoon for them to make it to Omaha. The corn in the fields alongside the interstate glistened in the midsummer sun and gently swayed in the breeze. Once they were off the interstate, they traveled for two hours down back roads and winding ways until they reached a bed and breakfast, nestled in the backcountry of the heart of Nebraska.

Abbie sat up straight in the passenger seat of Jackson's car as she took in the view before her. The bed and breakfast was simple yet elegant and quaint, with several porches and a white picket fence. Flower boxes lined each window on the upper and lower levels of the two-story historic mansion.

Jackson pulled the car around to the back porch. A friendly-looking woman who appeared to be in her late forties stepped outside, wearing an apron and wiping her hands on a towel.

"Are you ready?" Jackson asked Abbie through his teeth while smiling and waving a hand at the woman.

"Yes," Abbie said, and she also waved.

"Remember what we discussed—about who you are, where you come from."

"I've been practicing it in my head for twelve hundred miles." And with that, Abbie opened her car door, welcoming the sweltering Nebraska air as she shielded her eyes from the sun.

"You must be Sarah," the woman exclaimed as her plump frame walked down the steps to greet Abbie and Jackson. "I'm Bethany," the woman said, extending a hand to Abbie.

"Yes," Abbie said, trying to smile, "that's me."

Jackson approached both of them and held his hand out to Bethany.

"Jackson, right?" she asked, shaking his hand.

"Yes," he said. "So nice to meet you, Bethany."

"Well, come on in!" she said energetically. "Come get yourselves some sweet tea. I will show you around." She turned and led them up the porch steps to the back door of the bed and breakfast.

"What a nice place you have here," Abbie mentioned as Bethany led her and Jackson through the house after handing them each a glass of tea.

Jackson wasn't sure if Abbie was being sincere or playing the part of her new identity. Either way, he decided that her pleasantries were believable.

"Sarah, Jackson told me a little bit about your situation," Bethany said in a hushed, yet bubbly voice. "Don't worry, darlin', we've got room for you here for a while. And it just so happens I was looking for help around here, so this worked out well for me." Bethany continued talking as she bustled about, showing them the inn and explaining a little bit about the work Abbie would be doing. Bethany led them through the first floor, through the kitchen, showing off the formal dining room where she served meals to her guests. Bethany pointed out the fireplace in the sitting room as well as the baby grand piano tucked in the corner. Abbie was drawn to it. She had never seen one up close and hoped to be able to play it during her stay.

All three of them climbed the stairs to the second floor.

"Your room is up here on the left," Bethany said, a bit out of breath as they reached the second-floor landing. She opened the door to a small room with a cozy twin-size bed in one corner and a rocker and ottoman in the other. "There are clothes for you in the closet and in the drawers. Jackson guessed on your sizes, so don't blame me if they don't fit," she joked. Jackson's face turned a deep shade of red. He cleared his throat and awkwardly scratched his forehead. Bethany ended the uncomfortable silence between the three of them by clasping her hands together and saying, "Your car is coming tomorrow. That way you can come and go as you please. Stay until you get on your feet, but there is no rush."

"Thank you so much," Abbie said. "I really appreciate all of this."

Jackson could tell that Abbie was being sincere. He said, "I'll let you ladies talk. Sarah, I will bring in your things." Abbie smiled at him as he turned and walked down the steps.

Jackson heard Bethany speak in a low voice to Abbie. She said, "Oh, Sarah, he's handsome." He slowed to hear Abbie's response but couldn't make out what she said. He could feel his insides begin to ache as the time for him to leave Abbie was drawing near. He quickly gathered her bag of clothes and the manila envelope that contained everything Abbie needed to start her new life.

When Jackson walked back inside, Bethany was showing Abbie around the kitchen and briefing her on what she needed to do to help prepare breakfast each day.

"Oh, there you are!" Bethany sang as Jackson walked into the kitchen. "Here, let me take those upstairs," she offered with her arms held out. "I'll put his envelope in a safe spot," she whispered with a wink at Jackson. Bethany headed out of the kitchen but then stopped in the doorway and said, "I've got to get the dining room made up for dinner. I'll let you two say your good-byes. Jackson, so nice to meet you. Don't worry about this one," she said, winking at Abbie, "Sarah will be very well taken care of."

Jackson raised a hand at Bethany, "Thank you so much, and nice meeting you as well."

Bethany bustled away, and Jackson and Abbie were left alone in the kitchen. Jackson looked at Abbie, and he could tell by the way her chest rose and fell that she was scared.

"It's okay," he whispered as he moved closer to her.

Abbie quickly wiped a tear from her face and lowered her head a bit.

Taking a chance, Jackson touched a hand to her cheek. Abbie didn't pull away, but she didn't lean into it either. He lowered his hand, took a step back, and put both hands in his pockets.

"You're safe here. I promise," he said.

"Thank you," she whispered, wiping away another tear.

Jackson cleared his throat, took another short step toward the door, and said, "I left my business card in that envelope. In case you have questions, or if you need anything."

"Okay," she said.

"Well, I guess that's it then," he said, avoiding the silence. "Take care … Sarah."

"Thank you." Abbie stood in the middle of the kitchen, arms at her sides, looking helpless.

He took one last long look at Abbie and then Jackson walked out the door. He quickly got into the car and started the engine. As he turned the car around in the driveway to head out, he saw Abbie walk out onto the porch. She leaned one hand on the railing and raised another to wave good-bye to Jackson.

He raised a hand at Abbie from the front seat as he drove away, leaving his heart with her in Omaha.

21

HENRY

MEGHAN'S BODY TURNED UP in a marsh five weeks later near Williamsburg, Virginia. A man in his late forties was out walking his dog through the woods near his property in the early-morning hours when he noticed her. The leaves on the ground were still wet with dew, and daylight, though layering the canopy with its warmth, had yet to illuminate the forest floor below. It was nearly a miracle that Meghan's yellow dress, caked in mud, was even noticeable at that time of day.

Michael had kept in touch with Henry nearly every day since he sped away from Wilmington. Henry waited by the phone, praying that Michael had either found Abbie or come across someone who had seen her or Meghan. Michael's phone calls came, in between cities from as far south as Jacksonville and as far north as Boston. Henry was humbled by Michael's dedication to looking for Abbie. Long days were spent searching for her, followed by short nights of fitful sleep, often curled up in the cab of his truck, but Michael persisted—until Tracey called him with the news of Meghan.

It took thirty-six hours for the police to associate Meghan's body with her missing person report, and another eighteen hours for her parents to fly in and identify her body at the coroner's office. Meghan's death was hardly covered in the media, broadcast only once on the evening news out of both Wilmington and Richmond.

Henry was beside himself when Michael called and told him the news. His mind raced back to the memories of losing Annabelle. The idea that his daughter had shared the same fate as Meghan sank his heart into his stomach. Up until that point, he had feared it to be a possibility, but it all seemed too surreal. Henry waged war on the demons in his mind on a nightly basis, praying for Annabelle to come and tell him everything was fine but, at the same time, feared that if he closed his eyes, Abbie would appear in the same form her mother had for the past twenty years.

"I'm going back to Wilmington," Michael informed Henry the day before Meghan's funeral. "Henry," Michael said, slowly, quietly, "I'm not going to be able to get through it without you. Can you please come?"

"Yes." Henry's voice cracked when he said it. Clearing his throat and fighting back tears, Henry said, "I'll be there." He swallowed hard at the thought of attending the funeral of Abbie's friend while she was still missing.

So Henry drove back to Wilmington. Echoes of Annabelle's words rang through his head over and over, mile after mile, as he made his way to North Carolina. " ... *she needs you more than you need her* ..." Guilt and dread consumed him. Henry's physical world, which encapsulated Abbie from the moment she was born, somehow cracked, and she slipped through before he was able to catch her. When Abbie disappeared, Henry felt as though he had completely failed both his daughter and his wife. Annabelle had specifically sent Henry to protect Abbie. And now, their child was missing.

Michael was sitting on his porch with Sam and Bull when Henry's car pulled into the driveway later that evening. Henry got out of the car, suitcase in hand, and met Michael at the steps. The two men embraced, like father and son, unashamed of the tears that fell between them. Henry noticed a significant difference in Michael's appearance since he first met him. He looked ragged and worn. The happiness that he had previously seen in him had been replaced with sorrow.

Without words, Michael grabbed Henry's bag, and they walked into the house. The days ahead were, by far, going to be some of the worst they would ever experience, but, somehow, they knew they would get through it together.

22

ABBIE

THE STARS WERE PARTICULARLY bright that first night in Omaha. A calm, slightly cool breeze was unfamiliarly earthy, as the dust from the plains held onto its sails. Abbie hadn't realized how much she missed the scent of the sea and the taste of salt in the air that she had grown so accustomed to in North Carolina.

Bethany had gone home for the night, and the guests had all turned in. Abbie sat on the back porch, in jeans and a long sleeve cotton tee that she found in the closet in her room. She drew her knees into her chest and curled her bare toes around the edge of the step where she sat. She tucked her hands into her sleeves, wrapped her arms around her legs, and leaned her head back to view the sky.

For the first time in close to a week, she felt somewhat calm. Fear, dread, and doubt still took up most of the space in her heart, but she felt a stillness try to make its way inside. Abbie felt as though she was a million miles away from Michael, and at the same time, she sensed him there with her. Closing her eyes, she inhaled the air she knew she would never share with him and exhaled, imagining he would materialize before her from her very breath.

The late night turned into early morning. The stars began to fade, and Abbie's eyes adapted to the light that slowly swallowed the darkness away. Headlights flashed up the driveway as Bethany's car pulled in. Slightly startled, Abbie stood up to greet her as Bethany got out of her car.

"Oh, good, you're up!" Bethany said, delighted. "You can help me with breakfast." She pulled paper grocery bags out of the front seat and handed them to Abbie, ready to put her to work. Once their arms were loaded up, they went inside and into the kitchen to prepare the morning meal for the guests.

"Did you sleep well?" Bethany asked as they set the bags on the counter and began to unload them.

"I didn't sleep much, but the bed is very comfortable. Thank you."

Bethany put the milk and eggs in the refrigerator and then turned back toward Abbie and said, "Of course. I'll bet you have a lot on your mind, child."

Abbie shrugged, not wanting to reveal too much.

"We don't have to talk about it," Bethany said cheerily, and she was once again moving about the kitchen, pulling down place settings from the cupboards. "Can you put these around the table in the dining room?" Bethany asked with a smile, changing the subject.

"Absolutely," Abbie said, accepting the stack of dishes from Bethany. She set the table as Bethany gathered items from the refrigerator and cupboards to cook with. Abbie gently placed the antique plates on the tablecloth that was laid out on a long wooden table in the middle of the dining room beneath a beautiful crystal chandelier. She carefully positioned real silver flatware next to the plates. This small task, setting the table for guests for breakfast, was the first normal thing she had done in days.

"What's next?" Abbie asked as cheerfully as she could as Bethany held her arms around a large glass bowl, whisking up a dozen eggs as fast as she could.

"Have you ever made frittatas?" Bethany asked as she wiped her brow with the back of her wrist.

"Once or twice," Abbie answered.

Bethany stopped whisking, grabbed an apron from a peg in the wall near her, and tossed it in Abbie's direction. She then pointed to a pile of fresh veggies and herbs on the counter and said, "Those can be chopped up, if you don't mind."

Abbie got to work on cutting up the tomatoes, onions, asparagus, and mushrooms as well as a bit of basil and oregano. The aromas filled her senses, and she knew that when she smelled them in the future, she would travel back in time to that very moment.

"Sarah?" Abbie heard Bethany say.

"Hmm?" Abbie was lost in thought and didn't realize Bethany was trying to get her attention.

"Good grief, child, I said your name about three times," she laughed as she picked up a knife to help Abbie finish up the vegetables.

"I'm so sorry, Bethany," Abbie chuckled. "I think I was daydreaming."

"Oooh," Bethany said, her eyes glistening as she put down her knife and gave Abbie her full attention. "Are you thinking about Jackson?"

"Goodness, no." Abbie blushed.

Bethany resumed chopping. "Sarah, he's so handsome. And the way he looked at you! I could have sworn there was something between the two of you."

Abbie looked confused. "No, nothing at all," Abbie said innocently. "I just met him a few days ago. At the police station. And then he brought me here. That's it. I don't even know anything about him."

"Well, that's too bad." Bethany winked at Abbie.

"Tell me about yourself," Abbie said, changing the subject in fear she would slip up and talk about Michael. "Are you married?"

"No," Bethany said quickly, still keeping her friendly composure. "Used to be, but not anymore."

"I'm so sorry," Abbie said apologetically.

"Don't be," Bethany said with a slight head shake and a shrug. She quickly scooped up the vegetables and tossed them all in a bowl and then brushed off her hands over top. "He gave me two great kids that I wouldn't trade for the world."

"You have kids?" Abbie asked interested as she leaned up against the counter.

"Aaron and Iris." Bethany tossed a potato at Abbie and said, "Here, peel these up for some hash browns."

"How old are they?" Abbie asked as she continued to help Bethany prepare the meal.

"Iris is twenty-four, and Aaron is twenty-five."

Abbie smiled at Bethany, encouraging her to continue talking about her children. And continue, she did. Abbie was genuinely interested in getting to know Bethany but, at the same time, did not want to have to start a lifetime of lies just yet. She spent the next hour listening to Bethany talk while they finished up the frittatas and the hash browns.

The guests began to file down the stairs and into the dining room promptly at 8:00 a.m.

"Showtime," Bethany joked as they added the finishing touches to the food. They both made their way into the dining room. Abbie poured freshly squeezed orange juice into goblets and coffee into tea cups for the guests as Bethany served the meal.

Abbie naturally floated through the dining room, taking care of the needs of the guests. She enjoyed meeting and getting to know new people, as if she was back at the diner in North Carolina. Introducing herself as Sarah, she kept the details about herself brief but showed great interest in those that sat at the dining room table that morning.

Exhausted from the morning and the lack of sleep the night before, Abbie could barely keep her eyes open while she scrubbed the dishes in the sink after breakfast. Her eyelids were heavy, which she did her best to hide from Bethany, but to no avail.

"You look terrible, child," Bethany said matter-of-factly to Abbie as she brought another load of dirty dishes into the kitchen to be washed.

Abbie snapped herself awake as soon as she heard Bethany's voice. "I'm so sorry," she apologized. "I'm not usually like this. It's just that I haven't slept—"

"Oh, hush," Bethany said, gently taking the washrag from her as she placed a hand on her arm. "I can't even imagine what you could possibly be going through. How about you go lie down? Relax. I appreciate the help this morning, but you should rest."

Abbie hesitated as she looked around the kitchen at all of the work to be done.

"Don't worry about all this," Bethany reassured her about the cleanup.

"Are you sure?"

"Absolutely. Go." Bethany smiled as she shooed her out of the kitchen.

Reluctant yet thankful, Abbie trudged upstairs to her room. Her legs felt heavy, and she was out of breath by the time she reached her bed. As soon as she slipped under the covers, her eyes closed, and she tried to sleep. Every time she fell asleep, she longed for Annabelle to reappear and possibly bring her some peace.

Weeks went by before Abbie finally did dream of her mother. She was aching for a miracle, a sign that Michael and her father had found some sort of peace despite her disappearance. Abbie had cried herself to sleep every night with silent, desperate tears. She hadn't seen her mother in a dream since before the night of the abduction. Once she was finally able to drift off to sleep after a particularly long night of crying, Annabelle slipped into her dreams. Her mother was silent, calm, and beautiful. She simply held Abbie in her arms like a child and comforted her with whispers of reassurance that everything would be fine. Abbie's alarm went off at 5:00 a.m. She lay in bed for a few extra minutes, breathing in the serenity and clarity her mother's presence had provided while she slept.

She showered and dressed, and headed downstairs to help Bethany. Abbie had just begun to feel comfortable in her new skin as Sarah Walker, playing the part of a battered woman, afraid for her life. It wasn't too far from the truth, only she wasn't running from an abusive ex. She thought of Michael every second of every day since that last day she had spent with him. Being unable to talk about him made her feel as if she was dying inside.

Abbie was surprised to see that Bethany was on the phone.

"Oh, here she is, actually. Hang on a second," Bethany said into the phone as she looked up and saw Abbie. "It's for you." Bethany handed Abbie the phone.

"Hello?" Abbie said as her heart raced, wondering who would be calling her.

"It's me," she heard a voice on the other end of the line say.

It was Jackson. *Of course,* Abbie thought to herself. *Why would it have been anyone else?*

"Hi," she said as her heart sank.

"Can you talk privately? I need to share a few things with you and don't want to be overheard," Jackson said.

"Yes, I can do that." Abbie walked outside barefoot. Her heels walked on the bottoms of her jeans, which were soon soaked with dew up to her ankles. It was the first time she had heard from Jackson in over a month, so she was certain that what he had to say was important.

"They found Meghan, Abbie," he told her.

Abbie was speechless, filled with mixed emotion. She had prayed every day that Meghan's body would be found, but now that she had, it seemed so final. She had known it all along, but she was suddenly faced with the fact that people were going to eventually give up looking for her as well. But, in order for everyone to remain safe and sound, she tried to accept it.

"When?" Abbie asked.

"I just got word a few hours ago."

"Okay," was all Abbie could say.

Jackson continued. "This is actually a good thing, Abbie."

"Okay," she said again, flatly.

"Now that there is a body, we can make sure the evidence will point to Griffin Ford and Alex McCain as the killers. We won't need a witness." Silence hung between them. "You won't need to testify."

Abbie exhaled, a bit relieved. She was unsure of what to say. "So I guess that's it, then?" she asked, trying to keep her composure, knowing she would have to go inside and make up a story about why Jackson was calling her.

"I know all of this is tough to hear. And again, Abbie, I am so sorry for your loss."

"Thank you," she said, gracefully accepting his heartfelt apology.

"Don't hesitate to contact me with any questions or concerns."

"I will." Abbie paused and then asked, "Jackson?"

"Yes?"

She tried to keep her voice from cracking as she asked, "Are they looking for me?"

"Yes," he said, almost hesitantly. Jackson did not want to tell her the measures Michael was taking to reach her, and the work that Jackson had to do to make sure he was unsuccessful.

Abbie let out a long, labored sigh. "I had better get back," she told him.

"Take care," Jackson said.

"Same to you."

Abbie made sure she was composed as she walked back inside. She handed the phone back to Bethany and quickly busied herself in the kitchen.

"Everything all right, Sarah?" Bethany asked quietly.

"Yeah. I think so," Abbie said, measuring ingredients for Belgian waffles, trying to calm her nerves. "Jackson just had to give me some information about the charges that were filed on my behalf," Abbie lied.

Bethany believed her. "Do you want to talk about it?" she asked.

"No, I'm fine," Abbie said. As soon as she said it, she felt the color drain from her face. A surge of nausea caught her by surprise, and she doubled over the sink.

Bethany rushed to her side and quickly grabbed Abbie's hair away from her face. "There, there," she said, reassuringly. When Abbie was able to stand up straight, Bethany got her a cold cloth to wipe her mouth, as well as a glass of water.

"I am so sorry, Bethany," Abbie said, embarrassed. "I don't know what came over me. I just haven't been feeling well lately."

"I've noticed that."

"I guess I've just been a bit stressed out with everything," Abbie reasoned as she leaned against the counter.

"You've been going to bed awfully early, too," Bethany pointed out.

Abbie nodded, taking a sip of water.

"Sarah ..." Bethany cocked her head to the side, encouraging Abbie to think about what she was implying.

"What?" Abbie asked innocently, standing up straight.

Bethany laughed and gently waved a towel in Abbie's direction. "Aw, c'mon, Sarah. Think about it."

"Think about what?" Abbie asked, not understanding what Bethany was suggesting.

Bethany held up her hand and counted off her fingers as she said, "You've been nauseous, going to bed early, and let me ask you this," she said, holding up a third finger, "are you late?"

"Am I what? Ooh," Abbie's face grew serious as she realized what Bethany was asking. Her mind raced. She thought back to the last night she had spent with Michael. She hadn't been paying much attention to the time that had passed since she moved to Omaha, but she suddenly realized that she was, in fact, late. Her eyes darted to Bethany's as a hand flew to her mouth.

Bethany's eyes grew wide, and she said confidently, "Sarah, I think you might be pregnant."

23

JACKSON

JACKSON WAS PLACED ON a thirty-day unpaid suspension after he left Omaha and returned to Washington, DC. He knew it was coming. In fact, he expected worse. Glenn Harper had arranged a meeting with Jackson as soon as he returned.

"Let me explain why I did what I did," Jackson said, attempting to calm down his superior.

"I don't want to hear it," Harper said flatly. "You deliberately breached protocol, potentially jeopardizing this entire assignment. Lives were at stake. You repeatedly disobeyed orders and then refused to communicate with me."

Struggling to reason with Harper, Jackson said, "If I could just explain—"

"No! You cannot explain!" Harper shouted.

Jackson clenched his jaw as he struggled to remain silent.

Harper then looked Jackson in the eye and said quietly before seating himself at his desk, "I'm removing you from this assignment."

Jackson ran a hand down his face, fighting the urge to defend his behavior with Abbie. He felt as though she was too young and too vulnerable to have to go through what she had to endure alone. He also felt that he still needed to protect her, regardless if he was assigned to her case.

Jackson calmly walked out of Harper's office without saying a word. On his way out of the building, he stopped by Sloan's office.

"Jackson," Sloan said, surprised and a bit nervous as he stood up from his desk. "Look, man, I'm sorry, but I had to tell Harper what happened."

Jackson held out his hand for Sloan to shake as he said, "It's not a big deal, Sloan. You were just doing your job. In fact, I fully expected it. I don't regret what I did, and I would do it again if I had to."

Sloan nervously shook Jackson's outstretched hand. "Well, if you need anything while you're gone, just let me know," he said, referring to Jackson's suspension.

"I'm happy you said that," Jackson said slyly. "Because it just so happens I will need your help."

"Help?" Sloan asked, confused.

Jackson got straight to the point. "Who's assigned to Abbie Peterson now?" he asked.

"I am, actually."

"Good." Jackson had hoped that was the case. "You are going to keep me informed of the details of the case. And I am going to help you keep her safe."

Sloan hesitated.

"You owe me," Jackson stated.

"Yes, but—"

"Look, I spent more time with her than I should have, yes. Was I inappropriate? Yes. Do I have information that will help this case that I wouldn't have gained if I would have followed protocol? You bet. You need me, Sloan. It's your ass now if anything happens to her, right?"

Sloan couldn't argue with that. "Right," he answered.

"Good. I'll be in touch." Jackson walked out of Sloan's office before they had a chance to argue.

For the next thirty days, Jackson worked with Sloan, unofficially, on Abbie's case. The two of them gathered all of the intelligence they could to locate and apprehend Griffin Ford and Alex McCain. Jackson and Sloan also planned on contacting law enforcement in the Wilmington and surrounding areas to inform them that the US Marshals Service had Abbie Peterson in their custody and instruct them to call off the searches for her body.

The plan was nearly flawless. One month after Abbie and Meghan's disappearance the local news began to report on other stories. The girls' faces, which once plastered televisions in every home along the East

Coast, soon disappeared. The missing person reports turned into cold cases.

What Jackson didn't account for was Michael Hammond. During Jackson's suspension, he had learned that Michael was traveling across the country searching for Abbie. Once Meghan's body was found, and time had passed, Jackson figured Michael would give up looking for Abbie. But he didn't. Jackson admired Michael's dedication to looking for her, but it only made his job that much harder. He wasn't concerned that Michael would actually come across a witness from the night of, or any time after, Abbie's disappearance. He was concerned that Michael would come across someone like Griffin Ford or Alex McCain. If they, or anyone those two were associated with, got wind that Abbie still might be alive, it could be disastrous. Ford and McCain needed to believe that Abbie didn't survive out in the woods after she fled from the Suburban.

When Jackson wasn't working with Sloan on the case, he spent his time thinking about Abbie. Or trying not to, rather. He spent several hours a day outside, whether he was running, hiking, or trail riding. It was all he could do to keep from wondering, one moment to the next, if Abbie was safe and happy. He would never forget how scared and alone she looked the first time he saw her, curled up on the cot at the police station, covered in blood, dirt, and sweat, just hours after she had fought for her life. Each day that passed since he had left Abbie was yet another day he thought about going back to Omaha, scooping her up in his arms, and promising to always make sure she was cared for, protected, and loved.

Meghan's body was found not long after Jackson had returned to work from his suspension. Although it took several weeks for her body to turn up, he was relieved that Abbie would not have to testify in court once Ford and McCain were apprehended. Hearing Abbie's voice on the phone as he told her the news was nothing short of bittersweet. It pained him to hear the hope in her voice when she asked if her loved ones were looking for her, only to snatch the hope away from her. Jackson knew that Abbie was aware that his job was to make sure that no one would be able to find her. However, it didn't change the fact that it felt like he was breaking her heart.

It was six long months before Jackson spoke with Abbie again.

Summer faded into autumn, and autumn shed its skin to expose the bare bones of winter. Jackson and Sloan had been working around the clock, closing in on Ford and McCain, and developing a plan to apprehend them.

Jackson and Sloan were able to locate Ford and McCain before Michael came across them in his search for Abbie. In late January, Sloan was tipped off to the whereabouts of the men that had captured Abbie and murdered Meghan. A stakeout was organized near a motel in Charleston, nearly two hundred miles away from where Ford and McCain abducted Abbie and Meghan that summer. Two undercover patrol cars canvassed the area near the motel and reported back to Jackson and Sloan where they were camped out in a nearby SUV.

The officers and deputies involved waited for the perfect opportunity to rush in and arrest the criminals, who were holed up in the motel room. Ford and McCain didn't see the attack coming. They were, however, armed and dangerous. Police drew their weapons and ordered the two men to drop theirs, just after the motel room door was kicked in to make the arrest. A standoff ensued as orders were shouted, and weapons were aimed to fire. Ford and McCain eventually surrendered and were quickly taken into custody.

Jackson and Sloan transported the criminals to Washington, DC, from Charleston. Ford and McCain were restrained in the backseat of the SUV while Sloan drove and Jackson sat in the passenger seat. Halfway through their journey, Jackson heard whispers from the backseat.

"Hey," Jackson said. "Keep it down, please."

Ford and McCain were silent for a few minutes but then started to chuckle, aggravating the two of them in the front seat.

Jackson turned around in his seat. A steel, mesh cage separated the front seat from the back. He looked through it, faced the men in the backseat, and said, "I'm not going to ask again." Then he turned and faced front.

"What are you going to do?' Griffin Ford taunted.

Jackson felt his blood begin to boil. He glanced over at Sloan, who was staring straight ahead, trying to remain calm. Neither one said a word and kept driving. Laughter was heard from the backseat. Jackson felt his ears get hot, and he bit his tongue in order to keep his cool. Everything in him wanted to hurt the men that had put Abbie through hell that summer night. He took a few deep breaths in, exhaled, and then counted down the minutes until they would be in DC. It was late in the evening and would be even later once they reached the US Marshals Service headquarters.

"You should have seen them," Jackson heard Griffin say from the backseat.

Jackson refused to turn around.

"The blonde went down easy," he said, nonchalantly. "But that brunette, she was a tricky one."

"Is that a confession?" Sloan hollered over his shoulder to the backseat.

Jackson's knuckles turned white as he gripped the armrest. He closed his eyes, trying to remain calm. He heard them chuckling again.

"Enough!" Sloan warned. He could see that Jackson was about to lose it.

"It's a damn shame, really," Griffin continued. "They would have been perfect."

Jackson whipped around, looked him straight in the eyes, and said angrily, "Not another word." Griffin's eyes were wild. Jackson suspected he was most likely high on drugs.

Griffin Ford looked straight into Jackson's eyes. "I'm glad I killed them. They would have been trouble anyway."

Jackson clenched his jaw and stared into Griffin Ford's half-crazed eyes. Jackson obviously knew the man was lying about killing Abbie. Jackson could also see that Griffin knew Jackson was aware of the lie.

"You're both sick," Jackson said, with a quiet, angry whisper, and he turned around in his seat to face the road.

"You should have seen them!" Griffin called out. "*Begging* for someone to save them!" and then both men in the backseat laughed hysterically.

"Stop the car," Jackson said to Sloan.

"What?" Sloan asked, looking at Jackson.

"Pull over!" Jackson yelled. He couldn't contain his anger any longer.

Sloan obliged, but not without saying, "Wells, this is a terrible idea."

Jackson didn't care. *How dare they talk about Abbie or Meghan in such a manner?* he thought to himself.

Sloan maneuvered the vehicle onto the shoulder of the interstate. Jackson opened his door and leaped out before the SUV came to a stop. He jerked the back passenger door open, grabbed Griffin by the collar, drew his right arm back, and let his knuckles hit the man that ruined Abbie's life square in the jaw. Jackson kept hitting him, over and over, until he no longer had any strength left in his arm. Blood poured from Griffin Ford's nose and mouth. Alex looked frightened as Jackson slammed the door to the backseat. Without a word, Jackson got back into the front seat. As Sloan merged back onto the interstate, Jackson reached into the glove box and found some napkins to wipe the blood from his fist. He opened and closed his fist several times as it began to swell. Silence filled the vehicle for the remainder of the trip.

Chaos erupted once Jackson and Sloan reached Washington, DC, and dragged Ford and McCain inside the building. Harper was waiting as the four of them entered the building.

"What in the hell happened?" Harper shouted as soon as he saw the blood caked on Griffin Ford's strung-out, half-smiling face. That's when he noticed Jackson's bloody, swollen hand.

"Sir," Sloan protested on behalf of Jackson, "Had you been there, you would understand—"

"Wells!" Harper yelled, ignoring Sloan. "In my office. Now!" And he turned and marched down the hall. Sloan and Jackson exchanged anxious looks before Jackson followed Harper down the hall.

Harper took a seat at his desk once they reached his office. Jackson closed the door and sat down as well. Harper, however, irate as he was, couldn't stay seated. He leaped from his seat and began darting around the room.

"Damnit, Wells!" Harper said, pacing. "From the beginning, the *beginning* of this case, you have been out of control!"

Jackson refused to sit and let Harper shout at him. He stood up and defended himself by saying, "If it wasn't for *me*, and my actions on this case, our witness could very well be dead."

"Your *actions* have been completely unprofessional. I thought maybe your suspension this summer would have taught you a thing or two about the way we operate. But you aren't getting it. We don't just go around sleeping with witnesses and punching out criminals!"

"What?!" Jackson was outraged. "I didn't *sleep* with anyone!"

Harper stood before Jackson, hands on hips, and said, "You're done, Wells. I want your badge."

"You can't be serious," Jackson said, disgusted.

"Oh, I am serious," Harper said. "You're a disgrace to this entire department."

Jackson was speechless. He ripped his badge from his hip and tossed it on Harper's desk. He then unholstered his weapon and placed it next to his badge.

"You're making a huge mistake," Jackson said as he stormed out of the office and then out of the building. He was outraged at Harper's decision to fire him. Once he was in his truck, Jackson jammed his keys into the ignition, pulled out of his designated parking space, and then raced out of the parking garage. His blood was boiling as he headed out of downtown toward his house in the suburbs.

The squeal of his tires could be heard throughout his neighborhood as Jackson pulled into his driveway and threw his truck into park. He sat there for a while, out of breath and shaking. His mind raced and wondered what would happen to Abbie now that he wasn't assigned to her case. He was arrogantly convinced that no one, not Sloan or Harper, or anyone else, for that matter, could keep Abbie as safe as he could. The thought of harm coming to her tied his stomach in knots.

A plan formed in Jackson's mind as he sat there, in his driveway, stewing over what had transpired over the past couple of hours. He looked down at his knuckles and gave himself no other choice as to what to do next. He got out of his truck, went into his house, and packed a suitcase with a week's worth of clothes. He went back out to his truck, tossed the luggage into the front seat, backed down the driveway, and headed to the airport.

24

MICHAEL

THE DECISION FOR MICHAEL to sell the farm and hire a private investigator was by far the hardest thing he had ever done. Abbie had been gone for almost seven months, and Michael was out of his mind with desperation for her. He had returned home after two months of searching nearly every city along the East Coast. He was physically and emotionally exhausted, not to mention out of money. His landscaping business was failing with only Stephen to handle all of the work, and bills at the farm were piling up.

Michael was starting to realize that Abbie could, in fact, be dead, but he needed closure or some sort of evidence that she would never be coming home. Henry felt the same way. Michael and Abbie's father continued to communicate, but not as often as they had when Abbie first went missing. It had become too hard for Henry to be disappointed each time Michael called, and it was too hard for Michael to hear the sadness in Henry's voice. They agreed it would be best not to talk as often.

The sky was gray and bleak, and a chill carried its way across the farm on the day that Michael put the For Sale sign in his front yard. Winter had closed in on North Carolina, and all of the sadness that he had in his heart could be felt in the air.

"There's got to be another way." Clark Hammond initially opposed Michael's decision to sell the family farm. The two of them sat in Michael's kitchen, much like they did on the day that Michael told his father about Abbie for the first time.

"There is no other way," Michael explained. "My business is underwater. Stephen has been killing himself doing the work of three people for months. Paul is able to do some work now, but we were so backlogged for a while that our customers went elsewhere. I can't afford to pay either one of them, let alone myself. Another month or two, and I'll be in foreclosure."

The silence between the two of them was deafening. Clark sat with his head resting in his hands, which were propped up by his elbows on the table.

"I'm going to buy it back once I find her," Michael said, trying to reassure his father that the farm that had held their family together for generations would not be gone indefinitely.

"Michael," Clark said delicately. "Are you prepared to really know what happened to her? Are you prepared to go through what we all went through when Meghan was found?"

Michael sat down and hung his head between his knees. It took everything in him not to cry, but a few tears managed to spill to the floor.

"Oh, Son," Clark said and placed a hand on Michael's shoulder.

Michael looked up. "What if it was Mom?"

Clark sat up straight. He hadn't put Michael's loss into perspective until then. He chewed on his lower lip, also fighting tears. Clark began nodding, patted Michael on the shoulder, and then stood up. Neither of them said anything for a long time. Michael stared at the floor while he remained seated at the table. Clark stared out the window at the trees that had lost their leaves and the grass that had turned brown. The crops had been harvested, and the stillness of the farm settled his heart as he began to speak.

"Remember your freshman year of high school?" Clark said to Michael after his thoughts formed.

Michael looked up, confused. "Yes?" he inquired.

"You wanted to try out for the varsity football team, remember?"

Michael sat up in the chair and nodded his head. "You tried to talk me out of it," he chuckled, remembering how determined he was to prove his father wrong. "I was smaller than everyone else at the time, but I wanted to make the team." Clark nodded as Michael recalled what happened that year. "You told me to do my best but not to get my hopes up, because of my size."

"And wouldn't you know it—"

Michael stood up and said proudly, "I made varsity."

Clark smiled and crossed his arms over his chest and beamed with pride as Michael continued with the story.

"I was the fastest player on the team. I made varsity every year after that."

"I'm glad you didn't listen to your old man back then." Clark nearly choked on his words as he said them.

"Me too," Michael said, realizing the gravity of his father's statement.

Without another word, Clark grabbed his jacket from a hook by the back door. "Have a good night, Son," he said as he headed out the door.

Michael held the door for his father and watched as he left the driveway and headed home. Sam and Bull circled Michael's feet as he closed the door and locked it for the night. His thoughts were very clear about what he needed to do to find Abbie. As soon as he could sell the farm, he was going to hire the best investigator that he could afford.

That opportunity came one week later. An affluent gentleman in his early sixties drove past the farm on a quiet Sunday morning and knocked on Michael's door. Still in his pajamas, Michael wasn't prepared for visitors; however, Sam and Bull were happy to have the company.

"Hello," the stranger said as Michael, blurry-eyed, opened the door.

"Can I help you?" Michael asked.

"Hi," the stranger said, extending a hand to Michael through the door frame, "my name is Brody Garrity."

"Michael Hammond," he responded, shaking the man's hand. "What can I do for you?"

"I've been by your property a few times since it's been listed for sale. I'd like to discuss it with you, if you can spare the time."

Michael was taken aback. Had he known a prospective buyer would be on his doorstep that morning, he would have changed his clothes, showered, and possibly shaved. He ran a hand through an overgrown mess of hair on his head.

"Well, come on in," Michael said once the shock wore off. "Have a seat on the couch, and I'll be right back," Michael said as he hurried through the living room and headed upstairs to change his clothes. Sam and Bull greeted the stranger with wagging tails and licks on his open hand. "Sorry about the dogs," Michael called out as he ascended the stairs, two steps at a time.

Brody Garrity laughed as he petted the dogs and said, "I don't mind. I have three at home just like them."

Michael returned a few minutes later, quickly tucking a button-up shirt into a pair of jeans. "I've got coffee in the kitchen," Michael said. "Can I bring you a cup?"

"Yes. Black, please."

Michael went into the kitchen and nervously poured two cups of coffee. He looked around at the piles of dirty dishes and the dust that seemed to have accumulated on everything overnight. The past few months he had been so obsessed with finding Abbie that he seemed to neglect everyday responsibilities around the house. With a cup of coffee in each hand, Michael walked back into the living room. Brody was seated comfortably on the couch while the dogs relaxed at his feet.

"Thank you," Brody said, accepting a cup from Michael.

"What can I do for you, Mr. Garrity?" he asked, pulling the bench out from underneath the piano that sat near the couch. The memory of Abbie seated at that same bench, playing music for him, was at the forefront of his mind, and it began to cloud his thought process. Michael tried to block out the melody of the last song she had played for him and simply focus on what the man had to say.

"Well, I'm very interested in buying your property. I contacted your Realtor yesterday and asked about the price. When she told me what you were asking for it, well, I have to admit I didn't expect it to be so modestly priced."

"To be perfectly honest with you, Mr. Garrity—"

"Call me Brody, please."

"Brody. The thing is, I need to sell the farm."

The man on Michael's couch nodded and said, "That's what I wanted to talk to you about, Michael. I own three properties, much like this one, and yours is by far the most stunning. However, you have priced it a great deal lower than its fair market value. So, I knew there must be a story. Either that or you were out of your mind." The last sentence was spoken with a lighthearted laugh.

Michael also laughed. "I may be both."

Brody looked intently at Michael, waiting for him to continue.

"The thing is," Michael began to explain, realizing how crazy he sounded, but still said, "I need to hire a private investigator." Michael could tell that that was not the response Brody had expected to hear.

"For what?" the man asked, shocked.

"You see, I met a young woman this past summer. An amazing woman. Her name is Abbie. A few weeks later, she vanished. Without a word. Well, actually, both she and a friend of hers disappeared." He managed to keep his voice steady as he continued. "Her friend, Meghan, was found murdered a few weeks after that." Michael was silent for a few moments. He looked over at Brody, who was waiting patiently for him to continue the story. "It's been months and there has been no sign of Abbie. I've looked myself. The police have been involved in searching for her, but they are encouraging me to give up."

"Wow," Brody said as he sipped his coffee. "I wasn't expecting that."

"That's why I need to sell the farm. I've looked into how much this is going to cost me. I want to hire the best because I want her back. If I can't have her back, I at least need some closure. I won't be able to live with myself if I didn't do everything in my power to find her."

Brody Garrity, although a stranger to Michael up until minutes earlier, seemed to sympathize with him and wanted to help. He looked around the room, stood up from the couch, and said, "Do you mind showing me around? I'd like to see what I'm about to purchase."

"Really?" Michael was shocked. Brody Garrity and his offer were certainly an unexpected twist in his plans for that day. They spent the majority of the morning and part of the afternoon together. Michael showed him around the house and the farm, sharing stories of his childhood and the hopes he once had for his future.

The two of them were standing outside by the carriage house in the backyard when Brody made his offer to Michael. He asked, "Will you accept twenty-five percent higher than your asking price?"

Michael nearly choked. "Excuse me?" he asked.

"Do you not think that's a fair price?"

"Oh, no, no," Michael searched for words. "It's not that at all."

"I can have the money for you tomorrow," Brody said confidently.

All of a sudden, Michael felt completely torn about selling the farm. He would have given up the farm and so much more if it meant having Abbie back. However, when he looked around him, the farm was the exact place he wanted to bring her once he found her.

Mr. Garrity could see a look of regret begin to form on Michael's face. "Tell you what," he proposed, "I'll let you rent the carriage house for as long as you like."

Michael cocked his head to the side and gave Brody a bit of a confused look.

"I travel often and don't expect to occupy the residence more than a few days per month. In my absence, I'll be hiring several individuals that will handle the maintenance." He said it so casually, as if Michael had already agreed to the terms.

"Let's back up just a bit," Michael said, overwhelmed. He paused to collect his thoughts. Then he asked, "Why are you so interested in purchasing the farm?"

Brody thought for a few minutes and said, "You know, you won't believe me even if I told you."

Intrigued, Michael said, "You may be surprised."

"I'm from the area, and I've walked my dogs or driven by more times than I can count. I've always admired the setting, the backdrop, the way I always felt at peace when I walked by. Anyway, one particular afternoon this past summer I was walking by. I saw a woman standing at the end of your driveway. She was admiring it as well."

Michael gave Brody a curious look and was interested in hearing the rest of the story.

"I stopped and talked to the woman for a few minutes. I was telling her how fond I was of the place, and she looked at me and said, 'I think you should buy it'. I chuckled, of course, pointed out that it was not for sale, and she said, 'I still think you should buy it.'" Brody started laughing. "I thought it was strange, this gorgeous woman in a yellow dress, just standing there, telling me to buy one of the most beautiful homes and pieces of property I had ever seen. And then just a few short months later, I see the sign in the front yard that it was for sale. I knew I had to come by personally and discuss it with you."

Michael's brain kicked in to overdrive as soon as Brody mentioned a gorgeous woman in a yellow dress.

"Excuse me; I don't mean to interrupt," Michael said, "but can you tell me about the woman? The one you spoke with that day?"

"There isn't much to tell," he shrugged. "We talked for about five minutes, and then we went our separate ways."

"What did she look like?" Michael looked intently at Brody and felt a bit like he was interrogating his guest.

Brody thought for a moment and said, "She was probably in her early forties, big doe eyes, long brown hair, and tan skin. Like I said, she was gorgeous."

"And she had a yellow dress on," Michael was confirming, not asking.

"Yes," Brody said as he grew a bit suspicious about the nature of Michael's questioning.

"Did she happen to say what her name was?"

"Hmmm, we did introduce ourselves, but I can't seem to remember," his voice trailed off. "Anastasia? Annabelle? Annabelle. Yes, yes, I'm pretty sure she said Annabelle."

The hairs on the back of Michael's neck stood up as Brody said the name. He swallowed hard and closed his eyes, wondering if he was imagining everything that was happening to him.

"Is something wrong?" Brody asked, concerned.

Michael rubbed his eyes with the heels of both hands, scratched his beard, laughed, and said, "No. Everything is fine." He knew that trying to explain to Brody Garrity who Annabelle was may not be the best idea. Instead he held out his hand and said, "You have a deal. The farm is yours."

25

ABBIE

THE BITTER COLD OF Nebraska was unlike anything Abbie had ever experienced in Georgia. Shuffling from her car through the snow in the parking lot, Abbie opened the door to her apartment building and made her way up to the third floor. Her keys jangled in one hand as she carried a large paper bag full of groceries in the other. She stomped the snow off of her boots as she unlocked her apartment door. Once inside, she tossed her keys on the kitchen counter and set her groceries down next to it. She then removed her gloves, coat, and scarf, and slipped off her boots. She had worked a long day at the bed and breakfast with Bethany and was ready to relax.

But first, Abbie tiptoed down the hall to one of the bedrooms, opened the door, and flipped on the light. She walked over and gently placed her hand on the smooth wooden rail of a crib that stood in the far corner of the room. Abbie placed her other hand on her belly and smiled as tiny little kicks responded to her touch.

Her thoughts traveled back in time to when she saw the results of the pregnancy test that Bethany had purchased and urged her to take. When the test showed a positive result, Abbie was overjoyed, as well as scared to death. Abbie went from feeling completely hopeless and in despair to being filled with joy and anticipation. Her focus completely shifted from feeling sorry for herself and sad about the past to hopeful for the future. The fact that she was carrying Michael's child allowed her to keep a connection with the man that she loved more than anything, whom she may never see again. She was determined to give the best possible care and love to his child, so much so that Michael would be proud of her and the mother and woman that she had become.

The first few weeks of the pregnancy were rough on Abbie. Her nausea only grew worse, and on occasion left her unable to help Bethany with breakfast in the mornings. But by the noon hour, Abbie was usually able to come downstairs and help her with other tasks.

Bethany was very concerned about Abbie when she found out she was pregnant. Abbie recalled a particular conversation the two of them had concerning the baby's father.

"Are you going to contact him? To let him know?" Bethany asked Abbie a few weeks after a doctor had confirmed the pregnancy.

"The baby's father?" Abbie asked Bethany, referring, in her mind, to Michael. The two of them were outside on the back porch, sorting through vegetables they had just picked from the garden and washing them off with the hose.

"Yes," Bethany said, separating the squash from the tomatoes and cucumbers. "I'm so sorry, I don't want to bring it up because I know you want to keep that part of your life private, Sarah." She was referring to the fact that Abbie had never shared with her what had happened to her in the past. Bethany was still under the impression that Abbie had been in a battered women's shelter. Abbie had no plans to lie to Bethany or make up a story, so she simply never discussed it with her.

"It's okay," Abbie said, rinsing the dirt off of the bell pepper she had in her hand.

"Sarah? I hate to ask," Bethany hesitated, "but will you keep the baby?"

Abbie couldn't hide her astonishment. The thought never even crossed her mind that she wouldn't keep Michael's baby. Even if Michael was the monster that Bethany thought he was, Abbie couldn't imagine her life without the child growing inside of her.

"Oh, Bethany," Abbie gasped, kneeling in front of her on the concrete. "This baby is mine. I plan on doing whatever it takes to take care of him or her and to give this child the best life even though his or her daddy may not be a part of it." Abbie nearly choked when she said the last few words.

Bethany smiled and brought a hand to Abbie's cheek. She said, "This baby has the best mom anyone could ever ask for." The two of them immediately teared up. Bethany took Abbie into her arms, and they hugged.

By the time Abbie was five months pregnant, she had saved up the money that the US Marshals Service had provided, as well as what she had earned from working at the bed and breakfast, to afford her own apartment. With the car that was also given to her, she moved what little personal belongings she had across town to her own place. Bethany helped her find secondhand furniture and then hired both of her groundskeepers to haul the items up to Abbie's third-story apartment.

Abbie's first night alone in her own apartment in Nebraska was a turning point in her life. While she was staying at the bed and breakfast, she was in a state of transition, in between what she had left behind and what lay ahead of her. She was experiencing a new beginning, a state of independence, and she started to smile at the thought of raising her child right where she was. She tossed and turned that night, but for the first time in a long time, it wasn't because she was desperately missing home, but because her belly was growing, her ribs were expanding, and the child inside of her was gently kicking and stretching, slowly making itself known.

Abbie's thoughts snapped back to the present. With her hand still on her belly, she followed her baby's movements beneath her skin. She closed her eyes, inhaled deeply, and imagined Michael's arms around her, feeling the same movements she was while burying his face in her neck. She exhaled, opened her eyes, and swallowed hard as she pushed the thought from her mind. There were groceries to put away, laundry to do, dishes to wash, and bills to pay.

Morning came before Abbie was ready. It was still dark outside when her alarm went off, and she groggily reached over to silence it. She closed her eyes and searched for motivation to get out of bed. If it wasn't for her baby pressing on her bladder, she was certain she could have stayed in bed the entire day.

A half an hour later, she was showered, dressed, and ready to drive over and help Bethany with breakfast for her guests. She had only towel-dried her hair that morning, and the long strands turned to icicles as soon as she went out into the cold. As she drove across town, she adjusted the heat vents to point toward her. She tilted her head from side to side, attempting to dry her hair as well as warm up. She was still chilled as she pulled into the drive at the inn.

"Good morning, Sarah!" Bethany called out as Abbie blew in from the cold.

"Brr!" Abbie managed to say as she took her coat off and changed out of her snow boots to regular shoes.

"How's that baby?" Bethany asked as she rubbed Abbie's belly once she was in the kitchen.

"She's busy this morning," Abbie answered.

"She?" Bethany laughed. "Yesterday it was a 'he.'"

Abbie laughed. She hadn't found out the child's gender, and was waiting to find out until the baby was born. She poured herself a small cup of coffee and then began mixing ingredients for blueberry muffins while Bethany made a quiche.

The busy season was over, and they only had two overnight guests, so Abbie and Bethany decided to sit and have coffee with them during their meal.

"When are you due?" one of the guests asked Abbie while he cut into his quiche. He was an older gentleman, in his late sixties, who was there with his wife on an overnight getaway. The couple reminded Abbie of Kate and Karl Whitaker, with their bright smiles and kind faces.

"I've got about five more weeks," she replied.

"Do you have the nursery ready?" the man's wife asked with a smile.

"Yes, actually," she answered. "It's been fun, picking out everything for the nursery." Abbie was lying. The fact was, most of the baby accessories she had accumulated were all secondhand items that were given to her, mostly from people that attended church with Bethany. Nonetheless, she was grateful, and even felt a bit spoiled by the generosity of others.

Abbie noticed that the woman was eyeing her left hand, as most people did, and she hoped neither the man nor the woman would ask about the baby's father.

Knowing that Abbie was anticipating the subject, Bethany said, "Do you think we will get more snow?" She wasn't asking anyone in particular but more or less thinking out loud to take the focus off of Abbie.

Just then, they heard a car pull in the driveway. Unsure of who it could be, Bethany got up to look out the window. Abbie heard the car door shut and footsteps up the back porch. Bethany went into the kitchen to answer the door.

Abbie didn't think much of it when she heard Bethany say, "Oh my goodness, hello!" However, her ears perked up when she heard her say, "Sarah will be so happy to see you!"

She lifted her head just in time to see Jackson Wells standing in the doorway of the dining room. She hardly recognized him in the jeans and hooded sweatshirt that he was wearing. At first, she didn't know whether or not to be worried. He called with news of Meghan's death, so for him to arrive in person made her fear the worst. However, when he blushed and smiled at her, her fears subsided. She was thrilled to the see the very person who bridged the gap between her life in Omaha and her past. A smile spread across her face, and she stood up to greet him. As soon as she did, his eyes were drawn to her midsection. His smile faded and was replaced with a look of confusion. Abbie knew she needed to explain, but she was too overjoyed to see someone who knew what her real first name was. She threw her arms around Jackson, and he gladly embraced her.

"Let's go talk," she said to him as she pulled away, still smiling.

"Okay," he answered, a bit surprised that she was so happy to see him. The girl that he met several months earlier had blossomed into someone completely different. She was once broken, scared, and unstable, and, at the time, he was the last person she wanted to be near. He was not expecting such a welcome from her.

"What brings you here?" Abbie asked Jackson once they were alone. They sat on a sofa in the sitting room, facing each other. "Is everything all right? Did something happen?"

"No, no, nothing like that," Jackson said. He wanted to tell Abbie that he had come all the way to see her, to keep her safe, to help her and be there for her in any way that he could. He had rehearsed his speech on the plane and then again in the rental car on his way over to see her that morning. But he couldn't recall a single word once he laid his eyes on her. He thought she was beautiful before, but now she was simply stunning.

"What is it?" she asked, interrupting his thoughts, searching his face for answers as she tried to get comfortable on the couch.

"I'm sorry," he said. Shaking his head slightly, he leaned forward and asked, "You're ... um ..." He could barely spit the words out, so Abbie finished them for him.

"Pregnant," she confirmed. Jackson blushed once more as he nodded.

"Yeah, um, I guess I'm confused." He laughed uncomfortably and hoped Abbie would understand what a shock it was to him.

Abbie nodded, ready to explain the absurdity of her situation. "I found out a few weeks after you left."

"Oh," Jackson said, a bit shocked, realizing now that she was pregnant before she had been abducted. All at once Jackson felt a pang of guilt for taking her away from the baby's father, and how alone she must be feeling. He was unable to speak as his mind processed what she must have had to experience since he left her standing on the porch that day that past summer.

Abbie tried to fill the awkward silence by saying, "I'm excited. It was scary at first; I mean, I'm all alone, you know? But I'm as ready as I'm going to be, I guess. He or she will be here in a few weeks."

"Wow," he said. "Well, congratulations."

"Thank you."

"You look amazing." He wasn't sure how he let those words slip out, but he followed them up with, "I mean, it's nice to see you are doing so well. You seem very happy."

"I'm trying to be," she said, smiling. "There is no sense in dwelling on what my life won't be like. I hate that Michael won't ever meet his child." She put her hand on her belly when she said it and looked away from Jackson, holding back tears. "But, I can't risk anyone getting hurt. Right?" She looked to Jackson for reassurance.

"Right," he said quietly, wishing that he could give Abbie everything that she could ever want or need, including Michael. "The truth is," Jackson explained, "I came out here to see if you were getting along fine and if you needed anything."

Abbie looked confused, "Couldn't have just called?"

"Yes, well, I need to tell you something."

"I'm listening," she said nervously.

Jackson deferred from what he had originally planned to say, and instead said, "Griffin Ford and Alex McCain, the men who abducted you and Meghan, have been arrested and are awaiting trial. In the meantime,

I've been sent out here to protect you." It wasn't a complete lie, but it wasn't the entire truth either.

Abbie began to look worried.

"Nothing to worry about," he said, reassuringly. "Based on recent developments, my supervisor determined that it would be best to post a US marshal out here closer to you. To keep an eye on things for a while and continue to make sure that no one knows where you are." Once he started talking, he couldn't help the lies from spilling out. It was not his intention to make up such a story, but his plan completely changed once he saw that she was pregnant. Not that he didn't still feel exactly the same way about her, but he didn't want to put any unnecessary pressure on her to be with him. Instead, all he could do was let her know he was there for her, however she needed him to be.

"So what does that mean?" Abbie asked. "Are you my personal bodyguard?" she joked.

He laughed. "If you need me to be." He was half joking, half serious.

They sat talking for a few more minutes. Then Abbie said, "I should really get back to work."

"I don't want to keep you," he told her.

"Thank you for coming by."

They both rose from the couch, and Abbie led the way back through the dining room and into the kitchen, where Bethany was washing the breakfast dishes.

"I'm so glad you stopped by, Jackson," Bethany said, wiping her hands off on a towel.

"It was good to see you again, Bethany," he said, shaking her hand.

"Are you in town for a while?" she asked.

"Um, indefinitely, actually," he admitted, while avoiding Abbie's eyes as he blushed.

Bethany smiled as she watched him grow a bit nervous. She touched his arm and said, "Well, we hope you come by more often then." She looked to Abbie, hoping she would encourage Jackson to come back.

"Thank you," Abbie said to him, knowing that he knew those words had more meaning than Bethany knew.

"It was good to see you, Sarah," he said politely as he headed toward the door.

"You too," she said with a smile.

With a hand on the doorknob, halfway out the door, he turned around and asked, "Sarah? Are you busy tonight?"

She couldn't hide the shock on her face. Abbie wasn't expecting Jackson to ask her that, and it left her speechless.

"She's not busy!" Bethany piped up.

Abbie shot her a wide-eyed look.

"I'd like to take you to dinner," Jackson told her, "If you aren't busy."

"Um," Abbie stammered, "don't you need my help for dinner tonight, Bethany?"

"I can handle it. And you shouldn't pass up a chance with this handsome gentleman to treat you to dinner." Bethany winked and Abbie blushed.

"Pick you up at six?" he asked, looking at Abbie.

Abbie was having trouble speaking as she looked at Jackson. She wondered why he wanted to take her out to dinner. So many questions raced through her mind as she stared at him, unable to speak.

"She will be ready," Bethany answered for her.

"See you then," Jackson said to Abbie as he walked out the door.

"What's wrong with you?" Bethany asked Abbie, snapping at a towel in her direction.

"What?" Abbie asked innocently.

"A gorgeous man asks you to dinner, and you can't say yes?"

"It caught me off guard. I was not under the impression that he was interested."

"Are you insane? When he brought you here this past summer I thought for sure something was going on between you two."

"You did? Why?"

"That man had love in his eyes for you. He still does."

Abbie gave Bethany a puzzled look. She recalled the days she had spent with Jackson, and she had to admit, she was too consumed with grief, sorrow, and self-pity to remember many details about him. She knew he was kind, and took care of her while her world was crashing down around her, but beyond that, the memories of him were foggy.

"I'm not romantically interested in him, Bethany." She wanted more than anything to tell Bethany that her heart belonged to Michael, now and forever, but, of course, she couldn't.

"You know, it wouldn't be such a bad thing if you did, Sarah. Raising that baby is going to be hard work. Someone like Jackson could take care of both of you."

"Whoa, Bethany, he just mentioned dinner. I don't think I am in any position to be expecting someone to take care of me and my baby." Nor did she want to. She had been mentally preparing herself throughout her pregnancy to face the future with her child alone.

"I was a single mother, Sarah. Yes, I know, I always give you this speech, and I give you all of the encouragement I can, but to be perfectly honest, it's hard. If a man as good looking as Jackson wanted to swoop in and take care of me, I'd be damned if I had said no," Bethany said and laughed aloud.

Abbie couldn't help but laugh right along with her. Bethany inspired Abbie. She was one of the hardest-working women that she had ever met. As the two of them continued talking and cleaning up the kitchen, Abbie wondered if her mother would have gotten along with Bethany. She decided that if Annabelle was alive, she and Bethany would have been great friends.

Unlike Abbie's first date with Michael, she didn't put much effort into getting herself ready for her date with Jackson. She pulled on a pair of leggings, a long form-fitting sweater, and a pair of tall boots. She didn't bother with makeup, and she tied her hair back in a loose bun. She wasn't nervous, nor did she have first date butterflies like she had with Michael. If anything, she was hungry. It was just after six o'clock, and Jackson hadn't arrived yet. Abbie's stomach was growling, and she was growing impatient. He had called earlier to get directions to her apartment, and she wondered if he had gotten lost.

The buzzer to her apartment door made her jump, and she knew that Jackson had arrived. Instead of buzzing him in, she grabbed her coat and keys and met him on the first floor.

"Oh, hi," Jackson said as she came downstairs. "I could have walked you down," he offered.

"It's all right," she said; "no need for you to make that hike up there."

He held the door open for her as they stepped outside into the cold. Jackson had left the car running so that it would be warm for her.

"How are you feeling?" Jackson asked Abbie as they pulled out of the parking lot of her apartment building.

"I'm hungry," she joked.

"Me too," he said with a laugh. "You are a bit more familiar with the area than I am. Do you have any recommendations?"

"There is a good steak place not too far from here."

"Let's go there, then."

Dinner with Jackson was a lot less awkward than Abbie had anticipated. Bethany had gotten her worked up over nothing. Jackson simply wanted to catch up with her and make sure she was doing well. They chatted like old friends as she told him about life in Omaha as well as her anticipation for the baby's arrival.

"Jackson?" she asked as they drove back to her apartment later that evening.

"Yes?" he answered, turning his head toward her while also keeping his focus on the road.

"Am I safe?"

"Yes," he said confidently.

Abbie was silent for a few minutes. Then she said, "Can I ask you something else?"

"Anything."

"Did they stop looking for me?"

Jackson wasn't quite sure how to answer. If he said no, and told her about the lengths that Michael had gone to in order to find her, it may give her false hope and leave her feeling as though there were a chance they would be reunited. However, if he said yes, it would crush her, but it might also allow her to leave the past behind and not put herself or anyone else at risk by potentially reaching out to those that were desperate to find her.

Instead of answering yes or no, he simply stated, "You are loved."

Abbie knew she couldn't ask further questions. She rested a hand on top of her belly and stared out the window. Memories slowly began to return from when she and Jackson first met. It was all a bit of a blur, but she recalled how he stayed with her that night in the hotel room, propped up in a chair, completely uncomfortable, but more than willing to be there for her. She also remembered how he picked her up off of the floor, more than once, in her moments of complete despair. Abbie wasn't sure why she hadn't given those moments a second thought up until that point.

She looked over at Jackson and questioned if maybe Bethany had been right about him wanting more than just her friendship. Her thoughts were interrupted as they pulled into a parking spot next to her apartment building.

"Well, thanks so much for dinner," Abbie said, unbuckling her seat belt. "It was nice to see you again."

"Abbie?"

She paused. It was the first time in months that anyone had called her that. It stung more than she thought it would.

"You should practice calling me Sarah," she said flatly.

"You're right," he said, understanding that the pain in her heart was still very much alive. They were silent for a while, both of them unsure of what to say. Abbie wanted to scream at Jackson about how unfair it was that she wasn't able to raise her baby with Michael, but it wasn't his fault. Jackson wanted to apologize for all of the suffering she had endured and for her wounds that may never heal, but he knew his words could never fix it.

When the silence became unbearable, Abbie said, "I'm sorry. I interrupted you. It sounded like you were about to ask me something."

"I was going to ask you if I could walk you up to your apartment."

"You don't have to."

"Please. Let me be a gentleman."

"Fair enough." She obliged while she got out of the car, and Jackson led her to the door of her apartment building. She pulled out her keys and unlocked the main door.

"So which one is yours?" he asked as they stepped inside.

"My apartment?"

"Yes."

"All the way to the top," she said, pointing up the stairs.

Jackson stopped in his tracks. "Wait, are you serious?"

"Yes." She was a few steps ahead of him in the climb, and she held onto the railing, leaned backward slightly, and balanced herself to keep from toppling over by the weight of her belly as she continued up the stairs.

Jackson caught up to her and steadied a hand on her back. "Well this isn't acceptable."

"What isn't acceptable?" she asked, and laughed as they walked next to each other.

"Someone in your condition should not be walking up and down all of these stairs every day."

"Well, I've been doing it this long…" she said, her voice trailing off.

"What happens when you have a baby in a car seat, and several bags of groceries?"

"I guess I'll make it work," she answered, although she hadn't really thought about what she would do in a situation like that.

"I'm going to call your landlord tomorrow. See if we can't get you into an apartment on the first floor."

She let out a heavy sigh. "I appreciate the gesture," she said wearily, "but I'm due in a little over a month. I have no desire to pack up all of my stuff, the baby's stuff, and move it all."

"I would help you," Jackson offered.

"Jackson, I don't think you understand. I work all day. Usually twelve to fourteen hours a day. All I want to do when I get home is sleep." When they reached the top of the stairs, Abbie was out of breath, and she leaned against the wall next to her apartment door.

"Well, I can help you, Ab—Sarah. That's what I'm trying to tell you."

"Why?" she asked as she shifted from one foot to the other.

"What do you mean?"

"Why do you want to help me?" Her voice grew louder and a bit harsh as she continued to ask questions. "Why did you stay with me that night at the hotel? Why did you take me to dinner tonight? Why are you in Omaha?"

"Keep your voice down," he whispered as he stepped closer to her. Abbie looked away.

Jackson lifted a hand to her cheek and gently turned her face toward his. His eyes were soft and kind. "You know why," he whispered.

Tears sprang to Abbie's eyes as she looked into his.

"From the second I saw you, I knew that there was something about you that I wouldn't be able to forget. Not that you were broken, or desperate. I could tell over the course of those few days that you were the strongest woman I would ever meet in my life." He lifted his other hand and held her face in both of them. "You deserve the world. You deserve to be taken care of and not have to worry if you and your child are safe."

Tears spilled down her cheeks, and she looked down at her feet. "I can't," she whispered, and brought her hands to his. She carefully lowered his hands from her face, and as she did, he pressed his lips to her forehead. He held her there, for a small, perfect moment, and then she took a step back and turned toward her apartment door. Neither said a word as she wiped her tears with the back of one hand and unlocked her door.

Jackson reached for her hand, and her fingers slipped away from his as she stepped inside her apartment. She turned back around and faced him while she stood in the doorway.

"Don't waste your love on me," she said quietly. Then she closed her door, leaving Jackson on the other side, wondering what he could do to change her mind.

26

HENRY

BOXES OF ABBIE'S BELONGINGS sat unopened in Henry's living room for two weeks before he was able to open them. Kate and Karl Whitaker had made the drive from North Carolina to Georgia in March, more than eight months since Abbie's disappearance. The couple that owned the diner where Abbie worked, as well as the home she rented from them, felt as though it was time to pack away her things and return them to her father.

Karl and Kate arrived on a Saturday morning. The fog rolled down Henry's driveway and wrapped itself around tree trunks in the front yard. As the Whitakers' truck pulled slowly up the drive, the murkiness parted and drifted away. The two apologized for the circumstance of their visit. Henry helped Karl bring in the half a dozen boxes they brought with them. All three then sat around the kitchen table, with somber faces, drinking coffee.

"Michael speaks of you often," Kate told Henry as she placed a hand on top of his.

"Such a wonderful young man," Henry commented.

"Rumor has it he sold his farm," Karl added to the conversation, "to hire someone to help find Abbie."

Henry smiled. "Yes, the rumor is true. He called me last week to tell me. In some ways, I wish he wouldn't have done that. In other ways, I hope it allows us to at least uncover some answers about what happened to her. There isn't a single trace of her. Nothing."

175

Kate's eyes filled with tears, and she brought her hands together in her lap.

"I know," Karl agreed.

The kitchen grew quiet, and Henry stood up to pour his guests more coffee. The three of them spent half the day together, talking about Abbie, sharing stories of her carefree spirit, her charm, and her kind, selfless heart. Henry thanked Kate and Karl several times for making the drive to deliver his daughter's belongings. They told him how honored they were to do it.

The couple left Henry's house before midday. The pain of the reason for the visit was greater than either of them had anticipated. Although the two of them hadn't been there before, the absence of Abbie in her home in Georgia could be felt just as much as they felt it back in North Carolina.

Henry stared at the boxes, day after day, unable to look inside. Now, as he knelt down and carefully cut the tape off of the first box and opened it, his heart got stuck in his throat, and his eyes welled with tears. The first box contained pictures, some framed, some not. A few in particular caught his eye. There was one of Abbie and him on her high school graduation day. Looking back at that day, he thought at the time she looked so very grown up. But now, looking at her in her cap and gown, she was still just a child who had yet to discover the world. He sifted through loose photographs, and one of Annabelle brushed his fingers. He picked up the slightly tattered, delicate photo and took a closer look. His wife looked so much like Abbie. The picture was taken during their first year of marriage. She was sitting on a swing with her head tipped back and one foot in the air. She was smiling as her hair hung down her back and the sun hit her face. Henry had never seen a more beautiful photo. He set it aside and made a note to frame and hang it.

Settling himself onto the floor, Henry opened the second box. Tears flowed down his face as he lifted out articles of clothing. He could almost envision his daughter in the empty shells of where she should be.

His chest felt tight and heavy as he cried over the contents of the boxes. He scooped up several items in his arms and held them close to him, desperate to have Abbie back in her childhood home with him. In the midst of his despair, Henry felt a hand on his shoulder. It was soft, gentle, and all too familiar. He looked up to see Annabelle, as beautiful and young as the day he met her, sitting across from him, lifting his eyes to meet hers.

"Hey there," she said sweetly.

"Annabelle?" Henry asked, a bit shocked, wiping the tears from his face.

"Of course it's me, silly," she said, smiling at him with wide eyes.

"I've missed you so much," Henry said as he started to sob all over again.

"I know," she said apologetically. "I've been away. I've been taking care of Abbie."

Henry sat up straight. "Abbie?" He flew to his feet. "Is she alive? Or is she, um, with you?" Henry winced in pain and grabbed his arm as he prepared to hear the worst from her.

Annabelle stood and joined her husband. "No, darling, she's alive," she said, her eyes sparkling.

"She's ... alive?" he asked.

"Yes. Very much so." Annabelle placed her hands in Henry's and distracted him from the pain he felt in his chest and arms.

"Is she okay?"

"She is. She's having a baby."

"A baby?"

"Yes. A boy. You should see her. She's beautiful. Glowing. Strong."

"What happened to her? Why can't she come home?"

"Shh, don't worry, love. She's safe. She can't come home. She is protecting everyone by staying exactly where she is."

"Do you talk to her? Like this?"

"No." Annabelle smiled at him. "It hurt too much for her to see me when she first went away. I'm with her a lot, but she doesn't know I'm there."

Henry nodded. He couldn't help but focus on the pain he was experiencing and walked over to the couch to sit down. Annabelle joined him. It was getting harder for him to breathe, and he began to perspire.

"What's happening to me?" he asked her.

"Shh, just breathe. Lie down on the couch with me," she directed him. Henry obliged.

The two of them curled up on the couch together, in the middle of the afternoon, wrapped tightly in each other's arms. Annabelle calmed Henry by stroking his hair and kissing his forehead.

It suddenly dawned on Henry what was happening to him. He knew why she had come. Before he had a chance to start panicking, Annabelle began to speak.

"You are the love of my life, Henry Peterson," she whispered.

Henry wanted so badly to speak, to tell her he felt the same way. That he always had and that he would even after he died, just as she had. All he could do was pull her closer.

"The day you married me, I didn't think it was possible to love you more. You proved me wrong the day our daughter was born, and I saw you hold her in your arms for the first time," Annabelle continued.

He smiled, recalling that day.

"And then the day you took me home from the hospital for the last time," she continued. "Your heart was breaking, and yet you loved me enough to allow my final days to be at home with you and Abbie. I'm proud of the man you were then and now. You are exactly the man I wanted to raise our family with."

Annabelle was distracting Henry from the pain he was feeling. He knew she was trying to make the process of dying somewhat bearable. She was carrying him through death, just as he had carried her. Henry's thoughts were racing as he tried to focus only on Annabelle.

Annabelle continued to soothe him. "I know you're worried about her. I know you are scared. But I need you now, Henry. I need you."

Henry stared directly into Annabelle's eyes as they breathed their last "I love you" and drifted away together.

27

MICHAEL

HENRY'S FUNERAL WAS AN intimate memorial service in a small cemetery near his home. Although they hadn't kept in touch as often as Michael knew he should have, he made the drive to Georgia as soon as he heard the news of Henry's death. Kate and Karl, also saddened by the news, followed after Michael and attended the service as well. They stood with a dozen or so other friends, family members, and coworkers, in the chilly, late winter air, as they said their farewells to Henry. He was laid to rest next to Annabelle, at the top of a hill facing west. Tears stung Michael's cheeks as he and the attendees placed white roses on Henry's casket.

It was mentioned at the service that Henry had died of a broken heart. He was found by a neighbor on the evening that he passed, surrounded by his daughter's belongings and photographs of her and of his wife. Michael whispered a silent prayer for Henry that he may rest in peace. He also quietly vowed, as he had so many times in the past, to find Abbie.

A few weeks prior to the funeral, just after the sale of his property to Brody Garrity, Michael met with Patrick Solomon, a private investigator. After Michael explained the details of Abbie's disappearance, Patrick agreed to work for him. And, with the amount of money Michael was willing to pay him, Patrick agreed to work solely for Michael, around the clock, until he found Abbie. Patrick had twenty years of experience and a 99 percent success rate.

Initially, Patrick was able to set Michael's mind at ease. But in the weeks that followed, any leads that Patrick had come across led to a dead end.

"This is normal," Patrick Solomon reassured Michael. The two of them were having a conversation over the phone the evening that Michael got back from Georgia. Michael was exhausted, emotionally and physically, from the trip, and would have given just about anything to hear good news from the man he hired to find Abbie. He paced the floor of the carriage house as he fired questions at Patrick.

"Do you have any reason to believe she is alive?" Michael asked.

"I don't have any reason to think she's not," Patrick said.

"Tell me honestly. Is it easier to find someone who is alive or someone who is not?"

"The people that are the toughest to find are those that don't want to be found."

Michael was silent. He knew in his heart that Abbie did not disappear on purpose and that she would want him to be looking for her and to not stop until she was found.

"Here is what I do know, Michael. The fact that Abbie's body was not found with Meghan's, is a very good sign. Whoever killed Meghan didn't go to great lengths to hide her body, so I doubt it would have been any different had they killed Abbie."

"I guess that makes sense," Michael accepted.

"In the years that I have been doing this, all situations are different. Some people are easier to find than others. I have a long list of people and organizations I plan on contacting to try to track her down, including the US Marshals Service."

"The US Marshals Service?"

"Yes, they operate the Witness Protection Program. They may not give me any information if Abbie is, in fact, a protected witness, but it can't hurt to try."

"Okay," Michael said while letting out a heavy sigh.

"I'll be in touch," Patrick said, and then the two of them hung up.

Michael took Sam and Bull outside so the three of them could get some fresh air. He stood on the porch, overlooking the property. Brody Garrity had done an excellent job of maintaining the farm to Michael's standards. However, Michael wasn't sure he would ever come to grips with the fact that it was no longer his farm. It was late in the short winter season, but there was still a chill in the air. Michael put his hands in his pockets and tried to brush off the cold that bit at him through his long sleeve shirt. The dogs ran about and played, never minding the cold. Michael could see his breath in front of his face as he gazed up at the farmhouse. He pictured Abbie sitting on the balcony outside of the master bedroom, just as she had on the last day they spent together. Recalling her beauty as she sat reclined in his T-shirt sent a chill down his spine. Her spirit was still alive and well in his heart as well as in his home. A home that was, technically, no longer his.

Michael felt as though he let his entire family down, with the exception of his father, when he sold the farm. Generations of family history were lost in the name of a woman Michael had only known for a few short weeks, but had loved with all his heart.

Now that Michael had hired someone to look for Abbie on a full-time basis, and with little work to do at the farm, he needed to occupy his thoughts and time with something else. He whistled to Sam and Bull to head back toward the house. He began formulating a plan as he walked to his truck. He opened the driver's side door and allowed the dogs to jump in. Michael got in after them, and they headed down the driveway and then down the road. His truck ended up at Stephen's house. The two of them had barely been on speaking terms since that day at Paul's house, months back, when he had suggested to Michael that Abbie may have left voluntarily. Michael knew he needed to repair their friendship and mend any hard feelings that he had caused Stephen to have toward him. Sam and Bull waited in the truck as Michael knocked on Stephen's front door.

"Hey," Stephen said, a bit shocked to see Michael standing on his porch. They had seen each other only in mutual company since that day at Paul's house.

"Hey," Michael said humbly.

"You're back in town," Stephen said, referring to Michael's trip to Georgia for Abbie's father's funeral.

"Yeah. I just got in a little while ago."

"Come on in," Stephen said, holding the door open for Michael.

"I won't keep you long," Michael said as he stepped through the door and into the living room.

"You're fine," Stephen reassured him. "Paul is here too."

As soon as Stephen said it, Paul entered the living room from the kitchen. "Hey, Michael," Paul said, happy to see him.

"Hey. Wow, you look great, Paul." Michael was referring to the fact that Paul was walking, unassisted, on the leg that he had seriously injured the summer before.

"Thanks," Paul said. "The leg is pretty much back to normal."

"Have a seat, Michael," Stephen said. "Can I get you a beer?"

"Sure," he said, a bit surprised at the hospitality he was being shown after the way he had distanced his friends over the past few months.

"So, what's up?" Stephen asked Michael once the three of them were seated in the living room.

Michael leaned forward, put his elbows on his knees, and took a sip of his beer. He then looked at his friends and said, "I just want to apologize about the way I've been acting over the last few months."

"No need to apologize," Stephen said as he took a drink of his beer. "You've been going through some heavy things."

"Yeah, don't worry about it," Paul added. "We just hope you're okay."

Michael didn't know what to say. He stared at the floor. "The truth is," he said when he did finally speak, "that I don't know if I'm going to be okay from one minute to the next."

Paul and Stephen nodded in unison.

Michael looked up at both of them and said, "If you would have asked me last summer where I saw myself right now, I wouldn't have said I'd be here."

The room was quiet. Stephen and Paul didn't know what to say.

Michael continued. "I replay that last day with Abbie over and over in my head every day. And then the night she went out with Meghan ..." his voice trailed off. "I torture myself with what I could have done differently to have saved both of them."

"There's no way you could have known what would happen," Stephen said.

Michael nodded. "I know, but it doesn't mean I don't think about it all the time."

"I'll bet," Paul added.

"We're here for whatever you need, Michael. You know that, right?" Stephen said.

"That's sort of why I'm here," Michael explained. "I want to apologize to your guys for the way I treated you the last time we were together. And then for not being available after that. I've shut everyone out, and I really regret it."

"No hard feelings, Michael," Paul said.

"Yeah, we're here for you," Stephen said.

Michael had been friends with Stephen and Paul for nearly half his life, and he was always humbled by their forgiving nature and willingness to be there for him whenever he needed them.

"I was also wondering if you guys were interested in getting the business up and running again. I know I kind of dumped everything on you, Stephen, when Paul couldn't work, and then I took off," Michael continued.

"I think that sounds like a great idea," Stephen said.

"Paul?" Michael asked, "Are you ready to get back to work?"

"Most definitely," he answered.

"Great," Michael said. "Tomorrow I will call all of our old clients and drum up as much business as we can get back just in time for the season to begin."

"Sounds good," both of his friends said.

"Thank you guys so much."

"Hey," Paul said. "We heard you sold the farm. Is that true?"

"Unfortunately," Michael answered. "I ended up hiring a private investigator to find Abbie. On top of that, the business was in the toilet, and I had blown through all of my resources."

"Wow. A private investigator?" Paul asked.

"Yeah," Michael said. "He seems to think Abbie is alive."

"That's awesome," Stephen said.

"I need to stay busy during the investigation, and I miss my friends."

"Well, let's do it," Paul said enthusiastically.

The three of them finished their beers and talked for a short while before Michael decided to head back home. He hugged Stephen and Paul and thanked them both for accepting his apology and for being there for him. He felt truly blessed to have them as friends.

Sam and Bull were waiting patiently in the truck when Michael returned. He climbed in next to them, and they covered him in kisses.

Michael laughed as he gently pushed them off of him so he could see to put the truck in gear. As Michael drove back to the farm, he felt the weight of his burdens become lighter. A sliver of light began to shine through his world that had grown dark and empty.

28

JACKSON

A WEEK WENT BY before Jackson saw Abbie again. He was sleeping in his hotel room when he received a call on his cell phone at five o'clock in the morning. Half asleep, he nearly shot out of bed as soon as he saw that Abbie was calling him.

"Hello?" he said, trying not to sound groggy.

"Jackson? It's Abbie. I hate to bother you, but my car battery is dead. It's way too early to start banging on my neighbors' doors for help. Bethany really needs my help this morning, so I can't be late. Can you help me?"

"I'll be right there," Jackson reassured her. He threw on jeans, a hooded sweatshirt, and his shoes, and ran out the door. He arrived at her apartment, minutes later, jumper cables in hand.

Abbie was waiting just inside the main entrance of her apartment in order to stay warm while she waited for Jackson. As soon as she saw him pull into the parking lot, she stepped outside to meet him.

"Jackson, I can't thank you enough for coming. I'm so sorry to call you so early, but I didn't know who else to call," Abbie said apologetically.

"Don't apologize," Jackson said as he held out his hand for her keys. "I'm happy to do it," he said matter-of-factly. He didn't wait for a response. Instead, he got right to work on getting her car started. The last words she had said to him a week prior still stung, but he respected the fact that she had more on her plate than anyone should have to handle. Jackson had Abbie's car running a few minutes later.

"Thank you so much, Jackson," Abbie said gratefully. She stood in front of him, a bit awkwardly, not sure of what else to say. She knew she had hurt Jackson when she rejected him, and yet, he had still come to her rescue. He was there for her now just as he had been so many months ago.

Jackson could read her thoughts and knew what she was feeling. The last thing he wanted was for her to feel any amount of guilt for what she had said or what she was going through.

"You had better get going," Jackson said quickly, with a laugh, attempting to dispel any awkwardness between them. He wound up the jumper cables and headed toward his car.

"Thank you again," she said as she got into her car.

As she drove away, Jackson got back into his car and sat with the engine running while he warmed his hands. An idea began to form in his mind on a way that he could make life easier for Abbie. It was still early, possibly too early to begin making phone calls, but if Jackson wanted to see the plan through, he needed to take swift action.

By noon that same day, Jackson's plan was falling into place. He worried that the task at hand would not be complete by the time Abbie returned home, so he gave Bethany a call and told her to keep Abbie just a bit later that evening. Bethany agreed. Jackson could tell that Bethany held out hope that he and Abbie might have a chance at a relationship. Jackson also held out that same hope but knew that may never be a possibility.

Jackson was waiting outside her apartment building when Abbie returned home that evening. He rose to his feet as she got out of her car. Her coat hung open, as her midsection prevented her from buttoning it. Her eyes looked tired, and her ponytail was a bit disheveled.

"Jackson? What are you doing here?" she asked curiously as she met him at the stoop.

Jackson wondered if he would ever not be nervous around Abbie. Even when she wasn't trying to be, she was absolutely breathtaking. He suddenly second-guessed everything he spent the entire day doing.

"I did something for you today," Jackson began, "and before you find out what it is, you have to promise not to get mad."

"What do you mean? You didn't have to do anything for me," she said.

"Well, it was something that had to be done," he explained. "Come inside." Jackson held the door of the apartment building open for her, and she stepped inside. Jackson held out a set of keys for Abbie to take.

"What are these?" she asked him.

"Keys to your new apartment," he stated.

"New apartment?" she asked, confused, narrowing her eyes a bit.

"This is where you need to promise not to get mad."

"I promise," she agreed hesitantly.

"I called your landlord this morning and asked if a first-floor apartment was available. There happened to be one. I also know that you said you didn't have time to move, nor did you have the energy if you had the time. So I called a few moving companies and hired as many people as I could to move everything while you were at work today."

A look of shock spread over Abbie's face, and she wasn't sure if she heard Jackson correctly. She was having difficulty forming words, both to protest and to question.

"So that's where I want to apologize, Sarah. I knew if I would have asked you, you would have declined my offer. I also want to apologize for invading your personal space. But I think we both know that you and your baby will be much more comfortable on the first floor."

Abbie was speechless. Jackson lightly placed a hand on her elbow and encouraged her to step forward and follow him to her new apartment. Abbie walked slowly as Jackson led her down the hall, where he unlocked and opened the door to her new apartment.

"We did our best to make sure everything is in the exact same place as it was in your apartment upstairs," Jackson told her as they stepped inside.

Abbie gasped, and she lifted a hand to her mouth as she turned on a light just inside the door. "Jackson," she whispered. They both were silent as her eyes scanned the room. She kicked her boots off, but left her coat on as she walked into the kitchen and then down the hall and peered into the bedrooms.

Jackson stayed by the front door, waiting for her to approve or disapprove.

"It's unbelievable," Abbie said, still in shock, as she walked back down the hallway toward him. Abbie slipped off her coat and laid it over the arm of the couch. Just as Jackson said, it was as if her apartment on the third floor simply up and moved itself down to the first floor.

She peeked inside cupboards and closets and ran her hands over pieces of furniture, not quite believing that what he had accomplished was possible.

Jackson's heart raced as he watched Abbie move from one side of the apartment to the other, patiently waiting for her to react to what he had done. His eyes met hers from across the room. He gave her a half smile, and her shoulders began to relax. Tears filled her eyes, and she walked toward him. Jackson's racing heart nearly beat out of his chest when she slipped her arms through his, pressed her head into his chest and began to cry. He didn't say a word. He simply held her and let her cry.

When she was ready, Abbie lifted her head, looked into his eyes, and said, "This is by far the nicest thing anyone has ever done for me." Her arms stayed threaded under his, and he lifted a hand to her face as he wiped away her tears.

"I'm just trying to make your life easier, Sarah," Jackson said. He hated calling her that. To him, she was Abbie, a beautiful, charming southern girl with the biggest heart of anyone he had ever met. "If there is anything else I can do, please let me know."

Abbie hugged him tightly one more time and said, "I can't thank you enough. This is incredible. I really appreciate it."

Jackson didn't let his arms fall to his sides until Abbie moved hers away first. "You're welcome," he said, and he turned and walked out the door. He had almost walked out the main door to the apartment building when he heard Abbie open up her apartment door.

"Jackson," she called out to him.

He stopped dead in his tracks and turned toward her.

"Bethany gave me the day off tomorrow. Do you want to meet for coffee?"

"I would love that," Jackson said as a smile spread across his face.

"Great. I'll call you tomorrow." Abbie ducked back into her apartment.

Jackson couldn't believe what had happened just then, but he replayed the events of the evening over and over in his mind. Jackson knew Abbie may never fall in love with him, but he was perfectly content to simply be in love with her.

29

ABBIE

ABBIE SHIFTED UNCOMFORTABLY IN the high-top chair where she sat waiting for Jackson at Aroma's Coffeehouse. With her due date quickly approaching, it was becoming difficult to sit, stand, or even lie down comfortably. Her belly barely fit under the table before her, and she debated moving to a booth. However, the energy required at that point to relocate from her peaceful spot near the front window to a booth seemed more trouble than it was worth. Abbie was too busy adjusting her body in the chair to notice Jackson had walked in. She was just about to lift her frothy beverage from the table to take a sip when she saw him standing there. Startled, she nearly dropped her mug.

"Don't get up," Jackson said to her as soon as Abbie attempted to get out of her chair to greet him. She sighed and smiled as he bent down and gave her a polite peck on the cheek.

"Thanks for meeting me," Abbie said.

"Absolutely," Jackson responded. A waitress came by and took his coffee order.

The two of them sat in an awkward, uncomfortable silence at first. Abbie looked out the window. Winter had nearly passed, but a mix of slush and mud still plastered the road before them.

"What are you thinking about, Sarah?" Jackson asked her. The waitress came back with his coffee. He thanked her and then held the mug in both hands as he rested it on the table.

Abbie closed her eyes, breathed in, and said, "Summertime."

"Summertime?" he asked.

"Yeah," she said with a giggle. What she was really thinking about was Michael and her few weeks that past summer with him. She couldn't help but feel a bit of guilt for asking Jackson to get coffee. She certainly didn't want him to know the depths of her thoughts, so she remained evasive.

Jackson smiled back at her, knowing full well that was not what was on her mind.

"Why did you want to get coffee?" he asked her.

"I wanted to get to know you better," she started to explain. She looked around and then chose her next words carefully. "Remember back when we spent those few days together?"

"Of course."

"You were there for me in so many ways. I didn't make any effort to get to know you. I really regret that. You were so selfless and caring and didn't expect anything in return."

"I still don't." He took a drink of his coffee.

"I know." Then she lowered her voice and said, "I don't have anyone in my life that I trust completely. Bethany is my friend, but she doesn't know the truth about me. You are the only person that knows me. Truly knows me."

Jackson cautioned her with his eyes to not say much more about the topic.

Abbie nodded and steered the conversation away from talking about her past. "I want to know more about you—where you grew up, what your family is like, things like that."

"There's not much to tell," he said with a laugh. "My dad was in the army. We moved around my entire childhood. I was extremely spoiled. Too much for my own good. It caught up with me. I was humbled. I grew up, started my career, met you a few years later, and the rest is history."

Abbie laughed. "Well, that sounds wildly vague and mildly intriguing."

Jackson winked at her. He wasn't quite ready to give her all of the details of his past. He wasn't sure how she would react if he told her about Travis, and how he lost his best friend. Jackson was happy that Abbie was making an effort to get to know him, and he didn't want to do or say anything that would make her change her mind.

Seconds later, a man walked into the coffee house carrying a newspaper. He was in his forties, clean-shaven, and wore business casual clothes and loafers, much like what Jackson was wearing. Abbie wasn't sure what it was about him that caught her attention, but she couldn't keep from staring at him.

Jackson watched Abbie as her eyes followed the man across the coffeehouse until he sat down in a booth, far enough away from the two of them, but close enough that they could make out the headlines of the newspaper the man held up and began to read.

Abbie focused her attention back on Jackson and said coyly, "So you used to be spoiled, and now you're not."

"You could say that," he answered. Now Jackson couldn't help but notice that the man with the newspaper kept glancing over at him and Abbie.

Abbie asked Jackson a few more questions regarding his statement, but he didn't appear to be paying attention. He had a nervous look on his face that made her uneasy.

"Hey," she whispered in order to get him to make eye contact with her.

"Sarah," he said as he grabbed her hand from across the table. His eyes locked on hers as he said, "have I ever told you how beautiful you look? I can't wait for the baby to arrive."

Abbie was completely caught off guard and instinctively attempted to pull her hand away. But Jackson grabbed it, and held it tight. Tight enough to cause her to look at him and notice that his eyes were telling her that she needed to play along.

Jackson continued. "Let's go home so you can relax."

Abbie swallowed hard, put on a fake smile, and said, "That sounds lovely." She wasn't sure why she and Jackson needed to put on a façade at that moment, but she trusted him. He kept a firm grip on her hand and motioned for their waitress to bring the check for their coffees.

Jackson looked at her, this time putting both of his hands around hers, spoke a bit slowly so she would focus on his words and said, "It's very important for you to *not worry* and *trust me* that I'm going to make the next few weeks of your pregnancy as pleasant as I can."

"Thank you," she responded.

"I need to do a few things when we get home. Spring is coming, so I'd like to clean out the gutters." He tugged on her hand a bit so she would focus on what he said next. "Also, a family of sparrows built a nest in one of the rain gutters. They are becoming a real nuisance, and they need to *leave*."

Abbie's face went ghost white. It was the reference to the sparrows that made her realize that they weren't safe. She was shocked that Jackson had remembered what she had said about the sparrows when the two of them first arrived at their hotel after leaving the police station in Richmond.

"Well, then we had better get back to the house," she said, playing along.

Jackson quickly pulled a few bills from his wallet and left them on the table, and then helped Abbie down from her chair. As he was helping her put on her coat, the man with the newspaper approached them.

"Good morning, folks!" the man said to them politely.

"Good morning," Abbie and Jackson said in unison. Jackson took Abbie's hand in his and gave it another squeeze, indicating that the man standing in front of them was the one they needed to get away from.

"I hate to bother you folks, but I just got into town, and I was curious if you knew of any place to stay for the night?"

Abbie looked at Jackson as he said, "Not exactly sure, sir, but I'm sure one of the servers here can help you." Jackson stepped passed the man as he held Abbie close beside him.

"I see you're expecting," the man continued, regardless of the fact that Abbie and Jackson were attempting to leave the coffeehouse.

Abbie nodded politely and said, "Yes, thank you." They moved one step closer to the door, but again the man interrupted them.

"Boy or girl?" he asked, with a grin.

Had Jackson not been with her, Abbie would have not thought twice about having a conversation with the man. He seemed happy, friendly, and not at all a danger to either one of them. However, Jackson kept the two of them at a safe distance from him as they continued toward the door.

"Girl," Jackson lied. His response was friendly but hurried. "Thank you." Jackson held up a hand to signal politely to the stranger that they were leaving.

"Oh, that's wonderful," the man said as he clasped his hands together. He held the door open for Jackson and Abbie. Once they made it outside and began walking briskly down the sidewalk the man called out, "I'll bet she will be beautiful, Abbie."

Abbie gasped, and the two of them stopped in their tracks. Jackson whipped around and immediately put a hand on the gun he had holstered under his jacket.

"Abbie," the man said again as he walked toward them.

"My name is Sarah," Abbie said with a shaky voice. "Sarah Walker."

"Don't be afraid, Abbie," the man said, also putting a hand to his hip for the same reason Jackson had.

"Do not move!" Jackson yelled as he pulled out his gun and pointed it at the man.

"I know everything!" the man shouted back. "I'm here to take her back."

It was then that both Abbie and Jackson assumed that the man standing in front of them was sent by Alex McCain and Griffin Ford. Abbie screamed, and Jackson pushed Abbie away from him as the man drew his gun.

Jackson fired a single shot. The man fired back twice as he fell to the ground after Jackson's bullet hit him in the chest. Jackson also fell, after being hit in the arm and the belly.

Panic erupted in the streets. At first, Abbie thought the sound of the shots had impaired her hearing. But then she realized she was screaming so loud, she was unable to hear anything else. She ran over to Jackson and slid to the ground beside him. He was conscious, but pale and in extreme pain.

"You need to run!" Jackson urged her as she placed her hands on him.

"I'm not leaving you," Abbie said as she started sobbing.

"Abbie," Jackson said, "listen to me. Your cover is blown. You have to get out of here."

"No!" she shouted back. "Jackson, we have to stop your bleeding."

Strangers had begun to surround Abbie and Jackson, and within seconds, his head was propped up on a jacket, and a sweatshirt was being pressed into his belly, and another one was wrapped around his arm, both in an attempt to stop the blood loss he was experiencing.

"Is he dead? Is he dead?" Jackson kept asking over and over, referring to the man he shot, to anyone who would listen. "I'm a cop," he lied. "Find out who he is. Please."

"He's not dead," they heard someone say. "He's unconscious, though. Barely breathing. Ambulance should be here for you guys any minute."

"Find out his name," Jackson said again.

Abbie grabbed Jackson's hand and leaned down so that her mouth was by his ear. "I'm so sorry. I'm so sorry," she sobbed as she whispered in his ear.

"No, no, don't say that. Don't do this." Jackson reached up with his good arm and carefully grabbed her by the back of the neck. He pulled her forehead to his. Her tears ran down her face and onto his as he said, "I'd do it all over again. To save you. For just one minute with you. Now listen to me; you need to get out of here."

Abbie refused, shaking her head while it was still pressed against Jackson's.

Jackson began to black out.

"No, Jackson, stay with me. Stay with me!" Abbie pleaded.

She hadn't noticed that the ambulances had arrived until the EMTs were pulling her away from Jackson. As soon as he was on a gurney and being wheeled into the back of the ambulance, Abbie followed close behind. She clutched her belly as an EMT helped her into the ambulance next to Jackson. She was no longer crying, but Abbie still felt as though her heart had been ripped out as she sat next to Jackson, holding his hand. He was her only friend in the world, and she didn't want to lose him.

Abbie's attention was soon directed to the pain she was experiencing in her belly. She wasn't sure when the contractions had started, but as she looked down, she saw that her jeans were soaked.

"Are you all right?" one of the EMTs asked her.

With one hand on her belly and the other still holding onto Jackson, she started to cry again. She answered by saying, "I think my water just broke."

Part

3

30

ABBIE

"**What's your name? Ma'am?** *What is your name?"*

Abbie couldn't focus, couldn't think, and could barely breathe through her contractions. She and Jackson were separated as soon as they arrived at the hospital. She was wheeled into the labor and delivery wing of the hospital, and Jackson, to Emergency Trauma.

"We need to know your name," a nurse said to Abbie as she entered triage.

"Sarah," she stated. "Sarah Walker." In the midst of chaos, Abbie still practiced caution with her identity. It was only a matter of hours before her baby would arrive. She needed to make sure the two of them were kept as safe as possible, despite Jackson's warning that she had been found out.

"Is there anyone on their way to the hospital to be with you?" the nurse asked Abbie as an IV port was inserted into her arm.

"No," Abbie stated as she tried to breathe through another contraction. "It's just me."

"Is there someone you want to call?"

"Call?" she asked as the nurse strapped a device to her belly to monitor the baby's heartbeat as well as her contractions.

"Yes, is there someone else you want to call? A support person?"

Yes, she thought to herself, *I want to call Michael.* Knowing that was not a possibility, she told the nurse she wanted to call Bethany.

"How's Jackson?" Abbie asked when she could breathe again. "I came in with another man who was also shot. Is he alive?"

"They are operating on him now," another nurse said, reassuringly. She followed that with some words of encouragement. "You need to focus on yourself and your baby, Sarah. You've got a big job to do."

"I don't think I can do this," Abbie said as she started to cry.

The other nurse grabbed her by the hand, looked her in the eye, and said, "Yes, you can. And you will. You are about to do something amazing."

Abbie nodded as she breathed through another contraction. They were becoming stronger and closer together, making the pain unbearable at times.

An hour later, Bethany arrived. Abbie had just received an epidural and was resting comfortably in her hospital bed.

"I came as soon as I got the call," Bethany said as she scurried into Abbie's hospital room.

"Jackson was shot." It was the first thing out of Abbie's mouth.

"What?!" Bethany asked, bewildered.

"Go check on him, please, Bethany," Abbie pleaded.

"I can't leave you like this," she protested.

"I'm fine," Abbie said. "I don't want to have this baby until I know he's okay."

Bethany hesitated, but knew that Abbie wasn't giving her a choice.

"Don't have that baby until I get back," Bethany warned as she hurried out of the room to get information about Jackson.

Not long after Bethany left, a nurse walked in to check on Abbie's progress.

"Wow, I wasn't expecting that," the nurse told Abbie.

"What?" Abbie asked nervously.

The nurse gave her a reassuring smile and said, "This baby is ready to make an appearance. I'm going to get the doctor and a few other nurses in here, and then you can start pushing."

"Pushing?" Abbie asked as reality started to sink in.

"Yes," the nurse answered. "Your baby is crowning, and you need to start pushing. Just as soon as I can get a few extra hands in here."

Abbie started to cry. She spent several months preparing for this day, the day that she would meet her and Michael's baby, but now that the day had arrived, she had never felt more unprepared. The doctor arrived, and the nurses surrounded Abbie's hospital bed, ready for the baby's arrival.

Bethany came in just as the doctor and nurses were preparing Abbie for delivery. She grabbed Abbie's hand and attempted to calm her. "Jackson is in surgery. I spoke with one of the trauma nurses. They think he's going to make it. So, don't worry about him, Sarah. They will take care of him."

"Okay," Abbie said, still crying. "Thank you for checking. Stay with me please. I can't do this by myself. I thought I could, but I can't."

"I'm here," Bethany said calmly, the way Abbie's own mother would have calmed her had she been there.

"Thank you."

"Let's have a baby," Bethany said sweetly.

Abbie laughed as she cried. "Yes, let's have a baby."

As Abbie began to push, she felt her mother's presence in the room. She didn't see Annabelle, but knowing she was there calmed her. Abbie's mind raced through the events of the past year that had led her to where she was; leaving Georgia, meeting Michael, falling in love, Meghan's death, having to leave North Carolina, and meeting Jackson. For months she wished she could have gone back in time, noticed the signs of the danger that was lurking just around the corner, ready to take away all of the happiness in her life. She often wondered where she would be had she not gone with Meghan that night they were abducted. But as she lay there, pushing with all of her might, she knew that she was exactly where she was supposed to be. Regret had consumed her life, but as she pushed for the final time, and her baby was brought to her chest, pink and healthy, with wide eyes and a screaming set of lungs, she realized that everything had fallen perfectly into place.

"Your son is so beautiful, Sarah," Bethany said to Abbie.

"It's a boy?" Abbie asked, shocked.

Bethany nodded her head, and tears slipped down her cheeks.

Abbie began to sob all over again. Her heart had never been so full. As she stared into her son's eyes she promised to always love and protect him. Abbie allowed Bethany to sit next to them and kiss his tiny fingers and toes. Words weren't needed as they stared at him, mesmerized by both the stillness and the movements of the tiny child.

"I'm going to give you two some privacy," Bethany said after awhile. "I'll go check on Jackson."

"Thank you," Abbie said.

"Not a problem," Bethany said as she stood to leave.

"No, really, Bethany, thank you. For everything."

Bethany smiled, winked at her, and then left the room.

A few hours later, Abbie lay in bed cradling her baby in her arms, exhausted but determined to drink in every moment she could with her son. When the doctors and nurses had left, and just the two of them were in the room, Abbie spoke aloud.

"I love you so much. Your daddy would love you so much too. I'm so sorry he couldn't be here today. I'm going to tell you about him every day." Abbie kissed her sleeping baby's forehead as he lay swaddled on her chest. She gazed at him for as long as she could keep her eyes open, as if they were the only two people that had ever existed, until they were both asleep.

Abbie didn't hear Bethany slip into her room and sit down next to her bed. She opened her eyes as the baby began to stir. When she saw Bethany, they spoke in hushed tones.

"Hi," Abbie said to Bethany as she yawned. "How long have you been here?"

"Not long," Bethany said. "I didn't want to wake you."

"Do you want to hold him?" Abbie offered.

"I would love to," Bethany said with a smile.

Abbie handed her son to Bethany as his tiny hands stretched over his head while he clenched his eyes shut and yawned. He smacked his lips together a few times and opened his eyes once he was in Bethany's arms.

"He's perfect, Sarah."

"Thank you."

"Jackson is out of surgery," Bethany told Abbie. "He's sedated but stable. His doctor told me he will make a full recovery."

"That's a relief."

The two were quiet for a while, staring at the new life, just hours old, before them.

"What are you going to name him?" Bethany asked.

Abbie had known for several months what she would name her baby if she had a boy. "Henry," she told her.

"It's so nice to meet you, Henry," Bethany said sweetly to the baby as he looked up at her.

"Henry Michael Hammond," Abbie stated. When she said it out loud for the first time, all of the happiness and all of the pain of the past had collided with the hope for the future.

31

JACKSON

THE HOSPITAL ROOM WAS silent except for the hums and ticks of the monitors to which Jackson was hooked. It had been twenty-four hours since his surgery, and he was finally starting to become more alert. He tried to open his eyes, but the weight of his eyelids held them shut. Pain shot through his body, and he sucked in his breath as he tried to move his arms and legs. His eyes then flung open and darted around the room. Through blurry vision he thought he saw Abbie's face. He saw another, unfamiliar, face, and that person placed an instrument in his hand that would allow him to give himself more pain medication should he need it. He felt a touch on his right hand. His head and neck followed his eyes in slow motion as he looked to the right.

Jackson's eyes landed on Abbie. She was sitting in a wheelchair next to his bed, dressed in a hospital gown and covered in a blanket, holding his hand. She appeared to be exhausted, much like how she looked when he first met her at the police station in Richmond, only this time, she had hope in her eyes.

"Hey," he said in a cracked, hoarse whisper.

Abbie's eyes filled with tears. Her postpartum emotions were in full force as she held Jackson's hand to her lips and gently kissed it. A flood of tears ran down her face.

"I'm so glad you're okay," she managed to say with a smile.

Jackson's heart ached at the sight of her. He hated that she was so distraught over what happened to him, and he wanted nothing more than to take her in his arms and calm her. But he was too weak to move.

"What are you doing in a wheelchair?" he asked. His words came out slowly and a bit slurred. His tongue was dry and swollen, making speech difficult.

"I had my baby yesterday," she said.

A smile spread across his face, and he squeezed her hand.

"His name is Henry," she continued. "And he's perfect. He's sleeping in the nursery, so I thought I would come see you."

"Thank you." Jackson rested his head, closed his eyes, and allowed his hand to slip out of Abbie's.

"I'm going to let you rest, but I will be back."

Jackson nodded as he drifted off to sleep. When he woke up, Abbie was gone. The lights were dim, and he could tell it was night.

"How's your pain, Jackson?"

He groggily looked over and noticed a nurse standing next to him, checking his vitals.

"I feel like I got shot," Jackson joked as he tried to reposition himself to get comfortable. The nurse helped to raise his bed and adjust his pillows.

"Can I get you some water?" the nurse asked.

"Yes, please. What time is it? How is the other guy? The one who I shot? And there was a girl that came in as well. Is she still here? She had a baby."

"It's just past 11:00 p.m. Are you talking about Sarah Walker?" the nursed asked him.

"Yes," he said. "Is she all right?"

"She is doing fine. A detective is going to come by in the morning to get your testimony about what happened at the shooting."

"Okay," he said and closed his eyes. The nurse quietly left after awhile, and Jackson was alone with his thoughts. He tried his best to replay the events of the previous day in his mind. He remembered every detail from the time he walked into the coffeehouse up until he and Abbie left. Beyond that, the details blurred together.

Jackson carefully reached for the phone that was by his hospital bed. He dialed and then held the receiver to his ear when the other line began to ring.

"Sloan," he said when the other line picked up. "I need a favor."

"Jackson!" Sloan said on the other line. "I've been trying to get a hold of you."

"I've been a little tied up," Jackson said evasively.

"What's going on?" Sloan asked.

Jackson told him about Omaha, Abbie, and the shooting.

"Is this a joke?" Sloan asked after Jackson finished the story.

"I wish I was kidding," Jackson said.

"I'm booking a flight and will be out first thing in the morning."

"I'd really appreciate it. I need you to help keep Abbie's cover intact with the police. I won't speak with them until you get here."

"Have you heard anything about the other victim?"

"No, nothing. I'm guessing I will find out when I talk to the police."

"I'll be there tomorrow, Jackson. I'm glad you are all right."

"I really appreciate it, Sloan."

The two hung up, and Jackson fell asleep.

Sloan flew in on a 5:00 a.m. flight and was at the hospital by ten o'clock that same morning. Jackson was walking slowly up and down the hall with the aid of a walker and a nurse's steady hand.

"Wow," Sloan said to Jackson as soon as he saw him. "You look terrible," he joked.

"Good to see you too," Jackson joked back.

Jackson, Sloan, and the nurse made their way back to Jackson's hospital room. The nurse helped Jackson back into his bed, where he sat, propped up, talking with Sloan until the police arrived to get his testimony.

Sloan stood to greet the chief of police and another deputy when they arrived. He then closed the door to Jackson's hospital room for privacy.

"Let me introduce myself," Sloan began, taking control of the conversation while he remained standing. "My name is Matthew Sloan, and I'm with the US Marshals Service. As you know, this is Jackson Wells," Sloan said, gesturing toward Jackson, "a former US marshal."

The chief and the deputy looked shocked and were clearly not expecting to be meeting with members of the US Department of Justice.

"So this is how this conversation is going to go," Sloan continued. "We need to share with you some classified information. It is your duty to keep that information confidential. Jackson will then give his testimony."

The chief and the deputy simultaneously agreed, and Sloan began to explain what he had explained so many times to other law enforcement officers about Abigail Peterson and her affiliation with the Witness Protection Program because of her incident with Griffin Ford and Alex McCain.

Jackson began speaking after Sloan had finished. He said, "I was with Ms. Peterson on the day of the shooting. We were getting coffee when the victim walked in. I noticed that he seemed suspicious, so I signaled to the witness that she and I needed to leave. The victim stopped us on the way out and began to make conversation. Abbie and I walked out of the coffeehouse, and the victim followed us. He then yelled out a threat to Abbie. My instincts told me that she was in danger and that he was connected to the perpetrators Sloan and I had previously apprehended. I drew my weapon, he drew his, and we both fired shots. I don't remember too much after that."

The two officers were hurriedly taking notes while listening intently as Jackson spoke.

"We've spoken to a few other eyewitnesses, and your testimony confirms that you were acting in self-defense," the chief stated. "That's the good news."

"The bad news?" Jackson asked.

"The victim died on the way to the hospital," the chief stated. "Charges will most likely be filed by the family. I would suggest hiring a lawyer if and when that happens. As of right now, you aren't under arrest."

"Do we know the victim's identity?" Jackson asked.

"The identification that was found on the victim was that of a 'Patrick Solomon' from Raleigh. We don't know much about him yet. But chances are, he could be involved with the human trafficking operation as you suggested. We will get more details," the deputy said.

"Oh my god," Sloan said as a hand flew to his mouth, and his face went white. "Did you say Patrick Solomon?"

"Yes."

Sloan scratched his head as his mind began to race. "A few weeks ago a man came into the department. He was cleared by security and escorted into my supervisor's office," he said, referring to Harper. "He said he was a private investigator, and that his name was Patrick Solomon, and he was seeking information about Abbie. Of course, we didn't give the man any information and was denied even an acknowledgment of Abbie Peterson's existence. He didn't stay long. He seemed to understand that we couldn't give him any information whether or not we had any."

"Whoa. Hold on," said Jackson, holding up a hand. "Are you saying that the man that I shot and killed was a private investigator? Not a human trafficker?"

"It sounds very possible," the chief of police said.

"But I thought you just said you didn't give him any information," Jackson said, arguing with Sloan. "How did he end up out here, in the very place we are hiding Abbie?

"We didn't," Sloan said. He began pacing the room, racking his brain to figure out how Patrick Solomon could have known where Abbie was. "I have an idea," he finally said, and pulled out his cell phone.

Jackson's mind was racing. The knot in his stomach that had formed when the police officers told him the victim had died had only grown larger since hearing he was not trying to hurt Abbie but protect her.

"What have I done?" Jackson whispered as he closed his eyes and leaned his head back on a pillow.

"Harper," Sloan said into the phone. "Remember that man we met a few weeks ago? The private investigator looking for Abigail Peterson? I need you to sweep the room where we were talking. I think he may have bugged the room in order to listen to our conversation after he left." Sloan continued to explain to Harper what had happened in Omaha and how Patrick Solomon had found her and Jackson.

It suddenly dawned on Jackson why Patrick Solomon was ready to shoot him, in the middle of the street. He opened his eyes and said aloud, "He must have thought I was one of the men that had abducted Abbie. It was obvious she was scared that day, the way I was hurrying her out of the coffeehouse, but trying to act like she wasn't. He knew she was in witness protection, but there is no way that anyone would have known that I was out here with her, trying to keep her safe." He looked down and shook his head, regretting the poor decisions regarding Abbie's case.

Sloan hung up the phone and said, "Harper is going to look to see if that room is bugged and call me back."

"We really dropped the ball with this one," Jackson said.

Sloan couldn't help but nod in agreement. "This is a mess." He walked out of the room, leaving Jackson alone with the officers.

"Well I think that's all we need for now," the chief said. "We will be in touch." The two of them left the room as well.

Jackson wasn't alone with his thoughts for long. Sloan walked back into his room just after the police officers left.

"I was right," Sloan said flatly. "He placed a sound transmitter underneath the chair he was sitting in. After he left, Harper and I were discussing Abbie's case and where she was relocated. He heard everything. That's how he knew to come to Omaha."

"He was most likely hired by Abbie's boyfriend or father. Do you think he relayed any information back to them?" Jackson asked.

"I'm not sure," Sloan answered. "I think that if he had, one or both of them would have shown up by now."

There was a quick knock on the door, and a nurse peeked her head in, "Time for your meds, Mr. Wells," she said.

"Come in," said Jackson.

"Hello," the nurse said politely to Sloan.

"I should head out," Sloan said to Jackson. "I'll come by tomorrow."

"Thanks again," Jackson said to him.

Just as Sloan was heading toward the door to leave, Abbie had peeked her head into Jackson's room. Seated in a wheelchair, holding her baby, a nurse had wheeled the two of them down to see him. She was no longer in her hospital gown, but in loose-fitting loungewear that Bethany must have brought by for her. Her hair hung loose around her shoulders, still damp from her shower that morning. She smelled of lavender and vanilla as she breezed into the room.

"You look so much better," Abbie said to Jackson.

"Thanks," he answered. "Sloan, you remember Sarah?" Jackson said, reintroducing the two of them.

"Of course," he said. He gestured toward the baby and said, "Congratulations."

"Thank you," she answered. "It's nice to see you."

"You as well." Sloan smiled and waved to the two of them. He and the two nurses filed out of the room.

"This must be the little man," Jackson said to her, trying to conceal his emotions from the conversation that had previously taken place in his hospital room regarding the shooting and the private investigator.

"This is Henry," Abbie said, and positioned the sleeping baby in her arms so Jackson could see him.

"He looks like you," Jackson said.

"Thank you. How are you feeling?"

"I've been better," he laughed. "You?"

"We are good. We are being discharged today. I wanted to come by and say good-bye before we left."

"Thank you. I appreciate that."

"So do you think you are going back to DC? Or will you stay around here?"

"I haven't decided."

They were both quiet. Jackson wanted her to ask him to stay. She didn't.

"Well, in case I don't see you when you get out of here, I wanted to say thank you. I'm not sure what would have happened that day if you weren't there to protect me."

"It was nothing."

"It meant a lot to me. I also wanted to say thank you for all the other times you were there for me and all of your help."

"Not a problem." As they talked, Jackson knew there was a possibility that Patrick Solomon had contacted Michael about Abbie's whereabouts and that he was on his way to Omaha to be with her. He took a few deep breaths and decided he was going to enjoy as much time as he had left with her.

32

ABBIE

It had been two weeks since Abbie had brought her son home from the hospital. Henry had woken up every hour on the hour to be fed and changed. Abbie's spirit was breaking. She hadn't showered in days, nor had she slept more than two consecutive hours in over three days. Bethany was able to help for a few hours during the day, but Abbie was completely alone during the late night hours.

Abbie had just laid Henry down in his crib and crawled back under the covers in her own bed. Her eyes had only been closed for a few minutes, and she was slipping in between consciousness and sleep when she heard Henry start to cry. She forced herself to open her eyes and lift her son out of his cradle, again, to soothe him.

The two of them sat in the dark as Abbie rocked Henry. Tears of exhaustion rolled down her cheeks. She was a mix of emotions. She had never been so tired in her life, but had also never had such love and joy in her heart. After Henry's eyes closed, and he was content with simply sucking on his bottom lip, Abbie slowly rose from the chair, placed Henry back in the cradle, and tiptoed back to bed. Three hours of peaceful sleep later, Abbie heard a quiet knock on her door.

"It's just me," Abbie heard Bethany whisper from down the hall as her apartment door slowly opened. Abbie had given Bethany a key so as not to wake the two of them if she arrived while they were sleeping. Abbie was guessing that Bethany was dropping off a few groceries on her way to the inn to prepare breakfast for the guests. Bethany crept down the hall and peeked her head into the bedroom doorway to check on Abbie and Henry. Abbie opened one eye to see Bethany hold a finger to her lips signaling her to not get up, afraid the baby would awaken. Abbie nodded once, and Bethany motioned with her hand that she was going to leave.

Not long after Bethany left, Henry started to whimper. Abbie stretched, put her feet on the floor, and scooped up Henry. She knew she was in for a long day, but a bit of her energy had been restored.

By midday, Abbie had hardly had a chance to sit down. Between feedings, diapers, trying to feed herself, as well as trying to recover from the delivery, she began to struggle. At one point, she sat in the middle of the living room, closed her eyes, and focused on breathing in and out. She sat in clothes she had worn for two days, spit-up on one shoulder, and a gnarled mess of hair tied up on top of her head. Henry lay awake in a baby swing. His eyes darted around the room, and his tiny fists reached out before him, as he discovered the sights and sounds of the room.

As Abbie continued to sit and breathe, she heard a knock at her door. She wasn't sure who could have been knocking. Bethany was at work, her neighbors kept to themselves, and no one else had a key to the main building. Abbie opened her apartment door a crack and saw Jackson standing on the other side.

"I hope I didn't wake either of you by knocking," he whispered when he saw her.

"Hi," she said, surprised to see him standing there. "How did you get in?"

"I waited until one of your neighbors came home, and I followed them inside," he laughed. "I didn't want to ring the buzzer and wake up Henry. Or you."

"We are awake, unfortunately," she chuckled, suddenly aware of her appearance. "I wasn't expecting company," she said, tucking a few strands of hair behind her ears.

"You look great," Jackson said, and Abbie knew that he meant it.

"Come on in," she said to him. "I didn't expect to see you out of the hospital so soon. Shouldn't you be home, resting?"

"I was discharged a few days ago. I'm doing just fine," he replied.

"That's great."

"How are the two of you doing?"

Abbie laughed and then sighed. "We are doing well. Henry is amazing. But, to be perfectly honest, I was not prepared for how much work it is and how tired I am."

As if on cue, the baby began to whimper in his swing. Abbie walked over, picked him up, held him to her chest, and patted his back while swaying back and forth.

"Do you mind if I hold him?" Jackson asked.

Abbie looked up at Jackson, a bit surprised, and said, "Sure," as she delicately handed her baby to him. Jackson stood close to Abbie while she carefully handed the baby to him. He held Henry, a bit awkwardly at first, but then he relaxed and couldn't help but smile when Henry nuzzled into his arms.

"Why don't you go lie down?" Jackson suggested to Abbie.

"No, I'm all right," she said with a smile.

"I insist," Jackson said as he seated himself on the couch with Henry. "I came over to see you and offer my help. You look exhausted, beautiful, but exhausted. You said yourself you were tired. Now please, go lie down."

Abbie blushed, not only at the compliment but at Jackson's generosity. Still, she hesitated.

"Go on," Jackson said, shooing her with his hand. He cocked a leg up over his knee and leaned back on the couch with Henry still in his arms. "We need some male bonding time anyway," he joked and smiled at her. She smiled back.

"Well, all right, but just for a little while. An hour, tops."

Jackson didn't say anything, only motioned with his hand for her to leave the room again as he winked at her.

Reluctant, yet thankful, Abbie went to her bedroom to lie down. As she sank into the mattress and pulled the blankets up over her head, she thought about Michael. She wanted so badly for him to be the one in the next room with Henry. Jackson had a special place in her heart, but he could never replace Michael. Exhaustion took over her thoughts and soon she was asleep.

The smell of food cooking in the kitchen roused Abbie from her sleep. It was dark, and she wondered how long she had been asleep. As well rested as she felt, she knew it must have been several hours. She quickly got out of bed and walked down the hall to find Jackson in the kitchen, preparing a meal for her.

"I called Bethany and told her she didn't need to stop by tonight," Jackson told her. "I hope you don't mind." Jackson leaned down and pulled a casserole out of the oven.

"I didn't know you cooked," she said.

"I have quite a few secrets," he said as he winked at her.

Abbie laughed. "I'm sorry I slept for so long. Hopefully Henry didn't give you too much trouble."

"No trouble at all," Jackson said. "He's sleeping in the nursery. Fed and changed."

"Thank you."

"You're welcome."

"Are you hungry?"

"Starving. Mind if I jump in the shower?"

"Not at all."

Abbie was relieved to have the help that Jackson was providing, so she graciously accepted it. She allowed the near scalding water to soak into her hair and skin, and she stood in the middle of the shower, eyes closed, relaxed. For the first time in a long time, she wasn't overwhelmed with thoughts of how she was going to raise Henry by herself, keeping up with the lie about who she was and where she came from, or not ever seeing Michael again. She was calm. Her mind was at ease as she stepped out of the shower and wrapped herself in a towel. She wiped away the fog from the mirror and ran a comb through her hair.

Henry was awake when Abbie walked out of the bathroom. Jackson was holding him in his arms, bouncing him slightly as he fussed.

"Baby boy," Abbie cooed at Henry as she approached him and Jackson. Jackson inhaled the scent of her soap as Abbie stood next to him, placing a finger into Henry's tiny fist. "Shh, it's okay," she said, calming her son. She lifted Henry from Jackson's arms.

"Can I make you a plate of food?" Jackson asked her.

"Yes, please," she answered. "It smells delicious." Abbie sat down on the couch with Henry. The darkness of the evening, mixed with the light from a single lamp that was switched on, dimmed the room just enough to keep Abbie's mood calm and serene.

Once Henry was no longer fussing, Abbie placed him in his swing and joined Jackson at the dining room table. They were quiet as they ate, content with the pleasure of the other's company. Jackson had cleared the table when they were finished eating, and Abbie curled up on the couch next to Henry's swing. Her son had fallen asleep with his hand pressed into his cheek. Her heart swelled and, at the same time, sank as she saw the very image of Michael on her son's face.

Her serenity evaporated. She couldn't help the tears that came next. Jackson had just begun to wash the dishes and didn't hear her crying over the clanking of the pots and pans at first. Abbie did her best to hide her emotions. She tucked her hands inside her shirtsleeves, pressed them to her face, and choked back tears. Jackson eventually heard her sobs from the kitchen. He didn't bother to dry his hands off as he rushed to her side. Suds and water dripped down his arms as he knelt down beside her and brought her close to him.

"Hey," he said concerned, sweetly and quietly, "What's wrong?"

Abbie couldn't talk, couldn't breathe, much like the time she broke down in the hotel room when Jackson had been there to calm her down before. She didn't want to wake Henry and didn't want to concern Jackson. She wasn't sure how she went from being content and calm to an emotional mess. Abbie sank into Jackson and let him hold her while she cried.

"Abbie," he whispered quietly as he pressed his lips into her hair by her ear. He said her real name on purpose. As much as she tried to be strong and live her life as Sarah Walker, Jackson knew she was struggling. She cried even harder when he said it. They sat for a while, as Abbie cried, and Henry slept. Jackson held her close, kissing her forehead and gently stroking her hair.

"Tell me what I can do," Jackson said. He wanted so desperately to give her anything she needed. He would have dragged the moon across the sky for her if he could.

"I just want Michael," she said through her tears.

"I know," he said. "I know."

33

JACKSON

JACKSON DROVE HOME FROM Abbie's house that night, after she and Henry were tucked into bed. Abbie's tears had subsided, and the calmness he saw in her hours earlier had returned. She steadied her breathing and closed her eyes as he pulled the blankets around her, making sure she was comfortable before he left her apartment. He could still feel her heart breaking once he was back at his hotel and in his own bed. Selfishness tormented him throughout the night. But as the sun came up the next morning, his heart broke for her, and he wanted nothing more than to give her everything she wanted, even if what she wanted was someone else entirely.

For most of the morning, Jackson felt sorry for himself and the way he had allowed his heart to run wild, doing what he could to love Abbie, and to see her through the tough times she faced. By the afternoon, he set his feelings aside and began to focus on what he needed to do to make her happy. He paced around his hotel room, working up the nerve to make the one call he needed to make to give Abbie what she had wanted all along.

Jackson's hand shook as he pulled his cell phone from his pocket. "Sloan, I need your help," he said, after dialing his number. Jackson then presented a plan to Sloan that would bring Abbie happiness.

"I don't know, Jackson," Sloan said once he heard the plan. "I could lose my job."

"I know," Jackson said, slightly embarrassed for even asking the favor. He paused. Then he said, "You should see her, Sloan. She's miserable. She's trying very hard to move on and live her new life, but she just crumbles under the weight of the pressure to be someone she isn't." Jackson tried to keep his voice from cracking. "I've tried to be there for her. I've offered her everything I've got, and it's not what she needs. *I'm* not what she needs." He choked on the last sentence.

There was a long pause. Jackson took Sloan's silence as a sign that he was actually contemplating the plan.

"Sloan," Jackson said, feeling defeated. "Please." He sat at the foot of his hotel bed, head in one hand, the other on his cell phone, pressed to his ear.

"Okay," Sloan said reluctantly. "I'll do it."

Jackson stood up from the bed. He was in shock that Sloan actually agreed. They continued to discuss the details and what each of them needed to do to ensure that the plan would work and that everyone involved would be safe.

When they hung up the phone, Jackson busied himself by packing up his belongings and putting them in his suitcase. He moved quickly, not wanting to regret the choice he had made and abandon the plan he and Sloan had just created. Once he was packed, he walked out of the hotel room, luggage in hand, and headed to the airport without a second look back.

34

MICHAEL

MICHAEL HADN'T RECEIVED ANY news from Patrick Solomon in weeks. All of Michael's calls to the private investigator went directly to voice mail, and, after awhile, the voice mail box was full, so he was unable to leave any additional messages. At first, when his calls went unanswered, he held on to hope that Patrick was working hard and had a few leads as to where Abbie may have been. But, as time passed and Michael heard nothing, he began to feel taken advantage of. Michael thought maybe Patrick Solomon had taken his money and disappeared. Patrick, after all, was a man who knew how to find people, so Michael assumed he also knew the best way to disappear. The notion that that had happened clawed at him for days.

Michael had just gotten home after a long day at work and met Sam and Bull at the front door of the carriage house. He and the dogs sat on the porch for a while in the cool, crisp spring air. The silence of the evening broke with the sound of a truck making its way down the dirt road that led to the farm. The dogs perked their heads up when the vehicle slowed as it got closer. Sam and Bull leaped off the porch and ran to meet the truck as it pulled into the driveway. Michael stood up, curious as to who could be dropping by the farm that evening. Brody Garrity was out of town and wasn't due back for several more weeks. The truck itself was unfamiliar, so Michael assumed it was an acquaintance of Mr. Garrity who hadn't realized he was out of town.

The truck, with Virginia plates on the front, slowed to a stop. Michael squinted in an attempt to see who was in the driver's seat. It was a man he did not recognize. Michael waved a hand as he walked down the driveway to greet the guest. As Michael approached the truck, he noticed that the man sat and looked at Michael for several seconds before exiting the vehicle.

The man's shoes were the first thing Michael noticed when he stepped out of the truck. They looked expensive and well-polished. His shirt and pants were neatly pressed, and the man's chestnut hair was clean cut and neat. Michael stood across from him in his dirty blue jeans, work boots, and messy hair. Besides the man's shoes, Michael also noticed how tired the man looked.

"Can I help you, sir?" Michael asked.

The man cleared his throat and asked with an unsteady voice, "I'm looking for Michael Hammond."

"I'm Michael," he said, confused.

The man stuck out his hand and offered it to him. "I'm Jackson Wells."

"Nice to meet you. What can I do for you, Jackson?" Michael asked as he put his rough, calloused hand into Jackson's.

"I'm here about Abigail Peterson," Jackson said soberly.

Michael's face went white, and his hand fell from Jackson's. Unable to form words, Michael took a step back, fearing the worst.

"Can we talk inside?" Jackson asked.

Michael wasn't sure how he made it from the driveway into the carriage house, but he led Jackson inside and offered him a seat on the sofa in the living room. Michael sat across from Jackson in a folding chair, anticipating what he had to say.

"Is she alive?" Michael blurted out.

"Yes," Jackson said quietly as he looked at the floor.

Michael instinctively leapt out of the chair and clasped his hands together. He began to pace about and run his hands through his hair, firing off questions to Jackson.

"Is she okay? Where is she?"

Jackson stood and tried to calm Michael. "Have a seat, I will explain everything."

Michael sat down and attempted to compose himself. His heart was racing as he waited impatiently for Jackson to speak.

"I came here to tell you what happened the night that Abbie disappeared," Jackson began.

"I'm listening," Michael said. The two sat across from each other. Michael listened to every word.

"From what I understand, Abbie and Meghan left the diner where they worked together on the night they disappeared. They attempted to come home when the night was over, but they were followed, chased through the streets, and then abducted by two men. While they were being transported, Meghan was killed. Abbie managed to escape, unharmed, and was found by the police early the next morning.

"That's when I met her. I was working for the US Marshals Service at the time. The Richmond Police Department called me in to speak with her. We decided it would be best to put her into the Witness Protection Program. She was given a new identity, some cash, a vehicle, and a place to live.

"She wasn't able to contact anyone. It wouldn't have been safe. The men who abducted her and killed Meghan were extremely dangerous. So we allowed everyone to believe she had disappeared, even died. My team of associates halted the searches for her, the missing person reports that you filed, any trail that would have led to her, we covered up."

Michael looked shocked and confused, and he was unsure of what to say next.

"There's more," Jackson continued. "I had recently visited Abbie to make sure she was adjusting, and if her needs were being accommodated. A few weeks ago we were approached by a man I believed to be involved with the men who had originally abducted her. That man and I ended up drawing our weapons on each other; we both were shot. I lived. He did not. That man, Michael, was Patrick Solomon."

Michael sat up straight in the chair. "You can't be serious," he said in disbelief. The unanswered phone calls, the unexplained silence and absence from the private investigator quickly made sense to him. He couldn't believe Patrick was dead. Michael barely had time to process that thought when Jackson spoke again.

"I need to tell you something else," he said. His voice had remained steady and calm throughout the entire conversation, but Michael could tell by the look in Jackson's eyes that the next part of the discussion would be much harder to say.

"Okay," Michael said, not quite sure what to anticipate.

Jackson swallowed hard. "Michael, Abbie was pregnant before she left North Carolina. She had a baby a few weeks ago. It's your baby, Michael. A boy."

Michael had a blank stare on his face. He had waited so long to find out whether or not Abbie was alive. Jackson was not only telling him that she was alive, but that she had a baby. A son. *His* son.

"I know," Jackson said. "It's a lot to take in. It was a lot for her to digest as well. She is just now accepting the fact that she will never go back to her old life, that she's all alone, and now has a son to take care of."

"So, let me just try to understand what you are saying," Michael said as he rubbed his brow. "Abbie is alive, but she's in the Witness Protection Program?"

"Yes," Jackson answered.

"And I have a son?"

"Yes."

Michael broke down and put his head in his hands. His heart was filled with a renewed love for Abbie and their child, but it also broke knowing that he may never get the chance to meet or hold his son.

Jackson leaned forward, reached out, and rested a hand on Michael's shoulder.

"Why are you telling me?" Michael asked through his tears. "What am I supposed to do if I can't see them or know where they are?"

"That's exactly what we need to discuss, Michael." Then Jackson looked straight into Michael's eyes. "I can give you your family, but you have to leave with me, tonight."

"I'm sorry?"

"Abbie is trying to be strong, but she's falling apart. She needs to be strong for her son, but I'm not sure she can go on much longer without you. Abbie doesn't know I'm here. Quite frankly, I can't believe I'm here, but I would like for you to be reunited with Abbie and your son."

"I'm not sure I follow. I can be with them? Will they be safe?"

"I have all of the documentation that will provide you with a different identity should you choose to join your family in witness protection. But, like I said, you have to leave with me, right now. You won't be able to contact anyone to tell them where you are going."

Michael stood and began to pace around the room again. He stared out the living room window with his hands on his hips and allowed his thoughts to get lost in the darkness that stared back at him. He had no hesitations about leaving North Carolina to be with Abbie. He could only imagine the thoughts that had gone through Abbie's head when Jackson had presented the same scenario to her, to leave immediately without looking back. He would now do the same, for love, just as she had.

"When do we leave?" Michael asked calmly as he turned around and faced Jackson, who was also standing.

"As soon as possible," Jackson stated. "Pack a bag, and we can leave within the hour."

Michael nodded. He knelt down, and Sam and Bull sauntered over, covering Michael in kisses as he embraced them. Jackson waited patiently for Michael in the living room while he went into the bedroom and packed a duffel bag full of his clothes and belongings. The dogs began to whimper, sensing Michael's anxiety and knowing that something was happening that they didn't understand.

"Any chance they can come too?" Michael said, half joking, half serious, as he gestured toward Sam and Bull.

"We could probably make it work," Jackson said, smiling, as he reached down to pet each of them.

"Are you serious?" Michael asked.

Jackson laughed. "Load 'em up in my truck before I change my mind."

35

JACKSON

THE RUMBLE OF THE truck tires and the occasional click of the blinker were the only sounds heard for the first few hundred miles of the journey back to Omaha. Neither Jackson nor Michael had the energy to speak. Jackson was sure Michael was processing the news that Abbie was alive, she had been hiding in witness protection, and she had just given birth to his son.

Jackson knew he was taking a chance when he decided to go to Abbie's apartment the night he helped her take care of Henry and make her dinner. He had just gotten out of the hospital and was dying to see her and help her in any way that he could. However, by the end of the night, Jackson knew that Abbie's heart would never be his.

Sloan remained hesitant to help Jackson.

"There's no way I can justify him going into witness protection," Sloan told Jackson during another phone conversation after he had returned to Washington, DC.

"I know," Jackson said. "That's not what I have in mind."

"What are you asking, then?"

"I just need documents. A birth certificate. A driver's license. I'll take care of the rest. I'll go get Michael. I'll take him to Abbie."

"Jackson, this is dangerous."

There was silence on the line.

"What would you do, Sloan, if you were me?" Jackson asked.

More silence. Jackson caught himself holding his breath, waiting for Sloan to respond.

Sloan sighed and reluctantly said, "I'll call a guy I know."

Jackson exhaled. "Thank you. Really, Sloan, thank you."

"Hey, no promises, Jackson."

"I know. I owe you."

Two days later Jackson met Sloan in a parking ramp outside of the city where the two of them exchanged envelopes. One contained Michael's documentation for a new identity; the other held a large sum of money. Neither said a word during the exchange, and within minutes they each drove off in separate directions.

Now, in the truck with Michael, Jackson lifted the center console that contained the envelope from Sloan. He handed it to Michael.

"What's this?" Michael asked, opening it.

"The documentation I mentioned earlier for your new identity," he stated.

"Andrew Hayes?" Michael asked, reviewing the items that were in the envelope.

"From now on, that's who you are," Jackson said and looked in Michael's direction.

"And my son?" Michael asked, tucking the documents back into the envelope. "What's his name?"

"Henry Michael Hammond."

Michael felt the wind escape his chest. It was becoming more and more real to him that he would soon be reunited with Abbie and meet his son.

"Henry is Abbie's father's name," Michael said quietly. "He passed away while she's been away."

"I'm sorry," Jackson said, genuinely sympathetic. The two of them returned to their silence. It was becoming clear with each passing minute and mile that Jackson was making the right decision. Since he had met Abbie, he knew that she belonged with Michael. But now, after meeting him, it was clear that Michael belonged with Abbie.

They stopped at a hotel for the night when Jackson was too tired to drive. Michael stayed in the truck with the dogs while Jackson went inside and paid for two rooms. They then quietly snuck the dogs into the rear entrance of the hotel. Jackson and Michael didn't say much as they each went to their rooms. Both were exhausted from the events of the evening.

"Meet in the morning around eight thirty?" Jackson asked before Michael ducked into his room.

"Yeah, that sounds good."

Jackson nodded, somberly, and stepped inside his room. As he was about to close the door he heard Michael say something else, so he peeked back out into the hallway.

"Jackson, I really appreciate everything you've done. Not just for me and for today. But for taking such good care of Abbie and making sure she's safe."

Jackson smiled, swallowed the lump that formed in his throat, and managed to say, "Not a problem."

"See you at eight thirty."

They met the next morning, dogs in tow, and paper cups of coffee in hand, at eight thirty exactly, behind the hotel. Michael had showered, shaved, and changed out of his dirty work clothes he had on from the previous evening. He was dressed comfortably, in jeans and a T-shirt. Jackson looked much like he had the previous evening, in fresh, neatly pressed business casual attire.

Jackson noticed Michael's eyes were bloodshot and swollen, and rightfully so. Jackson had also been a bit emotional the night before, once he was alone in his hotel room. While he was certain Michael was overcome with happiness as he anticipated his reunion with Abbie, Jackson was having a hard time letting her go. The two of them hardly noticed the silence between them during the first few hours of the trip that morning. They were both occupied with their thoughts and didn't speak until after they had stopped at a gas station to refuel the truck. They stood outside, stretching their legs as Sam and Bull played in the grass. Jackson had gone inside, paid for the gas, and bought them each more coffee.

"You all right?" Jackson asked Michael as he handed him a cup.

"Yeah," Michael said quietly, accepting the coffee. "I mean, most dads have nine months to prepare themselves to be a parent. I've had less than twenty-four hours."

"You'll have a few more by the time we get there," Jackson said lightheartedly, patting Michael on the shoulder.

"All I've been thinking about is whether or not I'm good enough for them," Michael continued.

Michael's words made Jackson feel as though he had been shot all over again. He inhaled and then exhaled deeply as he forced all of his selfishness out of his body.

"You shouldn't worry about that, Michael," Jackson said. "I know for a fact you are all she wants." Michael turned to look at Jackson, a bit shocked. Before he could question Jackson's statement, Jackson said, "Ready to go?" Michael called after the dogs, and they loaded back into the truck.

They drove all day. Jackson started to get nervous once they were an hour outside of Omaha. He knew that the look on Abbie's face when she saw Michael would break his heart, but at the same time, heal it, knowing she was happy and taken care of.

The truck slowed as they approached the bed and breakfast. Jackson's heart raced as he saw Abbie's car parked in the driveway and he pulled in behind her. He looked over to see a nervous, yet ready, look on Michael's face. He was also wiping the sweat from his palms on the knees of his jeans.

"You ready?" Jackson asked.

"Definitely," Michael said confidently.

They each opened their door to the truck. They could hear piano music playing from inside the house as they approached the back door. Jackson's heart was pounding, and he was sure Michael's was as well. He looked over to see Michael doing the best he could to keep from tearing up. The woman that he thought to be dead was just inside the door, with his newborn son.

Jackson lightly rapped on the door, turned the doorknob, and walked inside. Michael followed behind. The piano music continued to play. Bethany was cleaning up the evening meal and humming along to the music that floated throughout the house.

"Jackson!" Bethany said, elated, as she put the dishes in the sink.

"Is Sarah here?" Jackson asked.

"Yes," Bethany answered. "She's in the other room." Her eyebrows narrowed, questioning the serious look on each of their faces. "Who is this handsome gentleman?" she asked, pointing to Michael.

"This is Michael," Jackson said. "He is here to see Sarah. Bethany, can you and I talk privately?"

"Yes, of course," she answered.

Michael looked at Jackson as if to request permission to walk into the next room. Jackson nodded in his direction and felt his chest tighten as Michael hurried away.

"What's going on?" Bethany whispered to Jackson with a worried look on her face.

"Let's go outside," Jackson said quietly and led Bethany out to the porch, relieved that he would not have to witness Abbie and Michael's reunion.

Sam and Bull lifted their heads and stared out the window of the truck and watched as Jackson and Bethany sat on the steps.

"I need to tell you a few things about Sarah," Jackson began to explain.

"Who is that man?" Bethany interrupted.

Jackson hung his head in between his knees. Then he began to tell Bethany everything. Using Abbie and Michael's real names, he explained to her that the man inside was the father of her child and that Abbie had never been involved with an abusive boyfriend, nor had she come from a battered women's shelter. Jackson also explained what had happened to Meghan and how Abbie entered the Witness Protection Program. He admitted that he was no longer associated with the US Marshals Service and that his return to Omaha was strictly an attempt to be with Abbie. Finally, he broke down and told Bethany about the night he had spent with Abbie, cooking for her and caring for Henry, and realizing that he knew he had to bring Michael to her.

Bethany couldn't fight the tears as Jackson spoke. She vowed to keep Abbie and Michael's identities a secret. She thanked him for everything he had done over the course of the past several months.

"Are you going back to DC?" Bethany asked him as she brushed away her tears.

"Yeah," he said sorrowfully. "I wouldn't feel right about staying out here."

Bethany nodded, patted him on the knee, and said, "You're a good man, Jackson. She won't forget what you did for her or how you were always there for her."

"I should probably go," Jackson said, and he, too, stood up.

"I'll take the dogs inside," Bethany offered, and Jackson opened the passenger side door of the truck to let them out.

"Thank you, Bethany."

"Are you coming inside to say good-bye?"

"No, I'll just head out now."

They shared a quick embrace before Jackson got in the driver's seat and started the engine. Bethany walked back inside. Jackson began to head down the driveway, much like he had when he left Abbie in Omaha so many months ago.

He did a double take as he saw Abbie race out the back door, leap off the back steps, and run toward the truck that was halfway down the drive. Jackson didn't hesitate as he parked the truck, flung the door open, and met her in the driveway. Abbie threw her arms around Jackson and hugged him tight as she cried tears of joy in his arms.

"Thank you," she sobbed. She said it over and over, "Thank you, Jackson. Thank you."

"Shh, it's okay," he told her, believing it to be true himself. He held her, one last time, and knew he had made the right decision. They pulled away from each other, both with tears in their eyes. "Take care of that baby," Jackson said with a smile as he walked away.

"I will," she called back, also smiling.

Jackson backed out of the driveway, one last time, again leaving his heart with Abbie in Omaha.

36

MICHAEL

T H E   M U S I C   T H A T   C A R R I E D   from inside the house to where he and Jackson were standing on the porch, brought Michael back to the previous summer, standing in the attic of the farmhouse with Abbie, as she played the old, dusty piano for him for the first time. Michael could barely speak as they walked into the house, and Jackson introduced him to Bethany.

Michael's head was spinning, and his heart was racing as he walked from the kitchen toward the sound of the piano coming from the other room. He made his way through a dining room and stood in the doorway of the sitting room where Abbie sat, lost in her thoughts, eyes closed, playing the piano in the corner of the room. Michael's breath escaped his lungs as he burst into tears and dropped to his knees at the sight of her, alive, right in front of him.

Abbie opened her eyes and saw him, knelt down on the floor, hands over his mouth, staring back at her. Unable to speak, her eyes grew wide, in disbelief, and she stopped playing, leaped from the piano bench, and raced to him. She too fell to her knees next to him, and they threw their arms around each other. They both sobbed, uncontrollably, as they held each other.

At one point, Michael slowly pulled his head back, which was buried in her shoulder, so he could see her face. He took her face in his hands and kissed her. She kissed him back as her tears continued to spill onto her cheeks.

"It's really you," he whispered over and over.

"How did you find me?" she whispered back.

"A man named Jackson came to my house the other night. He told me everything and asked me to come. I couldn't believe it. I thought you were dead, Abbie." Michael said all this as he touched her face and ran his hands down the length of her hair, as if he was making sure that the woman in front him truly existed and that she wouldn't vanish beneath his fingertips.

"Jackson? Is he here?" she asked.

"Yes, I think he and Bethany are outside talking. Abbie, he told me you had a baby."

"Oh, Michael!" she gasped, and started crying all over again. "He's beautiful. His name is Henry, and he looks just like you."

"Is he here? Can I meet him?" he asked as he, too, started to cry again.

"Yes, he's upstairs sleeping."

The two of them helped each other up off of the floor. Abbie grabbed Michael's hand and led him up the stairs and down the hall to where Henry was sleeping in one of the guest rooms. Abbie turned on a small lamp, and the dim glow of the light illuminated the room. Michael instantly fell in love with the tiny bundle that was swaddled and sleeping peacefully in the cradle before him. Abbie bent down and carefully scooped up the baby, without waking him.

"Would you like to hold our son?" Abbie said quietly to Michael.

"More than anything," he answered and held his arms out to take him. Michael cradled the baby and kissed his forehead, cheeks, and tiny fingers. He took a seat on the foot of the bed and stared for a while at the life that he and Abbie created. "Thank you," he said as he looked up at Abbie, who smiled and kissed him.

"Our son helped me through all of those months without you," Abbie said as she took a seat next to them. "I was so sad and lonely. There were many days I wasn't sure if I even wanted to live to see the next. But when I found out I was pregnant ..." her voice trailed off. "Everything changed at that point. Having that little life inside of me that was a part of you and a part of me kept me going every day." She rested her head on Michael's shoulder and put an arm around his waist. They sat for a while, staring at Henry and saying nothing. They both knew that there would be time for words, but in that moment, they were both comfortable with the silence.

Michael heard Jackson's truck engine fire up outside. Abbie lifted her head off of Michael's shoulder and stood up. She kissed his lips and said, "I'm going to say good-bye to Jackson. I'll be right back."

Michael stayed in the room with Henry, memorizing his face, hands, and his tiny movements as he slept. A small clock rested on a nightstand near the bed. As the second hand ticked by, Michael fell deeper and deeper in love with his son.

Abbie returned after awhile with Sam and Bull. "Bethany said all of us could just stay here tonight. We can go to my apartment in the morning." The dogs were exhausted from a long day of travel, and they curled up at the end of the bed, as if they were at home.

Bethany appeared in the doorway. She knocked lightly to get their attention but not to wake Henry.

"Hello," Michael said to her.

Bethany smiled. "If you want, I can keep Henry downstairs with me tonight. I'm sure you both have a lot to catch up on. Abbie looked in Michael's direction, to see if he had any objections.

"I'd like to hold him a little longer," Michael said.

"Okay," Bethany said with a smile. "I will come back up in a little while. Can I get you both anything?"

"No, thank you," Abbie and Michael said in unison. Bethany walked out of the room and went back downstairs.

"I feel like I have so much to tell you, but I'm not quite sure where to start," Michael said as Abbie sat down next to him.

Abbie laughed. "I was just thinking the same thing."

"You look so beautiful," he told her. She blushed. "I never stopped looking for you, Abbie. I did everything I could. Everything."

"That means so much to me," Abbie said to him. "What about my dad? How is he?"

Michael's face softened. He had dreaded telling her about Henry since he left North Carolina.

"Michael?" she asked, growing concerned.

"I'm so sorry, Abbie," He whispered. "Your dad passed away early this spring."

Abbie gasped. "No," she said as she brought her hands to her face. She cried, hard, heavy tears.

"I'm so sorry," Michael said. He gently placed Henry back into his cradle. He then pulled Abbie closer to him, and she pulled her knees to her chest on the bed. Michael's heart broke for Abbie as hers broke for her father.

A few minutes later, Henry began to cry. Bethany returned, hearing Abbie's sobs from the floor below, and quietly scooped up Henry.

"Let me help you gather up his things," Abbie said, wiping the tears from her face. Michael stood up as well and helped carry Henry's cradle downstairs to a room where Bethany planned to stay for the night. Abbie and Michael kissed their son good night and headed back upstairs, hand in hand.

Once they were back in the bedroom, Abbie shut the door behind them. She and Michael then pulled the covers back on the bed, and they lay down next to each other, as if they had been doing it the same way, each night, since the last night they had spent together. Michael pulled the covers up over them as Abbie switched the lamp off. They lay together in the dark, arms around each other, not taking a single moment with each other for granted.

Michael held Abbie as she cried for Meghan and her father and for the time that she lost with Michael. Michael cried for what Abbie had endured by herself for so many months. After a few hours of pouring their hearts out to each other, they fell asleep. Michael woke up at one point and noticed Abbie was propped up on one shoulder, silently staring at him.

"Are you all right?" he whispered as he pulled her close to him.

"Everything is perfect now," she whispered back. They kissed. "I spent months wishing I could go back in time," Abbie began to explain. "I had so many dreams about what was going to happen to me. To us. I ignored all of the signs that my mother had tried to tell me, my father, and you. I should have realized it, you know?"

"I'm not sure there is anything we could have done about it," Michael said reassuringly.

"I know that now," Abbie said. "The day Henry was born, I realized that I wouldn't have changed anything. Even if it meant I couldn't have you. I would rather have those few weeks with you, that one night with you, than to live my life never having it at all."

"Abbie," Michael sighed. "I love you."

"I love you too."

They kissed again, this time a bit more passionately.

Michael then said, "Abbie, I think your mother always knew it would turn out this way. You may feel like she was trying to warn you, or prepare you, but she always knew we would end up together."

"Why do you say that?" she asked.

He then told her about Brody Garrity, and how he met Annabelle during the summer, in front of Hammond Farm before Abbie was abducted, and her life changed forever. He explained to her that Annabelle told Mr. Garrity to buy the farm, long before Michael had ever dreamed of selling it.

Abbie smiled once Michael finished talking. "She knew all along," she whispered.

"She has taken care of you your entire life, Abbie."

"That is becoming more and more apparent every day."

"Look at how much she has taught you through all of this."

"I agree. I've learned so much from her."

"You are an amazing mother. Just like she was. You're the strongest person I know. I couldn't have asked for a better mother for my son."

"Thank you, Michael. I'm so glad you are here now. I missed you so much."

"I missed you too."

They kissed again, and this time they didn't stop. They made love, in the early hours of the morning, passionately and quietly. As their bodies came together they fell deeper and deeper in love. They held each other, as the morning sun streaked through the curtains, and Michael traced Abbie's skin with his fingertips.

"Abbie?" Michael asked.

"Yes?"

"Will you be my wife?"

"Yes."

37

ABBIE

ABBIE STARED FROM THE doorway of the sitting room as she watched Michael change Henry's diaper for the first time. She giggled a bit as he struggled, but her heart swelled as he smiled and made faces at the baby. The sight of her son with his father melted away all of the pain she had endured since the night she was abducted. She could tell Michael was more than happy to be a father, and he hadn't let Henry out of his arms since earlier that morning.

There were no overnight guests the night before, besides the two of them, but Bethany still served pancakes, bacon, and eggs. Henry lay swaddled against Michael's chest as he and Abbie sat at the dining room table.

"Cheers," Abbie said, toasting a glass of orange juice in Michael's direction.

"Cheers," Michael said, with one hand on Henry, the other on his glass. "To our first family breakfast." He grinned as he, too, raised his glass. Abbie had never felt more beautiful than she did when Michael looked at her. Her hair was swept lazily up off of her neck, and her face was swollen from the tears she cried the night before, but Michael's smile let her know she looked amazing.

Bethany busied herself in the kitchen, but Abbie and Michael both giggled every time they caught her peeking her head through the doorway.

"Why don't you join us, Bethany?" Michael called to her.

Bethany appeared in the doorway, wiping her hands on her apron. "No, no; you two enjoy your meal as a family together."

"Come on, Bethany, you are practically family," Abbie said. "You made too much food for just the two of us. Come. Sit. Eat."

"Well, if you insist," Bethany readily agreed. Abbie knew that Bethany was dying to sit and get to know Michael, so the three of them and the baby sat for most of the morning, eating and talking, laughing and crying, sharing stories and their hopes for the future.

As noon approached, Abbie helped Bethany clear the table while Michael tended to Henry. When they were alone in the kitchen, Bethany hugged Abbie.

"I'm going to have to get used to calling you 'Abbie' instead of 'Sarah,'" Bethany said.

Abbie laughed, "I was just getting used to you calling me 'Sarah.'"

"Are you happy?" Bethany whispered to her.

"I've never been so happy," she assured her.

"So Michael is the reason why Jackson didn't have a shot?" Bethany teased, winking at Abbie.

Abbie let out a nervous laugh. Then she said, "Jackson will always have a special place in my heart. He was there for me when he didn't have to be. I'm not sure I would have survived those first few days after Meghan was killed if he hadn't been there. I will always be in debt to him for that. I knew he was in love with me, but it wouldn't have been fair to him if he and I were together. I couldn't have loved him back with all of the feelings I still felt for Michael."

"I know. And he knew that too," Bethany said, starting to tear up. "That's why he brought Michael to you."

"I'll never forget what he did. He not only gave me Michael, but he always looked out for me, protected me, did everything he could to make sure I was happy and taken care of. I know I acted toward him as if I didn't notice, but I did. It broke my heart that I didn't love him back."

"No, see, I think you did love him. In a way. But he knew he would never live up to the standard Michael set."

Abbie smiled. "That is very true." She finished helping Bethany in the kitchen and then returned to the sitting room to find Michael lying sound asleep on the couch with Henry on his chest.

"Would you look at that," Bethany said with a happy sigh. "Absolutely beautiful."

Abbie smiled and fell even more in love with the two of them. She nudged Michael awake and suggested the three of them and the dogs go to her apartment.

Within the hour, Michael was helping Abbie haul armloads of bags, baby items, Henry, Sam, and Bull into her apartment. Her apartment was a far cry from the farm life Michael was used to.

"The place is a bit small," Abbie said sheepishly as she began to unpack Henry's diaper bag, and Michael began to look around the apartment.

"It's cozy," Michael said with a laugh as he stood in the living room. "I think it's perfect."

"We should look into a bigger place," she suggested.

Michael dropped the subject by saying, "My home is wherever you are, Abbie. Small apartment or a farm on one hundred acres. It doesn't make a difference to me."

Abbie believed Michael, but she couldn't drop the subject. She wanted new memories in an entirely different place that they could all discover for the first time together.

"Let's move away," Abbie said to Michael over dinner in her apartment that same evening. Michael stopped chewing his food and looked at her.

Michael laughed. "You really want to leave, don't you?"

"I think it would be nice if we had a fresh start as a family, don't you?" she asked him while taking another bite of her food.

"Can we do that?" he asked, taking her idea seriously.

"I have no idea," she giggled. "But I'm sure I can make a few phone calls and find out."

"Where do you want to move to?" he asked, intrigued at her idea.

"I wouldn't mind moving back down south," she admitted.

Michael smiled. "I think that sounds nice."

"I'm sure Sam and Bull would like some room to run around again," Abbie laughed. She watched as the dogs lay on the floor in the living room, on either side of Henry while he batted at his toys on the floor. Michael could tell that Abbie was serious about leaving Omaha, so the two sat and talked, while they gazed at their son and made plans for their future.

38

CLARK

THE SCREEN DOOR TO the carriage house slammed shut behind Clark, and he stood on the porch, hands on his hips. He raised a hand to shield his eyes from the late afternoon sun that was directly in his line of vision as he looked out over the farm. Michael had been gone for over a month, and Clark hadn't heard from him. The day after Michael left town with Jackson, Clark had driven over to the farm to drop off a homemade pie that his wife had made. Upon arrival, Clark had noticed Michael's truck was in the driveway but saw no sign of him or Sam and Bull. He wasn't sure what to think, but he left the pie on the counter in the kitchen, assuming Michael would return.

After a week had passed and Clark hadn't heard from his son, he grew concerned. Michael had left town before, to look for Abbie or to visit Henry, but this time felt different. Michael had always left Sam and Bull behind. The fact that the dogs were gone as well led Clark to believe that wherever his son was, he planned on staying away for a while. In a way, this set his mind at ease. Clark simply assumed that Michael had received information from Patrick Solomon regarding Abbie's whereabouts and that he had left abruptly to be with her. But weeks had gone by, and he still hadn't heard from Michael. And then the letter came.

Clark held the envelope in his hand as he stood on the porch. It was a letter from Patrick Solomon's attorney. The letter explained that Mr. Solomon had passed away and also included a check from Michael

235

Hammond that Patrick had never cashed. The amount of the check was the exact amount needed to purchase the farm back from Brody Garrity, which had been Michael's plan when he sold it to him. Clark paced back and forth on the porch a bit until he saw the car pull into the driveway.

Clark walked down the steps and met the car in the driveway as it came to a stop. Brody Garrity stepped out of the vehicle and greeted him.

"Clark?" he asked.

"That's me."

"Brody," the man said. "Nice to finally meet you."

"Likewise."

"Please, come inside." Brody motioned toward the farmhouse, and Clark led the way.

"Thanks for meeting me," Clark said once they were inside.

"Not a problem. You mentioned over the phone you had something for me?"

Clark handed Brody the letter. He opened the envelope and read its contents. Brody raised his eyebrows and began to nod his head.

"Michael and I had a deal," Brody stated what Clark already knew. "When he had the money to buy the property back, I told him I would sell it to him." Brody tucked the letter back into the envelope, looked at Clark, and said with a smile, "I'll arrange the paperwork."

"Thank you. I'm not sure when Michael is coming back home, or if he ever plans to, but he would have wanted the farm back in the family."

"Understood. Have you heard from him?"

"No, unfortunately. But I'm sure that wherever he is, he's where he wants to be."

The two of them exchanged a few more words before Brody left.

Clark made the quarter-mile trip back home, where he found his wife, Elisabeth, reading a book on the porch swing.

"How did it go?" she asked him, folding her book closed and resting it on her lap.

"It went well. Mr. Garrity has no issue with selling the farm," he answered her as he climbed the steps to the porch.

"That's wonderful," she said. "Dinner is in the oven. Should be ready in twenty minutes. Also, there is a piece of mail for you on the kitchen counter."

Clark went inside, curious as to what his wife was referring to. A letter was on the counter, just as she said. He picked it up and turned it over a few times, noticing it didn't have a return address. He slid the envelope open with his index finger and pulled out the neatly folded letter that was tucked inside. The handwritten words simply read: *I made varsity.*

Those three words were all he needed to rest assured that Michael was finally with Abbie. Clark tucked the letter in his back pocket, walked back out to the porch, and sat on the swing with his arm around his wife until dinner was ready.

39

ABBIE

AS THE SHEARS TOUCHED the nape of her neck, Abbie squeezed her eyes shut. She laughed out loud as her long hair was cut and fell to the salon floor. An hour later, she wore a shoulder length, bouncy bob and side-swept bangs. Abbie looked in the mirror at herself and admired her haircut. The subtle layers and bangs highlighted the angles of her face and accentuated her neck and collarbone.

"You're a brand new woman," the hair stylist said, delighted with her work and how it had transformed Abbie's appearance.

"Exactly what I wanted," Abbie said, knowing the hairstylist figured she was referring to the haircut itself, when what she was actually referencing was the way she looked almost unrecognizable.

Abbie and Michael had spent the better part of two months coming up with a plan to leave Omaha and move south. Abbie had contacted Matthew Sloan, who arranged for her family to be relocated to Birmingham, Alabama. Abbie had decided it would be best for her to alter her appearance, so she traded her long locks for a short bob and purchased a pair of nonprescription eyeglasses. Even she had a hard time recognizing her own reflection in the mirror.

She and Michael were to keep their identities as Sarah Walker and Andrew Hayes, with their son, Henry Michael Hammond. If people became suspicious as to why Henry's last name was different than either of theirs, they planned to tell people that they couldn't agree on which last name to give him, so instead they gave him an ancestral name, which wasn't completely false.

Abbie returned to her apartment after getting her hair cut. Michael had his back toward her in the living room, tending to Henry in his swing. Boxes of their belongings were stacked throughout the apartment, the contents of each clearly labeled on the outside. They had been packing for the past few days and hoped to be ready to move by the end of that week. The living room window was open, letting in the fresh, early summer air.

Michael briefly glanced in her direction but then swung around as soon as he saw how different she looked.

"Oh my goodness, Abbie," he said, a bit breathless. "You look absolutely stunning."

"Do you like it?" she said, a bit self-conscious, as she touched her hair.

"Yes, I do," he said, still amazed at the way she looked. He walked over to her, touched her hair and then kissed her. They both smiled.

The weekend came, and Michael and Abbie loaded all of their boxes and furniture into a moving truck. By Saturday afternoon Abbie turned in her apartment keys to her landlord, and then she and Michael headed over to the bed and breakfast to say their good-byes to Bethany.

Abbie started to cry when she saw Bethany standing on the porch waiting for them to arrive. Abbie and Michael got out of the vehicle, and Bethany stepped off the porch to greet them.

"Oh, don't start that," Bethany said as she laughed and, at the same time, also began to cry. She and Abbie embraced and held each other for a long time. Michael unbuckled Henry from his car seat, and soon the four of them were standing in the driveway.

"Thank you," Abbie said to Bethany, over and over as they hugged each other tightly. "You have been like a mother to me."

"I'm happy I've had the privilege to know you," Bethany said. "You as well, Michael," she said as she let go of Abbie and opened her arms to Michael and the baby. She hugged the both of them and kissed Henry on top of his head.

"Thank you for taking care of them," Michael said to Bethany. "I'd be lost without them."

"Your turn now," Bethany said to him as she gave him a quick kiss on the cheek. She took Henry in her arms one last time. She listened to him coo and squeal as the four of them shared their good-byes and spoke their well wishes. Bethany stood and waved from the porch as Abbie and her family backed down the driveway one last time.

They drove all night, in hopes Henry would sleep, taking turns at the wheel when the other grew tired. Michael held Abbie's hand as he drove, occasionally bringing her hand to his lips. Abbie pretended to sleep in the passenger seat, and she listened to Michael sing along to the radio. They had spent the past two months making up for lost time—laughing, crying, sharing stories, telling jokes, and making love.

As they put distance between themselves and Omaha, they grew more and more excited for their new life together. They wondered what their neighbors would be like and where Henry would go to school.

"What do you want to be when you grow up?" Michael asked, half joking, half serious. They were asking each other questions in the early hours of the morning, trying to keep each other awake. They could have stopped to rest, but the two of them were more than eager to reach their destination.

"Ahh, that's easy," she answered. "I'd like to be a music teacher."

Michael smiled. "Then I guess we better get you enrolled in school."

"I'd really like that."

The time and the miles went by quickly during their conversations. Even when they were silent, their thoughts were filled with what the other was thinking and feeling.

Michael was the one driving when the moving truck pulled into their new neighborhood. Exhausted but excited, Abbie sat up and leaned forward in her seat. She kept her eyes peeled and pointed out their new home as soon as she saw the numbers on the mailbox by the curb. They pulled into the drive and admired their surroundings. The house was a small Cape Cod with a fenced-in yard, perfect for their family.

Abbie climbed out of the truck and closed her eyes as she lifted her face toward the sun, which was already warm. She heard Michael's door close and then felt him behind her.

"Welcome home," he said, wrapping his arms around her as he kissed her cheek. Abbie put her arms over top of his and leaned in to him.

"Welcome home," she repeated back to him.

They slowly unpacked the truck and moved their belongings into the house. Sam and Bull took a nap in the grass after exploring the yard.

A few of their neighbors came by to introduce themselves and offer a helping hand. Michael and Abbie introduced themselves as Sarah and Andrew, as planned.

That night, after Henry was asleep in the nursery, and Abbie was unpacking dishes in the kitchen, she heard music coming from the garage. Michael had been outside for quite some time, unpacking the last few items from the truck and organizing the garage. Abbie headed out the back door, curious about the music.

"There you are," she said to Michael. His back was toward her, and he was tinkering with an old radio.

He spun around, a bit startled. He smiled at her. "Hey, look what I found," he said referring to the radio. "The previous owners must have left it."

"I like this song," she said, recognizing the tune, and walked toward him. It was an older blues song that she hadn't heard since she was a child.

"Then we should dance," he said to her and took her in his arms. He pulled her close to him, and she rested her head on his chest. They danced until the song was over, and then they walked, hand in hand, through the backyard.

A shed stood in the corner of the yard. As they approached, they heard several birds chirping. The noise was coming from a nest near the top of the shed.

Michael looked a bit concerned when he saw them. "Hmm," he said. "I suppose I should try to get that nest down tomorrow."

"Those birds aren't hurting anyone," Abbie winked, poking Michael.

"They're just sparrows," he said.

"I know," she smiled, "but they worked hard to build their home. I think we should just leave them be."

Made in the USA
Lexington, KY
28 August 2015